Allen Makepeace spent his childhood in South Shields, a north-east coastal town, on which the unnamed town in this novel is very loosely based. During his adolescence and early adult years he lived in Hexham, Northumberland. He became a schoolmaster and was a comprehensive school head and a schools inspector. Since retirement, Allen has written more than twenty non-fiction books under the name of W.H. Johnson. He has won awards and prizes from several bodies including South East Arts, and was a finalist in the Fenner Brockway Peace Prize for Literature. *And Such Great Names as These* was selected as 'the most promising novel' by the National Association of Writers' Groups.

ALLEN MAKEPEACE

AND SUCH GREAT NAMES AS THESE

Matador
9 De Montfort Mews
Leicester LE1 7FW, UK
Tel: (+44) 116 255 9311 / 9312
Email: books@troubador.co.uk
Web: www.troubador.co.uk/matador

ISBN 10: 1-905886-38-1
ISBN 13: 978-1905886-38-8

Contact the author at **www.johnniejohnson.co.uk**

Typeset in 11pt Stempel Garamond by Troubador Publishing Ltd, Leicester, UK
Printed in the UK by The Cromwell Press Ltd, Trowbridge, Wilts, UK

Matador is an imprint of Troubador Publishing Ltd

"Some speak of Alexander and some of Hercules
Of Hector and Lysander and such great names as these ...
(The British Grenadiers - 17th century military marching song)

1

Heroes.

Heroes, all of them, all of the ones on our side. Mr. Pybus never tired of telling them that and they never tired of hearing him say it.

Great heroes in a great cause, he used to say. Don't forget that. Mr. Pybus would look at them seriously. When he did that, what with his moustache and his big black eyebrows, he looked very like Kitchener. Everybody said so.

And, of course, the Durham Light Infantry and the Northumberland Fusiliers were the greatest heroes of them all.

But the English soldiers from other places were heroes as well and they'd have the beating of the Kaiser's men.

What about the Tyneside Scottish, sir? they'd ask him.

Yes, well, there's the Tyneside Scottish, them an' all, Mr Pybus would say. Funny, he never really said it but Mr Pybus didn't seem to like Scottish people so much.

Joshua used to wonder if that was because of the head master but then one day Mr. Pybus told them that Mr. McKie wasn't Scottish. He was of Irish extraction. That is, his mother and father had come to England from Ireland many years before. Mr. McKie had been born here in the town. In spite of his name and his mam and dad, Mr. Pybus told the class, Mr. McKie was really English. Or did he say, nearly English?

Anyway, the important thing was that our men were doing heroic deeds. Especially the DLI and the Northumberland Fusiliers and, yes, the Tyneside Scottish. And even the Tyneside Irish but they didn't mention them much either. They were Catholics.

And often they used to sing in class, all sixty of them.

'Come on now, you girls,' Mr. Pybus used to say, interrupting 'The British Grenadiers' or 'Hearts of Oak' or 'Toll for the Brave' or some such song. 'Come on now. Sing up, you girls.'

He never had to tell the lads to sing up. They always sang their hearts out. And once Mr. Pybus said, 'Joshua Slater, sing the first verse solo for us.' He had felt so proud that day.

But Joshua loved it best of all when they all sang up together. It made him feel like a soldier, all of them singing together.

Little Ernie Grayson, they put him in a handcart.
Put him in a handcart and took him to a quarry.
He couldn't have walked there, not if his life depended on it. Which it didn't.

And Little Ernie was so drunk he couldn't put one foot in front of the other.

So he lay on his back in the cart, his eyes closed and a daft sort of grin on his tearstained face.

And the fellers pulling him along in this handcart had had a drink or two themselves because they knew they were going to do something terrible. So they had daft grins on their faces as well but they weren't quiet like Little Ernie. Instead they cracked loud jokes and laughed loudly and they made all sorts of remarks which were not really funny. But which they laughed at though it was a kind of forced and unhappy laughter. But Dexter, he didn't laugh. He just walked along with his hand on the side of the cart and never looked once at Little Ernie.

And when they all reached the quarry, the Sergeant said to the Second Lieutenant in charge, 'He's fell asleep, sir, and there's no wakin' him.'

And the Second Lieutenant, who'd been second in his school batting averages only last summer, was shaking even though it wasn't all that cold.

'Just as well,' he said in answer to the Sergeant.

He told them to tip the cart so that the shafts stuck up in the air. And Little Ernie's body slipped down gently as they upended the cart and his heels rested on the ground and his little slack body lay quite at ease against the angled flat bed of the cart.

The Sergeant got the bottle out and filled two tin mugs.

'Hurry up, lads,' he said, urging them to take a swig and pass it on.

Then the officer lined them up.

2

'Remember, one of you has a blank,' he said, and his face was pasty white. 'Nothing to be nervous of.'

But only Little Ernie looked calm about the whole affair.

And it was over in no time.

Though the bed of the handcart was ruined.

And after the rifle fire and the sudden angry shriek of rooks, there was silence. They all stood still as if contemplating for the first time what it was they had been told to do. One of the soldiers, Alby Diggle, bent over and retched violently for several minutes though only the palest, thinnest, slowest dribble of vomit came and dripped onto his boot.

Marching back angry and shame-faced, the men were sure they'd never try to do what Little Ernie had tried. They wouldn't dare: they might get caught. So they would put up with whatever they had to.

Poor Little Ernie, poor little lad. Got fifteen miles back and nobody had challenged him. Until at Bethune, he was making for the railway station, thinking that was a good place to go to, and he bumps into a captain.

'Don't I know you?' the captain says. 'Weren't you my batman for a bit?'

(And a bloody awful one at that, he thinks.)

And then it all came out and they shipped Little Ernie back smartish up the line, back to his unit. He couldn't explain to them very satisfactorily why he didn't want to stay to be killed.

So after the Court Martial, they sent him under arrest to a barn.

'We'll let you know our verdict soon,' they told him. This was the way they always did it. Sent the feller off and chewed it over in his absence.

Outside, amid the crunch and crump of high explosive and the whizz and whirr of flying metal, farm lads and clerks lay together, silent, awaiting burial; riveters and barmen hung like bird-scarers on the wire; lawyers and lawbreakers were lost forever, buried under fallen trenches, and a prospective Olympic swimmer drowned in a puddle in No Man's Land.

Inside, the colonel spoke of what must be done while a lone persuasive major warned of mutiny. The way things were now, he doubted if the men would accept a traditional execution. But there might be a way around it, he said. So they reached a decision.

When they told him what they'd decided and after he'd wept a bit, Little Ernie said he'd appreciate it if Dexter from the supporting battalion could be there, be in the firing squad.

'Who's Dexter?'

'Feller that worked in the same shipyard as me. But he's in the supporting battalion and he's a corporal.'

So out of consideration they sent a runner down the communication trench to the other battalion and he found Dexter.

'The major wants to see you pronto,' he told Dexter.

'The major?'

'Aye. A lad you know's in a bit of bother.'

'A bit of bother?'

So the runner told him what was up.

Later, the major told Dexter that Grayson would like him there. But Dexter couldn't remember anybody of the name of Grayson. So they took him down to the barn to have a look at the feller inside.

'Oh, Little Ernie,' said Dexter who recognised him as a joiner in one of the shipyards he had worked in for a time when he was young.

He didn't know his second name but a few times, years back, they'd had a bit chat on the tram on the way to work. Or on the way home.

Funny, they'd seen each other just by chance not so long ago. They'd been in one of those estaminets in a village a few miles back. They'd had a drink or two.

So that's how Dexter got roped into Little Ernie's firing squad.

By invitation.

Not that Diggle would ever believe that. He thought Dexter must have volunteered. He wasn't even with their lot. Dirty sod, Diggle spluttered through his great ugly teeth, fancy volunteering to do something like that.

Anyway, it was all over in no time. Just another crumpled little bugger to join thousands of other across the wide miles, the narrow strip, they called the Front. But still it was a rare case – at least, it's thought to be – only a dozen or so like that though who's to know the truth of it? They hadn't made an example of Little Ernie, hadn't murdered him in front of the lads he'd come to

France with, in front of what now remained of the regiment. They didn't dare, not on this part of the Front, not with what had happened there, not in these war-torn days. But they went through with it for all that. Carried out King's Regulations. Or in part they did. They had him taken away, out of sight, with only a few men in a firing squad and allowing him Dexter for some perverse kind of comfort. A few men wouldn't kick up a fuss, they thought. And they conveniently mislaid all the papers relating to the matter. And they didn't even tell his mam and dad what they had done to their son. They sent a telegram. 'Killed in Action' it said.

Mr Pybus talked a lot about the war. But he was always telling them about the ones in the past as well. Fighting the French. The Black Prince. Richard the Lionheart and Saladin and his heathen hordes. And Drake and Nelson and Chinese Gordon. People like that.

'And you know what's important in war and life?' he'd ask.

And their hands would shoot up. And he'd take his time in choosing who would answer even though everybody knew what the answer was.

'Courage, sir,' somebody would say.

'That's right,' Mr Pybus would reply. And always he'd follow this up with another question. 'And ...?'

And someone else would be chosen to offer the usual answer. 'Staying power, sir.' And Mr Pybus would be delighted with the result.

He often told them about staying power. 'That's what you need in life,' he'd say when they started on their arithmetic, their nature study, their handwriting and especially when he prepared them for classroom drill. On a Monday he'd chalk out the place where each boy and girl was to put the right foot. 'Out in the gangway,' he'd tell them. 'Right foot on the mark.' And then it would be the exercises. 'Build you up will this,' Mr Pybus regularly told them. 'Make you fit and strong.' And they all believed him, all those who'd had scarlet fever and measles, whooping cough and chilblains; all those who went every day to the soup kitchens, all those from the worst tenements in town; all those whose fathers were ill with emphysema, whose brothers and sisters had died from tuberculosis. They all believed him as they puffed and panted, sweated and began to stagger as the drill lesson went on. 'Arms above your head … marching on the spot at a fast pace … bend down and touch your toes.' Until finally, red-faced, they were allowed to sit. 'Staying power, eh?' Mr Pybus would say as if proving a point.

But the thing was, Joshua loved it. He had staying power. He could run a mile, two miles nearly, without stopping for breath. And he liked Mr Pybus. And being at school as well. Sometimes, and increasingly, he'd rather be at school than at home.

A couple of days later Dexter nearly drowned in a shellhole, was lucky not to be sucked down into the mud. He could see an arm there where somebody had been a bit less lucky than him.

Then, after another few days, two of his best pals, standing right next to him, were killed.

But it was the business with the German officer a few days after that, that really made Dexter's mind up. They'd taken a trench one grey, drizzly morning and there he was, this German officer, slumped at the bottom of the parapet. 'Help. Please,' he was saying, speaking in English. His steel helmet was half off, the point of it indicating two o'clock. The tears were running down his cheeks into his old grey moustache. 'Help. Please,' he kept repeating, looking at Dexter and then down at both of his legs. Both off at the knees.

Before Dexter had made up his mind what to do, a little feller, a major in the Seaforths who'd just come on detachment with them, pushed his way in. He put his revolver up to the Jerry officer's head and pulled the trigger.

And before Dexter could answer the why and wherefore of that — was it an act of war or an act of mercy? A stray bullet took the Seaforth major in the chest. And what was that then? An act of retribution? Pure chance? Didn't matter. It would go on and on till the last man stood. That's how it looked.

'Fuck this,' Dexter said to himself. 'I've had me share of this.'

And even though a lot of them said that very often, they didn't all decide to do what Dexter decided. Because he made his mind up there and then to do just what Little Ernie had tried to do.

But he'd bide his time, he told himself, because he was determined to be successful.

Just as poor Little Ernie never was.

So that he ended up in a quarry in a handcart.

Because he couldn't have walked there,

Not if his life had depended on it.

Which it didn't.

So Dexter made his mind up. When the time came, he'd be off.

Running.

Joshua.

Running.

In the light of the early risen moon on a crisp February evening.

Grasps the cold metal of the lamp standard, rests his cheek on it, lets his eye travel up its fluted stem to the gas mantles, neglected these nights of blackout, criss-crossed with spiders' webs.

Oasis, he whispers to himself.

And glances back the way he has come. There is the lamp he ran past eighty-seven paces back. It is always or nearly always eighty-seven paces. Then, beyond, another lamp, this one on the corner. Somewhere even further back, hidden from view, is yet another, the first one he ran past when he left the house.

Or rather when *they* left the house for now he hears Billy, hears his nailed boots, thinks he hears him wheezing, puffing, and Joshua is glad he is beating him, glad that Billy is wheezing and puffing because Billy is bigger than him, a good three inches, and older too, exactly two years two hundred and ninety three days they have worked out.

'Come on, man, Billy,' Joshua calls into the dusk and now Billy is with him, sliding to a halt, the hobnails on his boots striking sparks. Joshua's momentary triumph disappears. If only his boots had new hobnails, struck sparks.

'All right, then?' Joshua asks and when Billy tells him yes, all right, Joshua feels once more triumphant because Billy is puffed out already and they have only just begun.

'See that fourth lamp?' he asks. He grabs Billy by the shoulders. 'Can you see it? The fourth one.'

'Yes.'

It was barely visible in this light. It was the next oasis, the last one in Alma Lane.

'Well just after that we're into Stanhope Street and that's busy. Shops an' that. And there's a lot of people about.'

Always people in Stanhope Street at this time of a Saturday night with the bargains just beginning. Daft really, all those people after bargains. Even when food was short as it had been all this last year. A lot of them, usually mothers or just bairns like Joshua and Billy out to buy last minute cheap stuff if there was any. Everybody with the same idea. At least, that was not altogether true. The fellers weren't out shopping. Most of them were out for a drink. They might have been working till five, some later. But Saturday night, no matter what, they'd have a beer or two and most likely a few more than that if there was any, if they were lucky, if there were supplies. And there were plenty of soldiers too. And ex-soldiers, one-armed, one-legged some of them.

Joshua was making for the butcher. His mother used to go but today she was not over well. She rarely was these days. Even so, she was overjoyed about Billy staying with them. She'd asked them, would they mind going to the butcher's tonight. Course not, Billy had said. And Joshua was delighted. Out in the blackout with the crowds, the noise, the shops. And a chance to test his running against Billy's.

'When ye get past the next lamp a road cuts across. Watch out there,' Joshua warned Billy.

Once a bike had come out fast and the rider's elbow had caught Joshua's shoulder and knocked him sprawling. Another time a stick cart had come racing out of the dark and it was just good luck it hadn't clipped him. He'd not heard it, never heard the clatter of the piebald pony's hooves, only heard it when it had rushed by him and the feller shouted at him, 'Get out of the way, ye daft little idiot. Wake yersel' up.'

You had to be careful.

'Really, from here,' Joshua said, 'it's better on the cobbles than on the pavement. It's all cracked. I once nearly broke me leg, trippin' on the pavement.'

It was a scrape; the flesh had been gouged out of his knee; it had bled quite a lot; he'd had a scab for weeks. But it was not true that he'd nearly broken his leg. Felt like it though, Joshua would tell himself.

'Anyway, I always go in the middle of the road from here,' Joshua said. He stood up straight, pulled his jacket down. 'Are ye right?'

'Yes.'

'Come on then.' And he could not help himself saying, 'Just keep up with me.' Because he knew now that Billy couldn't keep up with him. It wasn't that he didn't like Billy. He did. They'd just met for the first time a couple of hours ago and Joshua had liked him straightaway. He was a really nice sort of lad, no doubt about that, even though he spoke in a posh voice. And a clever lad. Cleverer than Joshua and any of the lads he knew. And he was famous. Everybody had heard of Billy Moffatt.

Off they set, Joshua's worn boot soles making scarcely any noise because they hadn't even one remaining hobnail. They had scarcely had any when his mother had bought them second-hand in the market. Now, their centres were worn into holes and for weeks his mother had been packing the insides with the cardboard of old boxes. Kept the wet out anyway though sometimes, when it was really wet, the cardboard soles had to be replaced every day, sometimes twice a day. But without nails, they were silent. Not like Billy's clatterclattering sharp iron on the cobbles behind him. All the same, Joshua consoled himself, Billy was falling behind again.

Couldn't he pray, Joshua asked himself, couldn't Billy pray to be a better runner? Mebbes he didn't want to be any better. But if he did, if Billy really wanted to be a better runner, could he not ask for something special for himself? Because he was special. Everybody said that. That was why he was here.

Joshua ran off course, darting across the cobbles from the crown of the road to touch the lamp coming up on his left, on the pavement's edge. He always did that, touched every lamp between the oases. He did it for luck. And then after a few paces he made once more for the centre of the road. He heard Billy's ironshods veering towards the lamp. He was going to touch it as well. Joshua glanced over his shoulder. Out of the corner of his eye he made out Billy's awkward run, saw his funny, angular shape, his elbows sticking out, his feet.

If he tried, surely Billy could do things for himself. Not just in the running line, but at school, in his lessons. Mebbes he could just say a prayer and his sums would come out right or his handwriting or his spelling. He could make it easy for himself. Surely. With his gift.

'He's a very special boy,' Joshua's mother had said. 'Billy Moffat's got a gift.'

She'd been explaining to him how they were going to have a visitor, just for one night, and they were honoured, should feel honoured, to have him.

'Out of all that chapel,' she'd said excitedly, 'they've chosen us to have him.'

Mr. Samways had taken her aside after morning service a fortnight before. She'd been rather nervous, because Mr. Samways was a chapel trustee and sometimes he used to preach. She was a bit afraid of him, with his thin, sallow face, his piercing eyes, his always rather severe expression. He very rarely spoke to her, just nodded usually. No wonder she was a bit uncertain when he came up to her. But she needn't have worried. He'd called her by her first name. He'd never done that before. Alice, he'd said, and he'd smiled. Could she put Billy Moffat up, just for the Saturday night? It would be much appreciated. Bite of supper was all he'd need. She needn't lay on a great spread. A great spread? Even she had smiled at that. To herself, of course. And then just give him his breakfast on the Sunday morning and bring him along to the service. And any bother about food, well, just let Mr. Samways know. He'd see what he could do. And he would, Alice knew that, even though she'd never dream of asking him.

'He's the most brilliant young preacher we've ever had,' Joshua's mother had told him. That's what Mr. Samways had said and he should know. He'd heard all the great ones on the circuit. John Evenden, Clifford Ellman, Tom Conway Bright. Name any of them and there wasn't one of them that Mr. Samways hadn't heard preaching. And Billy Moffat, he declared, topped them all. And him just a bit lad, a few weeks over thirteen.

'Fancy,' Alice said. 'And they want us to put him up.'

10

Her eyes had shone as she'd told Joshua the news. What an honour. She'd shaken her head in amazement, remembering again how Mr. Samways had come up to her and put his request, smiling at her.

'He asked me in the most lovely way,' she told Joshua. '"Alice," he said, "you've been a good member of this chapel for several years and we've never yet asked you to look after any of our visiting preachers."'

Mr. Samways had shaken his head as if in acknowledgement of such remissness.

'Anyway, we're going to make amends,' he'd said and he'd paused as if to raise her expectation even further. And then he'd told her.

She could scarcely contain herself.

'Billy Moffat,' she'd breathed to Joshua and her face, her beautiful face, had shone. 'Whoever would have imagined Billy Moffat coming here?'

That night, sitting in the outside lav with the candle's shadows chasing round the whitewashed wall, Joshua looked out of the open door into the back yard. The moon lit up the cracked cement, the crumbling brickwork; opposite was the door to the wash house. Over the back wall, across the lane, he could see the cracks of light in the windows of some of the houses. A woman shouted; a man shouted back; a little bairn cried somewhere. Nothing changed. The promise of Billy Moffat's coming hadn't changed any of that. He wondered what the boy would be like. Not as a preacher. But really like. When he wasn't preaching. When he was a boy. If ever he was. Because so many of those he saw preaching in the chapel weren't very cheerful. They talked about joy and exultation. Words like that. But more often they seemed either very sad or very angry. That night he was not sure what to expect but he had thoughts of a pale-complexioned lad with masses of golden curls. He couldn't imagine him moving about or playing or saying anything ordinary. If he said anything he thought it would be prayers or bits from the Bible.

'Are ye all right?' Joshua called over his shoulder as he ran over to touch the second lamp. Only two more and he'd be at the next oasis.

'Yes.'

11

He'd only asked so he could work out how far behind Billy was and to impress him as well.

Again, as he reached the middle of the road, Joshua could hear Billy across to his left, behind him, making for the lamp. Then, he heard clattering feet as Billy ran once more on the cobbles, thirty yards or more behind him.

Joshua couldn't picture him now, even though he was trying really hard. Strange. You know people well and sometimes when you try to think what they look like, you can't. Sometimes, when he was away from school, he would try to think what Mr. Pybus looked like. Yet he couldn't. Even though he saw him every day. You'd think you'd be able to picture somebody as important as Mr. Pybus when you saw him five days a week. What he did remember about Billy was that he wasn't golden haired, and he didn't have curly hair. And he didn't have a pale skin. When Billy had walked into the house with Mr. Samways a couple of hours before, Joshua had been a bit surprised. So even though he could not now remember what the boy looked like, at least he knew he wasn't as he had first thought he might be like. He was just tall and thin with a beaky sort of nose. He had high square shoulders and when he walked his feet stuck out.

Now racing towards them, came a pony-drawn cart, candles in jam jars fastened to each side of the front prop. Joshua pulled off the centre and ran on the spot at the pavement's edge. Past it went with a clip of hooves and a clatter of wheels.

'Didn't catch ye, did it?' Joshua laughed. 'Didn't knock ye down, eh?'

No answer. Joshua looked up the road. No sign of Billy.

'Billy?'

He couldn't hear Billy's studded boots.

'Billy?'

It was a breathless kind of answer, fainter than it should have been, for Billy was only forty yards or so away.

'I'll be all right,' he called. 'Just let me get my breath.'

Joshua walked back to where Billy stood with both hands outstretched holding the iron railings enclosing a narrow strip of garden of one of the little terrace houses. He was bent over, his head down, as if he was inspecting his shoes. Or as if he was going to be sick. Joshua hoped not. The people didn't like that sort of thing, being sick in the street. They might not even like seeing a young boy holding on to their railings, even if he wasn't doing any harm. Not even if he was Billy Moffat.

They waited two or three minutes, not saying very much. Just beyond, a few yards only, was the last lamp. Oasis two. Almost at the bottom of Alma Lane. Then they would be into the busier Stanhope Street. Even now, they could pick out its bustle. They could make out the tobacconist's, a faint light showing in the interior, and the second hand clothing shop. Next to that, but dark, there was a tailor, an old Jew. His blackout was perfect: he might be working behind it. At one of the grocers there was a long queue. They'd sugar and margarine, arrived not an hour ago. Up the hill and beyond, up the ribbon of shops that made Stanhope Street so lively, up only the slightest of rises, up there, that's where they were going, Joshua told Billy. They'd go under the railway bridge that spanned the street and with a bit of luck, there'd be a train going over when they went under.

'The noise, man,' Joshua told him and grinning at the thought of it. 'And the smoke comes down and gets in your eyes.'

After that, a hundred yards or so higher up and it was easy. All on the flat. Just across the road at the top, down a couple of back lanes, and they'd be there, at the butcher's.

'It's all on the flat when ye get to the top,' Joshua said as they set off.

They could not make so fast a pace in Stanhope Street. The pavements were crowded with shoppers and strollers. The road itself had two sets of tramlines here came one now, its rods whishing on the overhead wires, the driver clanging the bell loudly. Even with its lights partly obscured up and downstairs, it looked like some great ship easing out of the mouth of the river.

Between the tramlines and the pavement's edge were pony-drawn carts, handcarts with men at the trot between the shafts and pedestrians, careless of their safety in the gathering dark, insisting on walking there rather than on the pavement.

'Keep off the road,' Joshua warned Billy. He was beginning to feel rather proud of himself. Here was this lad, older than he was, taller than him, and Joshua was in charge of him. And famous too. Not just any lad.

13

It was always like this on Saturday nights; crowds of folk jostling, usually good naturedly; some in groups, sometimes standing talking; others making slow progress past the shop windows that were faintly lit up. There was always crowds outside 'The Star Vaults' at least, when there was beer, there was crowds pushing their way in, or barging their way out and here was the greatest noise, here the greatest chance of disorderliness, though usually it was cheerful banter. It was all push, all barge here, and you had to weave your way in and out. And there was no shortage of beer this night, war or no war.

'Crowded, eh?' Joshua laughed over his shoulder, trying to show Billy he was used to this. He didn't imagine that Billy had ever experienced anything like it, him coming from Hexham. Up there, they didn't have crowds like this. Not in the country. At least Joshua didn't think they did. He didn't really know. He hadn't been to Hexham. He'd never really been to the country. But it wasn't like this, he was certain.

Then they were under the railway bridge and a train did go over just as they were underneath. Joshua stopped and grabbed Billy by the arm and pulled him against a metal pillar.

'Put your ear against it,' he shouted, and both boys stood there, gripping the pillar, each with an ear to it. Then and only when the great rumbling echo, the shuddering tremor up their arms had passed on, only when the drift of smoke had curled lazily over the parapet and down into the archway, only then did they move on.

The crowd thinned out on the other side of the bridge; it always did. There were fewer shops here, and even fewer open. So Joshua broke into a run once more, but not so fast as before and Billy kept up with him.

How was Billy feeling, Joshua wondered. Not about tonight. Not about the running or staying at their house. But about tomorrow. Wasn't he nervous? When Mr. Pybus had told Joshua a few weeks earlier that it was his turn, that he was going to have to do a recitation in front of the class the next day – it was 'The Wreck of The Hesperus' and he already knew it well enough – he had scarcely slept all night. The thought of standing up in front of sixty others and reciting was awful. He'd done it, of course, but all the way to school he'd felt ill, and right through prayers and scripture, he'd thought he was going to be sick. Then, they'd had arithmetic and his stomach churned and then, just before eleven, Mr. Pybus had told them all to put down their pencils.

'Now Joshua Slater is going to recite a poem for us.'

And he had done it. He'd managed. He'd stood up and done it all right.

But Billy. Tomorrow he'd have a couple of hundred people, more perhaps, all looking at him, while he stood there and preached. They'd all be strangers to him. Except for Joshua and his mother and Mr. Samways and possibly one of two or the elders. And it wasn't just a few lines that he'd had to learn by heart; it wasn't 'The Wreck of The Hesperus'. How did he feel?

Joshua took a sideways glance but he couldn't tell how Billy felt. He couldn't make out his features now in the darkening street. Mebbes he was praying inside. Or mebbes reciting verses. That's what Joshua often did. Every Friday night his mother gave him ten new verses of the Bible and tested him on last week's.

He wondered what Billy was going to preach about the next day, wondered if he dared to ask, say to him, 'Hey, Billy, what ye preachin' about tomorrow?' but he felt that would be wrong, as if he was asking something private.

Now at the top, at the crossroads, they waited. There was a motor car on the other side of the road, gliding along so it seemed, behind a man with a hand barrow piled high with rags and secondhand clothing. Then, with a stab on the horn, the driver pulled out, rounded the cart and with a sudden spurt was gone.

'Have you ever been in one?' Joshua asked. He didn't know anyone who had a car. He didn't think he ever would.

Billy nodded his head.

'Five or six times,' he said. 'After meetings. There've been people at some of the places with cars.'

But not as many now as there had been. Petrol rationing was getting tighter.

Nobody at Joshua's chapel had a car. Joshua was sure of that. Not even Mr. Samways. He was going to ask Billy about riding in a car. Did he sink down in the leather seats? Did he know what all the dials meant? Did he feel really high up? High up in the sense of being high, up aloft, he meant. But did he also feel high up in the sense of thinking himself better than other people? He was going to ask but never did.

'Come on,' he said, leading the way over the road. Then they trotted side by side, turning to the right down the back lanes, just hoping somebody hadn't left a washing line out, strung from wall to wall. But it was unlikely. Especially on a Saturday.

They stopped in front of what was really a house window which gave right onto the pavement. A faint light from an oil lamp by the window and the gas jets over the fire place made it seem forbidding, cold. On the other side of the window sill, there was a bench with knives, bits of flesh and fat and a pair of huge hands wrestling with a tiny piece of meat.

The butcher, a heavy, jowly-faced man, saw the boys and leaned out into the street.

'Aye? What're ye after then?' His voice was coarse and loud.

Joshua wasn't sure quite what he was after. He never was when he came here. He never knew what he would find in the way of meat. He did know that this was no real butcher. You never saw any carcasses here like in the real butchers' shops on the days they had meat. You never saw a real butcher without his apron, without his hat. They didn't usually go half-shaven, weren't usually so pasty-pale though maybe it was the gas light or the oil lamp that made him look so pale, greenish even.

His mother had been vague too. She'd given no precise instruction. How could she when she did not know just what Joshua would find there?

After all, at a real butcher's you had to hand over your ration card. But she always sold her ration cards. She had to. Money was short. She couldn't afford real butcher's prices. And other food prices were sky high. What else could she do?

'Be polite, now,' was what she had said. It was what she always told him when he went on a message. 'Ask him for a nice piece.' She had meant as nice as he had; and she had meant as much as fourpence would buy.

'Just a nice piece of meat,' Joshua told him.

'Right'o, then,' the butcher grinned, rubbing his stubbly cheek with his grubby fingers. 'A nice piece, eh? What ye got in mind?' He waved a broad hand expansively to a table next to his bench. The glow of the gaslight from above the fireplace on the far side of the room or the sullen oil lamp by the window did not make it really possible to see the colour of any meat or even what kind of meat it might be. And there seemed few enough pieces, not much to choose from. One piece, almost on the edge of the table, might have been a chunk of meat or it might have been a sausage. There were no big, solid pieces, no joints, no breasts, no legs. There was nothing of the kind that they had passed in the three shops in Stanhope Street. Here there was just scraps, if the truth was known, from real butchers' shops.

'Come on, man,' the butcher said as if he had not all night to waste when there were others clamouring to be served. He put both hands on the window sill where pieces of the flaking paint stuck to his greasy fingers. He leaned well out of the window, his face almost touching Joshua's.

'How much ye got, son?'

'Fourpence.'

'Fourpence?' The man sounded delighted. 'You've got fourpence? Why, man, I've got just the piece for ye.'

He ducked back into the room and reached over to the side table.

'How's that then for your fourpence, eh? Ye'll do no better than that for fourpence. It's a lovely piece.'

In the man's broad hand it did not look very large nor did it hang together as one piece. It seemed to be made up of different parts, tenuously strung together with fine threads of fat or gristle.

'It's a lovely piece of meat, that,' the butcher said, shaking his head as if he was offering up a prime joint. 'I would've had it meself if you hadn't been taking it.'

Joshua had not said he was taking it. He wondered if he could ask if there was anything else, something more solid, more as if it was all together, like one whole piece. But this man, his bulk, his expression, his irritable way of speaking, put him off.

'Anyway, that's fourpence. I'll wrap it for ye.'

The butcher took a piece of newspaper from a pile on the floor.

'Ye'll have a lovely dinner with this th' morrer.' He smiled at Joshua. 'Your mother'll be pleased with ye an' all.'

The request Joshua had been framing died in his mouth. He reached in his jacket pocket for the money.

Then out of the blue it was Billy who spoke.

'Can we have some dripping?'

Joshua stared at Billy. He had not liked to ask. Not this man.

The butcher stopped his wrapping momentarily.

'Aye, certainly,' he said, stooping down under the bench again and coming up with a wedge of dripping between his fingers. He wrapped it in with the meat.

Joshua stretched out his hand with the fourpence in it.

'Hold on, hold on.' The butcher's tone had changed. 'What's this? What's this ye're givin' us?' He stared down in astonishment at the coins in the boy's hand. 'Fourpence ha'penny now,' he said, his tone outraged. 'We're not a bloody charity, ye know.'

Joshua half withdrew his hand. He was uncertain what to say. He thought it had been fourpence, the meat.

'Ye've got the drippin',' the man told him. 'Drippin's extra.'

'It's usually free, a piece like that.'

This was Billy again.

And, of course it was. With some butchers you might get a bone for soup as well and many would not charge you for that. And Joshua knew that. But not this man.

Again the butcher was leaning on the window sill, stretching his neck out into the street, turning now an angry face towards Billy.

'Oh, aye? Free is it? Well, it's not bloody free here. So ye can take it or leave the lot. There is a bloody war on, ye know.'

He could not go back now with nothing. What would his mother say? He could try the other butchers but for fourpence he might get even less than here. Frantically he searched in his pockets. He might have a stray ha'penny in there though he very much doubted it. But again, it was Billy who spoke.

'We'll leave it,' he said. 'Come on, Joshua.' He put his hand on the younger boy's shoulder. 'Come on. We'll go somewhere else.'

Before Joshua had time to answer, Billy had spun him around, away from the window.

But nowhere would they get anything as cheap as this, Joshua thought. Impossible. Fourpence worth of meat would not cover your little finger in the other butchers' even if it was three hours later and they were selling off the last scraps. He shrugged Billy's hand off his shoulder, preparing to explain this to him.

'All right, then.'

Joshua heard the voice behind him.

'Ye can have it this time for fourpence but I don't usually give away free drippin'! Don't forget that. This time ye can have it but don't expect no favours any other time.'

The butcher handed out the tiny parcel, scowling at both boys.

'I'm not runnin' a bloody charity,' he said again.

As he pocketed the parcel Joshua looked at Billy. He did not know what he ought to say. So he said nothing and neither did Billy.

Instead, they broke instantly into a trot, off into the back lane and into the dark.

Alice felt better now. Silly, she knew, getting worked up like that, excited, her heart thumping ninety to the dozen and her legs turning to jelly. She had no idea how long she had been standing there in the dark by the mantelpiece. It could have been ... well, she couldn't say how long. But she noticed she still had the gaslight chain in her hand. She had gone to turn it down and had just stood there never moving, holding the chain, thinking about Billy. It was absurd, she told herself. He was just a boy like any other, like Joshua. Except that he spoke so beautifully, so quietly and politely.

When the boys had first gone off to the butcher's Alice had sat a while in the quiet. There was just the hiss of the gas; an occasional clatter of footsteps along the pavement outside; somebody calling her bairns in: "Haway, youse lot. Time to come in. Haway now, Jimmy. Haway, our Mary," and once the rag and bone man's pony and cart had clip-clopped past. But Alice had little thought for any of that. She'd just sat, trying to catch her breath. The sudden palpitations; it was just excitement she told herself but you'd have thought they would hear the beating of her heart upstairs.

Now she tugged lightly on the chain, just enough to light her end of the room again. It was neat enough, she was sure. When Mr. Samways had come in she could sense him sizing up the furnishings, seeing if it was good enough. She had been relieved when he gave a

19

nod and one of his little tight-lipped smiles. She was so proud that one of the town's most important citizens had approved.

They would not be long, she knew. And even if it was dark, they'd be safe; you couldn't imagine anything happening to Billy or anybody with him.

It was wonderful to be able to do something for the chapel, she told herself. Once, only once, apart from the day recently when Mr Samways praised her, some woman had told her she was a valued member of the congregation. Much valued, in fact. She'd been so proud of that. Though she couldn't bring herself to believe it. Some of them scarcely spoke to her. They were a clannish lot up here. Sometimes more than sometimes she wished she'd never come, never left the South. She should have braved it out. Yet how could she? And she mustn't start thinking about the past. Must keep thoughts of Edwin out of her mind. Edwin. Edwin ... She shook herself as if to throw off all of these thoughts, throw them off, drive them out of her mind as she had done nearly every day for the past ten years. She'd never go back, never could; she'd have to stay up here. But she mustn't dwell on that. Not tonight.

A couple of hours ago, when he came with Billy, Mr. Samways, quite unasked, had brought some cheese and a few ounces of butter. There was some milk as well and she'd put a drop of hot water in it so the boys would have a hot drink before they went to bed. In the morning, she'd warm up some dripping and dip them some bread. And there was an egg each that Mr. Samways had given her and tea. Before Mr. Samways took Billy to his train she'd ask him if he'd like to come back to the house for his dinner. If he had time. There'd be meat and potatoes and turnip. Maybe he'd like that. But she was sure in the back of her mind that, if Billy was going to have his dinner before going home, it would be with Mr. Samways. There was no food shortage there, she knew that. But she'd ask anyway.

'I'd better put the kettle on,' she told herself and picked it up from the hearth. It was full and she placed it in the centre of the fire, just resting on the edge on the bars. It would be ready boiled by the time the boys came back. She went into the scullery for the teapot and came back with it, tipping the old leaves onto the fire.

After that she took a fine white tablecloth. It had only been used two or three times. It was a special-occasion cloth, a lovely cloth. A woman she used to clean for had given it to her. In each corner some flowers had been sewn in different coloured threads. Out of the drawer at the end of the table she took the knives. Then, she placed the loaf on its board in the middle of the table.

There. All ready. She glanced round approvingly. At the limp curtains; at the worn rugs which covered no more than three quarters of the bare boards; at the chest of drawers, cheap years before; at the second-hand chairs; at the glass pendants on the gas mantles. How she liked the glass when the light caught them and the colours came off, the colours of the rainbow, sparkling. She gently touched one of them and it turned with its own grace, the spectrum of colour rainbowing her cheek, her shoulder, and going on to dance on the wall. She smiled to herself. Then, once again, her heart seemed to race and she had to sit down. Her brow was hot and she leaned back in the chair, closing her eyes. She hoped the headaches weren't going to start again. These last few months had been desperate. She never mentioned to Joshua how she felt.

But then it was Edwin again. Thoughts of Edwin. Coming in again as they always did. Edwin. Edwin.

She saw his face as he lay there. They had tried to persuade her not to look.

'I wouldn't bother, pet,' the man at the mortuary had said. 'I really wouldn't bother.'

But she had summoned up her courage, what little she had ever had.

And she remembered now, as she had every day for the past ten years, the skin, beetroot-red on one side of his face, the swollen cheeks and mouth, the faint rim of dried blood round his nostrils.

'What's up here?'

Wally Robson sounded indignant. Was it bairns fooling around? He could see a young lad at the pavement's edge. Kneeling over a vague shape. If it was them bairns again, he'd skelp their backsides. They got bloody daft this time of year. Winter often kept them in but when it was warmer they were out in the streets messing about. They upset the wife with all their noise and carry on. Not that it bothered him. It was her. When they bothered her, she got onto him. And she'd go on and on.

Wally had heard a shout and a clatter and he was out of the door as fast as he could, ready to send them on their way. He had picked up the torch he kept handy in the passage. When he saw the kneeling boy, he made his way over, ready at the same time for some bit of cheek or daftness.

'What's happened here?'

As the torch came on Joshua turned his face away from Billy, just for the moment. To Wally Robson he looked frightened.

'He's been knocked down. A lad on a bike. He didn't see him.'

Wally was going to ask who hadn't seen who, who hadn't been seen, but didn't bother. This wasn't the time for those kinds of questions.

'What were ye doin'?'

'Goin' home.'

'Let's have a look at him then,' Wally said, directing the torch and peering down into Billy's face. 'Can ye hear us?'

Billy nodded feebly.

Wally knelt down, blew out his cheeks as if undecided what to do.

'How'd he come to get knocked down?'

Joshua swallowed. It was his fault.

'We were runnin',' he said, hoping that that would be a satisfactory answer.

'In the middle of the road?'

Joshua couldn't tell if the man was interested in his answer. He seemed too busy staring into Billy's face and prodding his arms and chest and legs.

'I'm not over conversant with first aid,' he said at last, more to himself rather than to either of the boys. He sat on his heels for a moment, his hands on his thighs as if making up his mind what to do next. The torch beam pointed up to the sky.

'Well,' he said at last, 'Ye cannot lie here all night, that's certain. Let's have ye in the house.'

He handed the torch to Joshua and picked Billy up easily.

'Go on in,' he said, leading the way through the front door and into the room. 'Hey,' he shouted. 'Are ye there?'

It is warm in here, Joshua thought. Very nice. Nice room.

A woman came bustling in from the kitchen, and stopped suddenly, staring at her husband with Billy in his arms.

'Oh dear God,' she said, rubbing her damp hands down the front of her pinafore. 'Is it a bairn? Is he all right?'

Wally made no answer. Instead he laid Billy down carefully on the clippy mat in front of the fire. He pushed aside a comfortable looking armchair and he saw his wife's eyes on Billy's feet resting on the frill at the bottom.

'Can ye move your arms, son?'

Billy moved his arms slowly above his head.

'Good. What about your legs?'

They were all right as well. Joshua felt relieved. It was his fault, he told himself. He should have warned Billy not to cross there. The bike had come out fast and just caught him slightly, just enough to knock him off balance.

'Look at his head,' Wally's wife was saying. 'Look at the back of it.'

Wally cradled the boy's head in his hands and turned it gently so that his wife, bending over, could inspect the injury. Blood was oozing over Wally's fingers, dripping onto the mat.

'It's bad,' Mrs. Robson said. 'It's cut bad.' She looked anxiously at the mat. Wally stared at her long enough to silence her.

'Get us a towel or somethin' to put round his head. Stop the bleedin' a bit.'

She went off to the scullery.

'Is he goin' to be all right?' Joshua asked.

Was Billy going to die, he wondered. All this blood. He'd never seen so much. How much could anybody afford to lose? If you lost a lot, you could die.

'Oh, aye, he'll be all right,' Wally said, smiling rather uncertainly. 'We've no worries on that score. We'll have to get him up to the infirmary, but. Looks to me like they'll have to do somethin'.'

Mrs. Robson, anxious for her furniture, came in with three towels. She gave one to her husband and the other two she spread, one on top of the other on the mat just where Billy's blood was still soaking in. Wally tied his towel round Billy's head. His wife eased the boy's boots away from the chair.

'Ye've nothing to worry about,' Joshua said, feeling a strong desire now to laugh at Billy wearing what looked like a turban.

'I don't feel very good,' Billy said very quietly, scarcely moving his lips as he spoke. His eyelids suddenly fluttered and closed. His face was a grey putty colour. 'Is he all right?' Joshua asked yet again, looking first at Wally and then at his wife. Was this what dying was like? Did you just not feel very good? Did you go pale? Did you look as if all your blood had run out? Onto a clippy mat in front of a fire? When you were dying, did your eyelids flutter and then close? And when they were closed, what did that mean?

'Get's me coat. Hurry up,' Wally snapped, laying Billy's head back gently on the towels. 'Hurry up,' he ordered his wife almost as if he was enjoying telling her what to do.

'Are ye goin' to go to the infirmary with him like that?' she asked him.

'I am,' Wally answered. 'Only place to go.'

Mrs. Robson, standing over her husband and the boy on the floor, shook her head in despair. All that blood and mess, she was thinking. My mat. And the chair cover with his dirty boots.

'Go an' get next door's handbarrow,' Wally said. 'Ask them if ye can borrow it.'

Off she went at a trot and Joshua could hear her knocking hard at her next door neighbour's door. Then he heard their voices.

'D'ye know his mam and dad? Know where he lives?' Wally asked.

And Joshua, ashamed, somehow feeling that a host should not allow his guest to fall into such a condition, muttered, 'He's stayin' with me. At my house.'

'Are they waitin' for ye at home?'

Joshua nodded. 'Me mam. She's expectin' us back.'

'Why, ye'd better let her know what's up,' Wally told him. 'She'll be worried if ye're late.'

Joshua was only too glad to get out of the house, almost as though, if something happened to Billy, he couldn't be held responsible if he wasn't there.

Alice struggled awake. But she had just sat down. Or it

24

seemed so. These days she just had to sit down and she'd be off to sleep. Always tired.

Urgent knocking. The front door. That's what must have wakened her. She struggled out of the chair, reaching out to the table's edge to steady herself. She closed her eyes, waited till she felt ready to go to the door.

More rapping. A shout.

'Mam.'

Joshua. And Billy.

Taking a deep breath she went slowly into the lobby and opened the door. She forced a smile. Wouldn't do to welcome a guest if you looked miserable.

But Joshua stayed outside, standing like a stranger on his own front step.

'Come in then,' Alice said.

And then, Billy? Where was Billy?

'Where's Billy?' she asked. She looked up the dark street as if she expected to see him hurrying out of the shadows. 'Is he not with you?'

When she looked again at Joshua she could see the streaks of tears on his cheeks.

'He's had an accident, mam.'

She heard Joshua speak, heard the sound, the words. A bike. Mr. Robson. Blood. Infirmary. But Billy was due to preach tomorrow. Alice felt suddenly dizzy. The street outside, the terrace of houses, the street lamp slipped sideways. She staggered.

'I'll be all right,' she said as Joshua called out to her. 'All right,' she repeated, turning to go inside.

Joshua took his mother's arm. He guided her across the room and eased her down gently into a chair.

'Tell me again,' Alice said when she had recovered.

Joshua went over what had happened.

'Mr. Robson, d'you say? There's a Mr. Robson taking him up there?' she asked as if for confirmation.

'Yes,' and as if he had just remembered, Joshua took the small packet of meat out of his pocket.

'Shall I put it in the scullery?' he asked.

Alice nodded absently.

Joshua went through to the scullery and put the meat in the

25

cupboard. When he came back, his mother was sitting on the edge of her chair, her right hand to her face, her index finger in her mouth. Joshua went over and stood by her.

'What are we going to do?' she asked him. She didn't really feel up to this.

He had no idea how to answer.

'I don't know.'

She took her hand from her face and sighed deeply.

'Will he be able ... tomorrow ... ?' she faltered as though unwilling to formulate the question in case the answer was too brutally awful to accept.

'I don't know,' Joshua said again.

'We'll have to go up there,' his mother said though it was obviously the last thing she wanted to do. 'He might be all right. They might just put something on his head and let him come back.'

She felt feverish but she'd have to see the boy. Perhaps they were just waiting for her to bring him home.

'He'll probably be all right,' she said.

But Joshua remembered the blood, how it had trickled so quickly through Mr. Robson's fingers and how pale Billy had looked when he lost consciousness.

Dexter ... wondering what they would be doing back at home ... wondering what he would be doing if he was at home instead of sitting under the same stars at the back of a trench, his boots soaked, his puttees soaked, his pants, jacket, shirt all soaked ... and more waste today, just like every day ... men, boys, fathers, sons ... even one man a grandfather ... just waste and hurt and fear. Two years here and he was still afraid. You didn't get used to it. How could you? You'd be some kind of a monster if you could get used to this every day ... he had seen a photographer the other day, a brave enough feller, risking his life ... if the folks at home ever saw what he was taking pictures of, if they really saw the truth of it, the war would be over in hours ... they'd no idea at home.

Quarter to ten chimed on a far-off clock just as they were

26

going into the infirmary. Joshua had seen pictures in books of palaces and castles and great cathedrals but he wondered if anything could match the echoing vastness of this building with its high, shadowy, vaulted ceiling. The floors in the main corridor were tiled in patterns of brown, cream and black and the lino-covered floors of the corridors leading off, and there were so many of those, were pale green but reflected the ochre-coloured walls. That the lino was worn through and patched, the paintwork scarred and peeling, the tiles cracked and in places missing, and that a huge black stove stood cold and blank against the wall, made no impression on Joshua. This was awesome, a place of power, of magic. Especially coming into it from a faltering journey through the blacked-out streets.

The nurse they chanced upon, crackling in her starched cap and an apron which came down well below her knees, had no smile for them. Perhaps a smile wouldn't be right in this gaunt place.

'Yes?'

Alice bit her lip, smiled hesitantly and tightened her grip on Joshua's hand.

'We've come to see Billy Moffat.'

The nurse frowned.

'He came in just a short while ago,' Alice said helpfully, although she was disappointed that the nurse had not instantly recognised the name. The nurse looked at the woman with the worn overcoat, and the scuffed shoes; she looked at the poorly dressed boy by her side.

'Is he a relative?' she asked.

'He's staying with us,' Alice said.

'He's a preacher,' Joshua blurted out, proud to be the friend of such a distinguished patient.

A few more brief exchanges and the nurse went off to make enquiries, returning in a short while.

'He's asleep,' she reported. 'He's had a nasty knock but it's not serious.'

Alice sighed with relief.

'When's he coming out? Can he not come tonight? He's staying with us.'

The nurse looked at the clock high up on the wall. It was

going on for ten. What was this woman thinking of?

'Tonight?' she said, clearly exasperated. 'He's certainly not comin' tonight. Anyway, he'll be here two or three days from what I can make out.'

But tomorrow.

'What about tomorrow?' Alice stammered, feeling what courage she had ebb away as she realised the consequences of what she was hearing. 'Will he be able to come out in the morning? Even for a couple of hours?'

The nurse shook her head.

'Out. Of course not. Can't just come out of infirmary like that. I've just said. He's stayin' in.'

'But he's preaching tomorrow,' Alice said as though that would explain everything and would act as a key to the problem. 'At the chapel. He's Billy Moffat.'

'He won't be allowed out,' the nurse told her, not hiding her impatience. 'I can't imagine how you think he could be.'

Joshua looked up at his mother, her bewildered face, her mouth opening and no sound coming out.

'They won't let him out, mam,' he said.

The nurse, her face stern, stared hard at Alice.

'D'ye understand? He won't be allowed out,' she said, turning away and striding down the corridor.

Alice had not moved. She still wore the stunned expression which had come over her face when she had first realised what was happening. She stared uncomprehending at the nurse's back. Her lips moved silently as though she was trying to formulate some kind of statement, as though she was going to try to persuade the nurse, though now well down the passage, to release Billy. But though her lips worked no sound came.

'Mam,' Joshua said, tugging at her sleeve. 'Come on, mam. He's not comin' out tonight.'

The day Dexter eventually took off he was given a bit of encouragement and help. It seemed that way to him, anyway.

Jerry'd started up with howitzers very early that morning, five o'clock or thereabouts, and they'd all kept their heads down. There wasn't much in answer coming from our side.

Then later, their machine guns opened up stutter-stutter, firing just above ground level so that if you chanced a look over the parapet whatever happened to you was your fault and served you right.

About eight o'clock, as expected, over they came in huge numbers, a massive wave of them, new Bavarian reserves all keen to do well and there was no wire to hold them up, their gunners had seen to that. And on they came as if nothing could stop them.

Then out gets at least a couple of hundred of our brave lads, up and out of their trenches. And they run like hell, Dexter with them, because truth to tell it's better to live to fight another day. Or at least to live. So off they go, all ranks, making for the rear. They're all in a sweat of fear, their bowels churning, threatening, as they run.

At one point there was a couple of sergeants, old regulars, with rifles and they were pointing them and shouting.

'Get back in line and fight, you bastards,' they were yelling and they were grabbing at some of those running past them but eventually, even they knew it was no good so they joined in the run.

And there was Captain Willows, his revolver in one hand and his swagger stick in the other, and he was yelling his head off as well.

'You men, stop this. Stop this. Stand and fight.'

Captain Willows. Not an officer you'd forget. After you'd been up the line for eight or nine days and they sent you back for a few days' rest, you hoped that Willows wasn't with your unit. If he was, it was lectures, parades, bayonet drill and blanco and bullshit. And him being a generally nasty bastard, putting you on charges, that kind of thing.

And here he was now, Captain Willows, ordering them to stand and fight. But a big feller coming by, just ahead of Dexter, wasn't having any of it. Not him. He remembered Willows. And he didn't even raise his rifle above the waist but he let Willows have one round that took his jaw off. The soldier shouted something. Dexter heard him but could not make out what it was. They both went on running with the rest of the mob while Captain Willows lay there and went on dying with his revolver in his hand and his swagger stick underneath his body.

At six o'clock, though the darkest clouds were parting, there was not yet even the faintest streaks of light in the sky when Alice went through to the bedroom. Joshua was fast asleep, the blanket barely ruffled, as though he had not moved since first he had gone to bed. His clothes he had folded neatly on the chair by the washstand. By contrast, Alice's bed, though she had not slept in it, looked almost untidy. When they had come back from the infirmary, she had thrown her coat, hat and cardigan down there and had not made any attempt to put them away. Joshua stirred as his mother leaned over him.

'Come on,' she said, shaking him by the shoulder. 'Time to get up.'

He turned and lay on his back, opening his eyes to look at his mother. The events of the previous night came back to him. He remembered what his mother had said when they were walking back home. They would have to explain to Mr. Samways what had occurred. They would have to go to his house early because there would have to be some change of programme at the chapel. There would be so many in the congregation to hear Billy Moffat, so many who would be disappointed. Joshua struggled up into a sitting position, rubbing his eyes with the heel of his hands.

'We should've gone last night,' Alice said as though she knew what Joshua was thinking. 'Should've called on our way back from the infirmary.'

But how could they have done? All that way in the dark, tripping over the cobbles, walking into things in the blackness. They couldn't have done. She knew that.

Now she intended to visit Mr. Samways by half past seven at the latest. It would not give him much time but perhaps he had a sermon tucked away somewhere that at the worst he could use. But it was more serious than that, Alice told herself. It wasn't simply a matter of Mr. Samways having to fill in for a missing speaker: he would be filling in for Billy Moffat. They had rarely had such a prize speaker, rarely been so honoured. And never had Alice ever had such honour. Now it was snatched away from her. She had been chosen not just by Mr. Samways and the elders: it was more than that. She had been chosen in a very special way. And now rejected. Punished.

By half past six they were out in the still black streets. On weekdays men would be out at this time, on their way, most of them, to the shipyards, others to the pits or the chemical factories. They would make their way along the terraced rows, their bait tins under their arms, clattering along in their heavy boots, calling out to each other in their coarse voices, ignoring the possibility of others still abed. But on this Sunday morning, not a soul stirred, and Joshua and Alice had the world to themselves.

'I ought to be grateful,' Alice told herself, gathering her coat tightly at the neck against the morning chill. She had to tell herself so often how lucky she was. Had to try to convince herself. She would sometimes bring to mind a sermon she had heard about others less fortunate than she was. She might not like these sad and grimy brick streets; might not like the grey cobbles, especially on those days when they reflected lead-like in the drizzle; might not like the smoke-filled air, the grit in it that you could taste, feel in your mouth. And the people. Their crudeness, their drunkenness and violence.

'I ought to be grateful,' she repeated, glancing down at Joshua walking beside her. They'd had sermons about the darkies in Africa and places and the lives they led. At least she'd never starved; hadn't seen her family die one by one in a plague of some kind. Once, a missionary had told them about the heathens in some place or other — she couldn't remember where it was — and the way they murdered their little girls because they couldn't feed them. Someone from the London Missions had scandalised the congregation one night talking about young girls in London and how they made their living, going out with men. Alice had been horrified but at least not scandalised and whilst the others after the service had talked in hushed and outraged tones, she had merely breathed silent thanks that at least she had been spared such a life. And she had prayed and prayed her thanks. It never occurred to her to pray so intently for the darkies and the murdered babies and the young prostitutes of London but at least she was willing to express her gratitude that she hadn't been born in their circumstances. And so this morning, yet again, she reminded herself of how fortunate she was, how grateful she ought to feel. Sometimes, she persuaded herself of her blessings. Though not for long.

Where Mr. Samways lived was called The Village. It was on the outskirts of town and seemed purified of the smoke and grit which those living in town constantly breathed. The houses were set around a green and a pond and it required no stretch of imagination to believe it to be miles away from the slum streets, the blank brick terraces, the acrid smells from the chemical works, the glass factories, the coal mines, and the busiest river in Britain, building the greatest ships in the land. The Village was centuries away, worlds away from all of that.

The houses here were those of men who made money from the chemicals, the glass, the coal and the great ships. Theirs were grand houses, built not of brick, but of a grey substantial stone. Their houses had white porticos and verandahs and conservatories. Their steps were washed by servants; their windows cleaned by servants; their grass cut, their hedges trimmed by other servants. Some of these men owned motor cars, visited London regularly, had shooting rights and shares in racehorses. And while he had no motor car, no shooting rights, no racehorses, Mr Samways, whose dye-manufacturing company had flourished along the river for so many years, was accounted one of the town's wealthiest inhabitants.

Alice put her hand on the heavy iron gate to Mr Samway's house. There was a notice there - 'Tradesmen's Entrance' - and an arrow pointing to the right. Momentarily she wondered which gate she ought to use. She was conscious of her threadbare coat, of Joshua's shabby boots.

'Are we goin' in, mam?' Joshua asked, for his mother seemed very hesitant, standing there as though she was going to change her mind.

She made no answer but quite suddenly opened the gate and they made their way up the wide gravelled drive to the front door.

'It's very early,' she said, as though she was looking for an excuse not to awaken Mr. Samways. Now the moment had arrived and she dreaded what he might say to her.

She tugged the bellpull. Away somewhere in the depths of the house, they could hear a ringing.

Joshua turned and looked down the garden. The grass was neat, trimmed, the hedges solid and square. He made as if to wander away from the front door to look more closely at the rose arbour but his mother put her hand on his shoulder. She wanted him near.

'They're a long time,' he said.

Alice made no reply. For the last hour, when she had not been telling herself how grateful she ought to be for the life she led, she had been trying to work out how she would explain matters to Mr. Samways. She had let him down though it was not entirely her fault.

There was a rattling of bolts behind the front door. Then it opened. A smiling girl, done up in a white cap and apron, prepared to say 'Good morning,' said it, completed the greeting just before the smile left her face. This was the kind of problem she always worried about. These people, the woman so poorly dressed, the boy too; should she send them round to the back? These weren't the kinds of folks who normally came to the front door. They were not beggars, she could see that. But all the same, they weren't invited company.

'Good morning,' Alice said, the words coming out in a rush. 'Can I see Mr. Samways, please?'

The girl moved from foot to foot. She wished the housekeeper was nearby. She would know how to deal with them. Her worst dream was that one day somebody she knew, somebody from her own street, from her own family even, might call. Just out of the blue. Like these two.

'It's about the chapel,' Alice went on. 'An emergency.'

'Wait here a bit,' the girl said, her voice desperate, going off down the passage, uncertain whether she should have asked them inside.

In a short time, another female figure appeared. At first Alice thought it must be Mr. Samways' sister but instead it was a short, stubbily built woman in a black bombazine dress.

'Can I help you?' she asked. Her voice was brisk: she was going to stand no nonsense.

'I've come to see Mr. Samways,' Alice told her. 'It's important.'

'How d'ye mean?' The housekeeper's mouth set itself into a tight line as though she was preparing herself to disbelieve anything she was told.

Alice shook her head from side to side, fumbling for words or for the nerve to speak them.

'It's about the chapel.'

The housekeeper's mouth tightened even further.

'Mr. Samways is an elder of the chapel but I don't think ye should bother him now. Not at this time of day. He's havin' his breakfast. Can't ye talk to him at the chapel? He'll be there this mornin'.'

From the way she moved Alice could see that the housekeeper was preparing to shut the door, clearly expecting that her answer had resolved the matter.

Then, in the shadows of the stairway at the end of the passage, there was a movement.

'Who is it?' The voice was sharp, authoritative.

It was Mr. Samways.

'What's the matter?' he asked, coming into view round the foot of the stairs.

He was chewing as he came. Bacon, Alice guessed. Egg perhaps. Though she did not dwell on that. Her mind flicked back to the matter in hand.

'Good morning, Mr. Samways,' she said. She squeezed Joshua's hand and he took the hint.

'Good mornin', Mr. Samways,' Joshua said.

'What's on this morning?' Mr Samways asked. He was already dressed for chapel. Black jacket, striped trousers. Waistcoat with a heavy gold Albert. White shirt with winged collar. Dark tie. 'What's up?' He was holding a gold half-hunter in the palm of his hand as if to tell them that his time was precious.

Now he stood on the doorstep, his housekeeper retreating a few respectful paces behind him, but retaining the dubious look she had worn since she had come to the door less than a minute earlier.

Mr. Samways fixed his pince-nez, peering at his visitors.

'Is that you, Mrs. Slater?' he asked, scarce able to believe that she could be there, in The Village, at his front door, at this time on a Sunday morning.

'We've had a bit of trouble,' Alice said, the words coming out in such a rush that Mr. Samways could not make out what it was that she intended to say.

'You've had what?'

'A bit of trouble,' Alice repeated, this time more carefully.

'Trouble?'

'It's Billy. Billy Moffat.' Alice put her head down not daring to look at Mr. Samways. 'He's had an accident.'

Mr. Samway's sharp, black eyes narrowed. He nodded at Alice, indicating that he wanted details.

'He's been knocked down,' she told him. 'He's in the infirmary.'

'But what about today? Surely he's going to be able to come to chapel?'

Alice swallowed hard. She wasn't sure. They would have to go back to the infirmary. She didn't tell Mr. Samways what the nurse had told her. But anyway, Billy might have improved in the night.

'He was poorly last night,' she faltered, 'but after a good night's sleep ...' and she went on to explain what had happened. She stammered out the story, licking her dry lips, never looking directly at Mr. Samways until she had finished.

He made no immediate response, just stood there in the doorway, taking off his pince-nez and appearing to clean the lens between finger and thumb.

'In the blackout?' he said at last. 'Running the streets at that time of night?'

We were running, Joshua thought, that's just what we were doing, Mr. Samways.

'They'd been for the meat,' his mother said.

There were bargains on Saturday nights, Mr. Samways knew that well enough. No need to tell him about Saturday night and going for the meat. Not that he had ever done that. But his own father had done. He'd told the story many a time. And it showed how far they'd come. But this stupid woman and her boy ... They'd been waiting for months for Billy Moffat to come to the chapel. People in other chapels had asked how it was that they'd managed to get him and Mr. Samways had smiled and winked and tapped the side of his nose. It was a triumph. He looked at Alice again and felt the anger inside. What would people say? He knew all right what some of them would say. Not to his face, of course. And they'd have a damn good laugh behind his back as well.

Mr. Samways perched the pince-nez back on the bridge of his bony nose, staring grimly at Alice and Joshua.

'We'd best get down to the infirmary,' he said. It had occurred

35

to him that he might be able to rescue the situation. He turned to the housekeeper.

'Telephone for a taxicab,' he told her. 'Tell them who it is. And tell them it's urgent. Ten minutes.'

Telephone ... taxicab ... Joshua heard the words and a surge of excitement as though an electric charge jolted him. Telephone ... taxi cab. He wondered if he might see the woman use the telephone. And then perhaps he would see the taxicab. It was going to come to the door at Mr. Samways' command. But the housekeeper went away down the passage and was lost to view. He did not hear her speaking on the telephone.

Mr. Samways had also gone into the house, telling them to wait where they were. They could hear his voice but were unable to make out what it was he was saying. After a few minutes he came back, struggling into a heavy black overcoat. It had a collar of black fur. Joshua did not know what kind of fur it was but he did know that only rich people could afford it.

'We'll have to get him out of there,' Mr. Samways said to Alice, as though his mind was made up. She only hoped that they could do so although she had the utmost faith in Mr. Samways.

Standing above them on the top step, Mr. Samways stared at Alice, wondering how it was that he had allowed himself to be persuaded that she ought to be given some opportunity to prove her worth. He had told the others she was too vague, too weak a vessel, not to be trusted with such an important guest. But they would have their way and he wasn't going to argue over such a minor matter as to who would put up a visitor. That was the sort of thing that interested them, of course, Cross, Ainscough, Robinson, people like that. It made them happy to make that kind of decision. Oh, they'd said, like a lot of mother-hens, it might be just the right thing for her. Put her right. And she was all right with children. And a nice enough woman, they'd said. And a nice little lad she had. On and on, give the woman a chance. They were as much to blame as her. If they'd only listened.

'Here's the taxicab,' Joshua shouted seeing the black car coast up to Mr. Samways' gate.

'Shh,' Alice said, squeezing the boy's hand: nobody in The Village ever shouted, she was sure.

Without a word, Mr. Samways strode down the steps and,

passing Joshua and his mother without a glance, led the way to the gate. There was no sound but the crisp crunch of gravel underfoot and the running engine of the taxicab at the gate.

It would stay in Joshua's mind all his life. The driver was wearing a cap with a shiny peak and a uniform and gaiters. He got out of his seat and opened the rear door. Mr. Samways ignored him, seizing hold of the handle of the front passenger door and climbing in without a word. Then Joshua heard the word 'Madam' and the driver beckoned the two of them into the rich leather upholstered interior.

It did not matter, at least not to Joshua, that no-one spoke. For him what mattered was the car itself, its shine, its smell, its comfort, the very feel of it, the dials, the little silver flower container with the rose buried in a spray of London Pride. But it was not the precise details that would remain with him, just the whole sense of that first remarkable ride in a motor car, driven by a man in what looked like military uniform.

Pity, he thought, that there were not more people in the streets to notice them but it was still too early. But one or two were about. Joshua tried to catch their eye as they glided by, and when he did so, he smiled at them. It did not concern him that his mother sat tensely on the edge of her seat or that Mr. Samways sat stiff and silent in front of him.

All too soon they were in the main hallway of the infirmary and the taxicab which had brought them there in so short a time had already driven away through the gates. In daylight the building seemed even more daunting, the corridors stretching off left and right until they were lost in a blur of shadows. Even Alice felt dwarfed by the scale of the place. And chilled by it, too, not solely because the imposing black stove against the wall was still not lit but because the ochre of the walls also emphasised the lack of warmth. Already, despite the early hour, women were scrubbing floors and washing windows and the sharp smells of carbolic and vinegar rather than suggest cleanliness only served to hint to visitors that they should not be carrying in their dirt from outside.

It was typical of Mr. Samways that he should take instant command. He collared a nurse and sent her off for the Matron as fast as she could go. And when the Matron came, scarlet faced and out of breath, he explained, without any preliminaries, why he, excluding Joshua and his mother from his remarks, had come to the infirmary at this early hour. Others might have been given shortshrift but the Matron knew Mr. Samways of old. She led the visitors straightaway to Billy's ward.

On each side of the ward, its high narrow windows affording little light, the beds were closely cramped. There was an overriding smell of sweat and that special sickly sweetness that comes from cramping eighty men, suffering from all manner of ailments, in such a confined space. At the far end, in a corner, they found Billy, lying on his back, his head heavily bandaged, his face pale, and his eyes barely open. He smiled vaguely and tried to speak though no sound came.

The Matron walked to the head of the bed so that she might more closely inspect the boy.

It was obvious that Billy, though not seriously injured, was not ready to leave the infirmary that day.

'If it had been an adult we could possibly let him out,' the Matron told them. 'But he's only a bit lad. We can't take the risk.'

Alice moved to the bed to squeeze Billy's hand. She smiled down at him tenderly.

'Right,' she heard Mr. Samways say. 'No point hanging about then.' Even he had to admit that the Matron was right. He gave Billy only the briefest of glances. But for Alice he had a bleak scowl.

She felt sick at what she had done. All her fault. She opened her mouth to say something, to explain yet again how it was that the boys had been out of the house, but Mr. Samways and the Matron were already halfway up the ward. Alice grabbed Joshua by the arm.

'Come on,' she said anxiously. 'We've got to go.'

As he was propelled up the ward, Joshua turned to look at Billy. He waved but there was no answering wave. Billy was asleep again.

When Alice and Joshua reached the entrance steps, they found Mr. Samways standing there, still with the stony expression that had not altered since he first saw them.

'I'm waiting for my taxicab,' he said in a way that indicated that he wasn't expecting them to share it with him. For a moment he looked as if he did not intend to say any more, but then he turned to Alice.

'You've ruined one of the great days on the chapel calendar,' he said. His words came out clipped and suffused with anger.

As he spoke, white spittle formed on his lips and as he continued speaking little specks shot out, some of them landing on Alice's sleeve.

'We've got a congregation really looking forward to hearing that boy. And you've ruined it. Ruined their day. They've been really excited about Billy Moffat coming to speak to them. And all you can do is send him roaming the streets all night so he can get knocked down. You ought to be ashamed of yourself, woman.'

He finished speaking and turned his back on Alice and Joshua.

'I'm really sorry,' Alice began, but it was obvious that Mr. Samways had no intention of listening to her excuses. She took Joshua's hand in hers. 'I'm really sorry,' she said again as they walked past Mr. Samways but still he made no reply.

The next morning about five miles back a couple of the Provost Marshal's men stopped him.

He had no movement papers, just his paybook.

'What you doing back here?' they asked him.

'I'm looking for me unit,' Dexter told them.

What unit was that, they wanted to know, looking at him, unshaven, in his muddied greatcoat and his puttees torn and wrinkled.

He told them, looking at them all blanco, clean-jawed, stern-faced twenty year olds squinting down at him under the flat peaks of their caps.

'Got stuck in the dressin' station after the "do" yesterday. Got a cut on the wire.'

He'd thought that would be a good enough excuse. Three days ago he'd had a dressing put on his arm after he came back from the wire.

But they'd not heard of any particular "do" yesterday, not a big one.

You wouldn't be likely to hear anything back here, he nearly said. Instead he stayed with his story.

'Ye know what those places are like,' he said. 'Those dressin' stations. Sheer bloody chaos. Keep ye there hours if you're not seriously hurt. Just waitin'.'

But these lads knew nothing about field dressing stations, hadn't been, either of them, as close as that to the front. So they sent him on his way.

2

That was not the start, that business with Billy Moffat. The neighbours, chapel-goers, any who knew her, weren't surprised. She hadn't been well — that's how they put it — for months really. Now, she rarely went out. The cleaning jobs in people's homes that had been so regular had come to an end. In the day time, the curtains were closed as soon as Joshua went off to school and her voice, now plaintive, sometimes wailing, would carry to next door, to upstairs, to anyone passing by the window. All day long, praying, weeping.

And when Joshua came home at night, her face was red and swollen. He would tell her what he had done during the day, what had happened at school, ate whatever she had prepared for him for she had, in spite of her devotions, enough time to get potatoes ready and a soup perhaps and occasionally on Monday or Tuesday a thumbnail piece of meat left over from Joshua's Saturday visits to the butcher.

But chapel was out for both of them.

'Are we not goin' back?' he used to ask Alice.

And she would shake her head, unable to answer 'Never' or 'They don't want us'. For she had never heard from Mr. Samways or any of the elders or anyone else. She had committed the unforgivable sin. She had let them down. She had deprived them of Billy Moffat. All she did know was that after a few days Billy Moffat's father had come down to collect his son from the infirmary and that Mr. Samways had arranged for a taxicab to take them to the railway station. Alice had visited Billy in infirmary on the Monday but after that visit the Matron had spoken to her and asked her not to go again. She upset the lad, Matron told her. Perhaps Mr. Samways had reasserted himself; more likely the frantic prayers that Alice had insisted in saying over Billy's bed had persuaded the Matron that even for a boy preacher enough was enough.

'We've got a new world map.'

Mr. Pybus was unrolling it, holding it by one hand under his chin until, opened out, it covered his knees.

'And look here,' he said, waving his free hand airily across the surface in front of him, 'this in red. See it?'

He paused like the proprietor of a well-stocked emporium, smiling at the class as though he was about to reveal a personal triumph to them.

'This in red? Eh? Well, it's all ours. Belongs to us. The British Empire.'

Any other day Joshua would have been enthralled. To learn that he was heir to all that, that others owed so much to him and his fellow Englishmen, would have entranced him. Even today, his neighbour, Michael Lawrence, with no elbows to his jacket sleeves, swelled with the pride of ownership. The four other occupants of the Windsor desk were equally impressed. All these darkies they had beaten. India. Africa. Jackie Udall eased his feet in his brother's castoff boots. Betty Wright stopped picking at the purple-daubed spot on her face; Ernie Pattison's open mouth betrayed his black and broken teeth; and Alan Hogg ran his hand through the fringe in front of his close-shaven scalp. The whole class, every one of the sixty boys and girls, treated the information with proper respect and wonder.

'Think of these people before we went,' Mr. Pybus told them. 'Poor, benighted savages.'

But Joshua's thoughts were elsewhere. His mother was the problem. She had been crying such a lot these last few weeks. When he got up in the morning her eyes were red and puffy and when he came home at dinner time and tea time, he could tell that she had been in tears again. Yet he never felt able to ask her what was wrong although he judged that it had to do with the chapel and their banishment from it.

But there was the praying. For weeks now he had become accustomed to hearing her after he had gone to bed. The last week, however, she'd prayed even more loudly than ever before. And he had heard her not only imploring God, appealing to Him but, the last three nights, even abusing Him and His Son, as well as the elders of the chapel and Mr. Samways. The only thing Joshua could do was pull the blankets over his head and stick his fingers in his ears though he knew that when he took them out again, he would hear the continuing tirade.

What was wrong? She used to clean at half a dozen houses but that had come to a stop. He wondered if she slept at night. There were constant shouts and knocks on the walls from the neighbours. At one point last night he heard a knock at the door and later after she'd answered there were loud arguing voices.

What was wrong with her?

'Not all darkies either,' Mr. Pybus was saying. 'Up there,' he pointed at Canada, 'they were Frenchmen.' Now he moved to Australia and New Zealand. 'They're ours too. And they're white.'

Mr. Pybus paused to take a deep breath, heightening the drama of his tale. It was important to him, to these bairns, to know what Englishmen were doing for people in other places, people without advantages. He tugged at the ends of his generous moustache, preparing to launch into the next stage. He would just be brief today, give a broad picture, let them know of Wolfe's victory, the gallantry at Rorke's Drift, the treachery of the Indian prince at the Black Hole of Calcutta, the lack of civilisation before the English reached Australia and New Zealand. He would give more detailed accounts of each event later in the year.

'The White Man's Burden,' he was saying when there came a knock on the glass pane of the classroom door. A kind of involuntary spasmodic shudder went round the room. It was Mr. McKie. He rarely came unless somebody was in trouble. Then it was six of the best. Or at least that is what all of the children seemed to believe. They used to say that if you put a horse hair across your hand, it would split the cane. They had often talked about that but who ever had a horse hair on him at the right time? And anyway, Joshua had often told himself, if the cane split, it might nip your hand as well as all the other damage it did. These thoughts about canes and horse hairs always passed through Joshua's mind when Mr. McKie came in.

And his worst fears, almost the stuff of nightmares, were realised because today Mr. McKie had come for him. As Mr. McKie bent confidentially towards Mr. Pybus, Joshua heard his name mentioned, saw Mr McKie turn away briefly from Mr. Pybus and look for him down the rows of desks. After more whispering between the two men, Mr. Pybus stood up straight.

'Joshua Slater. Go along with Mr. McKie.'

'In my office,' Mr. McKie added.

Joshua's knee jumped involuntarily, his legs felt limp and rubbery as he made his way past Michael and Jackie who stood in the narrow gangway between the rows of desks. Sixty pairs of eyes on him. Why him? Why me?

Mr. Pybus said nothing until Joshua was near the door, on the point of opening it.

'Right now ... The White Man's Burden ... everybody ... now, pay attention ... don't take any notice of him ... right, now ... The White Man's Burden ...'

And Joshua closed the door on Mr. Pybus, his Empire and his Burden.

The walk to Mr. McKie's office was no more than thirty yards. It seemed to take a lifetime. Why was he being called? He'd done nothing wrong; he was convinced of that. Was there anything in the last two or three days? Not that he could think of.

Mr. McKie had reached his office before Joshua had closed the door of the classroom. Reaching the green door, the boy was unsure whether he should knock. After all, Mr. McKie must know he was there. So had he shut the door because he was not ready for him? Was he getting out the cane? Did he have to move furniture before caning? Or was he busy with other important things? Should he knock? He had never been in there before. He scarcely knew Mr. McKie. He didn't usually speak to any of the children until they were in the top class. Next year, of course, Mr. McKie would teach him. He was not looking forward to that. He knocked at the door.

'Come in.'

Joshua opened the door and Mr. McKie was sitting behind his desk. Strange how, anxious as he was, Joshua had time to take in the brown painted walls, the two or three pictures, a book case full of books, a pile of copy books on the desk, a brass ashtray containing Mr. McKie's pipe. He looked around for the crook-handled cane. He had heard so much about Mr. McKie's cane. Horse hair, he thought.

'Sit down, Joshua.'

The voice was softer than he had expected. It was not Mr. McKie's morning prayers voice; it was not Mr. McKie's afterprayers announcement voice; it was not Mr. McKie's quiet mysterious voice to teachers that he used when he interrupted lessons as he had done just a couple of minutes or so earlier.

'Now, lad,' Mr. McKie said, reaching over and picking up his pipe. 'I've got to have a word with you.' But he seemed in no mood to hurry up with what it was he had to say. Instead he focused his attention upon the bowl of the pipe, tamping down the grey ashes and then reaching in his pocket for his tobacco pouch.

'Your mam's not been over good lately,' he said at last, keeping his attention on the tobacco in the palm of his hand.

'She's not been well,' Joshua told him.

But she had his meals ready and got him ready for school and she talked to him at night and heard him recite his verses. She was not ill in bed.

'She's not ill in bed.'

'No, I know that well enough. She's not ill in bed, I'm aware of that, but she's not been over good.'

Was it the praying? Was she ill? Sometimes she used to say she was dizzy and other times, she'd struggle for breath, holding her hand to her chest.

'She's been taken ill this morning,' Mr. McKie said, not looking Joshua in the face now, still devoting his whole attention to the pipe and the tobacco.

Joshua waited. There was more surely.

'Well,' Mr. McKie said as if it was time to come out with it and stop beating about the bush. 'They've taken her away.'

Taken her away?

'No need to get upset.' Mr. McKie was tapping in the tobacco with the end of a penknife.

Taken her away? Where?

'She's all right. Nothing for you to get too worried over.'

Where? Who'd taken his mam away?

'You see, when folks aren't too fit, they've got to be looked after. Taken care of.'

Where's she gone, Mr. McKie? Who's taken her away?

It wasn't a time for tears. Joshua did not feel like crying. He wanted answers. And then it struck him. When he went home tonight she wouldn't be there. Would she ever be there again? Would he ever see her again?

'They've taken her up to Pirton.'

Pirton? It was on the other side of town.

'There's like a hospital there,' Mr. McKie explained. 'And a place to stay.'

Mr. McKie still wasn't satisfied. He stared at his pipe, scratched at the tobacco with his index finger.

'Is she in hospital?'

Joshua's mind suddenly jerked across to Billy, lying in the infirmary bed.

'Yes. She'll be well looked after,' Mr. McKie licked his lips. 'There's a gentleman from the Town Hall'll come for you later today.'

What for? What's he coming for me for?

'Your mam can't look after you now, you know. She can't do that when she's in the hospital. So you'll be going up there with her.'

To the hospital?

Why send him to hospital? He wasn't ill. And was she going to be there for a long time? Is this what Mr. McKie meant?

Do I have to go to hospital?

Mr. McKie cleared his throat noisily, reached into his pocket for a box of matches.

'You won't be in the hospital wing, son,' he said hesitantly, as though picking his words with care. 'You'll be in the male ward. Your mam'll be in the female ward.'

Male ward? Female ward?

'Male is men, female ladies,' Mr. McKie added unnecessarily. Joshua knew that. What he didn't understand was 'ward'. Male ward, female ward. At least, he understood it. What he did not understand was why they were to be separated. 'It's the workhouse,' Mr. McKie said, as a kind of afterthought.

Workhouse?

'Look now,' Mr. McKie said standing up and at the same time putting his matches back in his pocket and his unlit pipe in the bronze ashtray. 'I've got to go and teach. You just sit here and there'll be somebody along to see you.'

When he saw the look of incomprehension on Joshua's face, he added, 'From the Town Hall. He'll straighten things out for you.'

And with that Mr. McKie was gone, the door closing hurriedly behind him, as though he was glad to get away. Even Joshua could see that. He even began to wonder if that was why they so rarely saw Mr. McKie. Perhaps he did not like being with people, explaining things to them.

He looked around the room again. It was so small; it had so little in it that he felt he knew it and had known it for years. He gazed out of the window at the high blank brick wall only feet away. Beyond that, there were houses and shops and the biscuit factory, but Joshua could see nothing but the wall.

His mother, he thought. Mam. Hospital.

He did not get out of the chair that Mr. McKie had told him to sit in but occasionally, when he heard footsteps outside in the passageway, he would swivel round on the pink cushion and look at the door expectantly. But the only one to come in, and then only after half an hour, was Mr. McKie.

'Playtime,' he said, walking past Joshua and going to the window sill. He picked up the handbell and took it out. Joshua heard the bell ring first at one end of the corridor and then at the other. Then came the rush of feet, voices, shouts from the yard on the other side of the building.

When Mr. McKie came back in a few minutes later he was accompanied by a tall, thin man in a grey overcoat. In one hand he carried a bowler, in the other a case.

'This is the lad,' Mr. McKie said, pointing at Joshua.

The newcomer looked at him, said nothing.

'This is Mr. Newton from the Town Hall,' Mr. McKie explained. 'He's come to sort things out.'

Joshua stared up expectantly at Mr. Newton but the man from the Town Hall was talking to Mr. McKie.

'I'm not sure if he'll come back here. Pirton Elementary's mebbes more convenient.'

'Aye,' Mr. McKie agreed. 'I'm sure it is.'

'Anyway, we'll decide that in the light of things.'

'Yes,' Mr. McKie agreed again.

'We'll away then,' Mr. Newton said, making for the door.

Joshua looked up at the headmaster who nodded down at him, indicating that he should go with Mr. Newton. He was unsure what he should do now; he felt that he ought to say thank you, though for what he did not know; he wondered if he ought not to offer his hand the way they did at chapel on Sundays, but Mr. McKie only made for the door and said something briefly to Mr. Newton. It was too late to say goodbye or thank you. The door closed with Mr. McKie behind it.

Days later, still on the wander, eating in different messes bold as brass and then going on, no questions asked or not many, he was in a biggish village just outside Bethune.

A barrage opened up. Jerry sending stuff in from forty miles back and way off target, making a mess of the place they were never intending to touch. The Frenchies were emptying their tills and putting the shutters up; scarcely anybody on the streets, not a soldier in sight until a couple of Gloucesters came staggering out of a building serving as a company office. One of them was in a bad way, held up by the other feller. You'd wonder at it really, seeing him so badly hurt, blood all over his tunic and legs and you could see he'd be more at home working in a ticket office on the railway or looking after his herbaceous border or taking the missus to a church social. Not the sort of chap you'd expect to find all bloodied up.

'There's two more inside,' the feller carrying him along shouts across at Dexter, sheltering in a doorway over the road.

Not much choice really. Dexter went over. They'd had a bad hit. Smoke and dust everywhere, walls down, roof in. He put his hand over his mouth so he could breathe, went into the smoking passage, dust working its way through his fingers, into his hair.

It wasn't so bad in the room they were using as an office. The corporal lay across a trestle table piled with documents, booklets, files, a tin mug half-filled with tea. There was a slow ooze of blood and brain from a hole in the top of his head.

On the other side of the room, his outstretched legs almost hidden in a scatter of cardboard files, another soldier sat with his back to a cabinet. His eyes were open and he looked so surprised at what had happened, the noise and the roof falling in all of a sudden just like that. There wasn't a mark on him. Dexter went over and knelt by him.

'All right?' he asked. 'You all right, mate?'

48

But the man's life, whatever little had been there, just floated away.

There was nobody else.

On the table there were some blank leave passes, travel warrants, an ink pad, a company stamp. There was a pen in the corporal's hand, a fine black fountain pen with a gold nib. You'd think he was just going to start writing. In one of the drawers there were a few francs. And both the dead men had French money on them.

It wasn't looting.

They were all useful things to someone in Dexter's situation. Necessary for survival.

He pocketed them.

They'd come across the schoolyard, through the iron gate and along the path by the side of the school wall so fast that Joshua was almost out of breath before they reached the main road. Mr. Newton's long legs covered the ground at such a lick that Joshua had to go at a half-trot, just to keep up.

Only when they reached the tram stop did there seem to be any chance for questions because so far Mr. Newton had seemed to have no time to say anything or even to listen to anything. He did not look as if there was anything exceptional happening. It was as if he was always going into schools and collecting up young boys whose mothers had been suddenly taken into workhouses or hospitals. So only now had Joshua any opportunity to ask a question.

'Is me mam all right?'

But Mr. Newton's face was blank.

'I've really no idea. I've not seen her. I don't work at the workhouse. I couldn't tell ye.'

The workhouse: the word was insistent, and Joshua shuddered at the thought of the place. He had seen workhouse people. The men who stayed there went for walks some afternoons. He used to see them sometimes. They were paired off in a long crocodile like children in a school yard. Some of them, the ones who staggered as they walked, stretched an arm out, resting a hand on the shoulder of the man in front. Sometimes they used to laugh very loudly and if they were too noisy, and started to shout at each other as they walked, they were checked by the men in charge who were themselves very often inmates. It was just the same when they waved their arms about or pulled faces. They were told off because they were supposed to keep quiet, look straight ahead, not bother other people. Supposed to march in silence like soldiers. Supposed to enjoy their walk, to pay attention to the red brick houses, to the cobbles, the railway bridges and the grimy, smoke-stained sky. Often they were coarse and ugly, often out of shape; their tongues would stick out; their eyes would roll; their heads would loll from side to side; some of them limped or had withered arms; some had bumps on the sides of their heads. And even those who were in no way misshapen – and there was the occasional handsome face with the beauty of an angel – even those were made to look clumsy in their stiff grey suiting. The only real difference in their dress was in the colour of their peaked caps: each man wore one but it might be black or brown or grey or any shade of these colours.

The women came in separate groups, swollen bellied often even if long past child bearing, tangle haired many of them, not very clean. Obviously not very clean. They never mingled with the men, never saw each other from one week's end to another.

They weren't all like that, Joshua knew. When they'd passed these groups, him and his mam, she'd always reminded him that they were 'Poor unfortunates' and that they were to be pitied and needed help. And there were others there for other reasons. She'd tell him about men out of work, laid off from the shipyards, crippled in mines, diseased through no fault of their own. These men came to the workhouse with their families, though these men and women too saw each other only for a couple of hours on a Sunday. Even the very old, when they could no longer pay their rents and look after themselves came here, couples parted after lifetimes together. And these were also 'Poor unfortunates' his mam told him.

Joshua thought of his mother: he thought of himself.

Is this how it was to be?

'Is she in the workhouse?' he asked Mr. Newton.

'I can't say. She might be or she might be in the hospital wing.' Mr. Newton sounded impatient. He was not paid to answer questions.

Their tram rides, for they had to make a change at the market, took nearly forty minutes and all that Mr. Newton offered in the way of conversation in all that time was, 'We get out here' and 'Here we are'.

At last they reached their stop. Mr. Newton gave one grim nod of the head and stepped down from the tram. Joshua followed.

'Are we here?' he asked.

Mr. Newton grunted something and strode ahead purposefully.

From the outside the hospital had the appearance of something rather elegant. There was a kind of tower on the roof, with its own sloping slates, and on the ridge, right on the top, there was a fancy iron railing. Joshua recalled a picture in a book at school. It was about a rich French family who lived in a house with a tower like that. Just beyond the hospital, hidden by high brick walls, as though the builders had been ashamed of them, were the workhouse buildings.

The grounds of the hospital were perfectly kept: there were long, smooth-shaven lawns; borders lined with tulips, whites, yellows and reds, and on the bends, daffodils, oceans of these. Only when he got inside the building did the illusion fade for the paintwork was neglected, the windows were dirty, the heavy grey lino torn and stained. Just as the infirmary had been when they had gone to see Billy Moffat.

Mr Newton marched into an office with Joshua behind him. He made a few brief remarks to a man sitting at a table and then, without more than a curt nod to Joshua, he left the office.

'Take him over to the other side,' the man at the table said to a young lad who was standing by the desk.

Joshua is led from this dreary building, along narrow passages and then outside to a gate in the wall. And as soon as that gate opens, as soon as he sets foot in that desolate yard, he feels, he sees the difference. Almost immediately, twenty, thirty men perhaps, pass him in a headlong rush, in a panic, in a retreat, fear in every face for they know their fate, know what their pursuers will do. They cannot save themselves.

When they find they can go no further, when they are completely exhausted, some of the men turn their panic-stretched faces to the enemy. Others hurl themselves to the ground and curl up in tight balls, their arms covering their heads, their eyes squeezed shut. And now they all wait in silence, wait for the end. Then rifles are raised and volley after volley is fired; grenades are hurled; bayonets seek out and stab. No-one is spared.

'They never tire of it, man,' Joshua is told by Thomas, the young lad who is escorting him from the hospital building. He leads Joshua across the asphalt yard in the direction of the dormitory building. 'They go down to the rec when they're on their walks. They watch the soldiers.' The rec is where the recruits learn to drill and fight, to shoot, to bayonet, to throw grenades. If they are well-behaved the fellers from the workhouse are allowed to watch them. Then they smuggle back what they have learnt, these new and useful skills, and incorporate them into their games.

Like our schoolyard games, Joshua thinks, wondering if even now Willy and the others were playing similar games.

And now the slaughtered pick themselves up. In turn they face the enemy. Now it is their turn to chase and corner the defeated, their turn to annihilate. It is like this every day. Wave after wave slaughters or is slaughtered. There are never too many to kill or be killed. There is an endless supply of men. No-one is too old or too young here.

Not all of them fight. Around the walls some stand alone, mutter, address unseen questioners: perhaps these are the shell-shocked. Others in small static groups out-shout each other: perhaps these are the commanders. In the centre of the yard a man with a cleft palate rages at a platoon of three who cannot quite get the hang of things, cannot yet turn right when told, nor find left nor right, nor march in step, nor come to a halt smartly though the clubfooted private perspires as he tries to do his best.

They pick their way through the battlefield and enter the dormitory building with its heady smell of unwashed flesh and urine. Thomas, the escort, is handsome; he is kind; he has been here all of his seventeen years; he is four feet tall with a massive distorting hump on his back; he has taken over so efficiently from Mr. Newton who ghosted out of Joshua's life ten minutes ago.

When Joshua sits on his newly allocated bed, one of seventy in this dormitory, and when he bursts into tears and weeps and weeps for nearly half an hour, Thomas puts an arm round him and comforts him.

'Ye'll get used to it,' he says. 'Ye'll get to like livin' here. There's some really grand folks here. Nice people. They're not all like these.'

Joshua puts the heels of his hands to his ears, screws his eyes up tightly. If he can make it black, he might be able to stop thinking about this place, about his mother. She's in the women's ward, they've told him that, but nobody has said what is wrong with her and nobody has said when he can see her. But he tries to black it all out. When he opens his eyes again, it may all be a dream.

Later, in where they call the refectory, furnished with trestle tables scrubbed so often that they smell of old bristles and soda, he sits at the boys' table. He answers questions about himself but most of all he hears the other boys' reasons of why they are here. They are anxious to talk about themselves, trying to explain away, excuse, successions of unknown fathers, drunken mothers, mad uncles. They tell long, involved stories, horror tales. Yet they seem not much moved by them, not at all alarmed or appalled at what has happened to them and what has brought them here. It seems as though they are talking of other people, that the events have not really concerned them, as though they tell their tales simply because of their interest, although they must have told them countless times. They each of them know the others' stories so well, anticipating endings, adding details, even offering corrections and amendments. These accounts have become the histories no longer of any sole individual. What Joshua is hearing is a whole multi-patterned story that belongs to all of them, that all share, so that each boy round the table has a life story of wanton neglect, cruelty, folly, madness; each one is a bastard, each one a child of drunkenness, each one a victim of every imaginable vice.

'It's best when the Catholics come,' one of the boys announces as they sit at supper tea, bread, margarine, a small piece of cheese. 'You have a fine night with them.'

Catholics? He has been trying not to weep, trying not to think about his mother, trying not to imagine living here for ever and ever.

Catholics? The word shakes him out of his self-preoccupation.

'Aye,' another one says. 'Grand when they come.'

They tell him that once a week some Catholic priests come and spend the evening with them. They get a cup of cocoa that night and the Fathers give them a singsong.

Joshua remembers what he knows about Catholics. He has heard enough in the chapel and from his mother. They are dirty and ignorant. They are lazy as well. They won't work if they can get away with it. All of them bone idle, he remembers being told. They're Irish and they don't know any better. And there's all their scruffy bairns. And they're not to be trusted because they think they can do as many bad things as they like and their priests let them off on Sundays so there's no holding them. Thank God there's not many round here, he had heard their next door neighbours saying one day, just the one family in Sage Street who look respectable enough, one of the sons is at the seminary training to be a priest. But their priests are just as bad as they are.

'Are they comin' here?' Joshua tries not to sound anxious.

Are they trying to make them Catholics? Ever since the business with Billy and Mr. Samways, Joshua hasn't been to chapel. But that doesn't mean he's not a Christian. What if the Catholics come and try to change him from Christianity to their religion?

He hopes they aren't coming tonight. No, they are not, they tell him. It is a small relief.

He can't remember how many times he has burst into tears today. He cried in the office when Mr. Newton left; he sobbed when he crossed the asphalt yard; he had wept bitterly, sitting on his bed and waiting to be told to go for his supper.

Suddenly all the chattering of over a hundred men ceases and the silence ripples from the entrance at the top end of the refectory where the men sit until finally it settles on the boys' tables. All through the room mugs are held half way to lips or are quietly replaced on table tops. There is not the slightest whisper yet there has been no command for silence. The only signal has been the appearance of a short, squat, motionless figure, standing in the doorway. He stands there for perhaps half a minute and makes not one word or one sound and it seems to Joshua as if the whole community of seated men and boys have drawn one collective breath and are waiting there for permission to resume speaking, eating and drinking.

And then the man, grey-haired, grey-suited – there is little else that seemed to describe him – leaves the door and walks deliberately between the rows of benches. His face never gives the slightest flicker, never the remotest suggestion of what he is thinking. He gives no look at any of the men but as he passes them they are clearly relieved that he has not stopped at their table. Those who have been passed by pick up their tin mugs, but the conversation when they begin is hesitant and muted.

'It's the Master,' one of the lads whispers. 'Mr. Forsyth.'

The Master stops at the head of Joshua's table. Now he can make out more distinctly the particular features, the heavy black eyebrows, the eyes themselves almost black, the dark jowl, the red, moist lips.

'All right?' he asks the table.

'Yessir,' the boys reply in unison.

His dark gaze roves down one side of the table, up the other. He stares at Joshua.

'New boy?'

'Yes.' His voice falters.

The lips tighten.

'Sir,' the Master says.

'Yes, sir,' Joshua replies. He is afraid of this man. His black eyes frighten him.

'What's yer name?'

Joshua gulps; his mouth dries up.

'Stand up, lad.'

He struggles to his feet, rests his fingers on the table top and then puts them to his sides so that their shaking will not be noticed.

'Come on, lad. Yer name. Haven't got all day.'

Joshua licks his lips, swallows hard.

'Joshua Slater.'

The flat of Mr. Forsyth's hand suddenly banged down hard on the top of the trestle table. The mugs, the tin plates, the knives and forks dance on the table.

'I'm not being addressed like that, Slater,' he shouts. 'Don't ye know who I am?'

The fear that now seizes Joshua, that seems almost to turn his insides to water, that makes his legs shake, robs him once more of speech. His mouth drops open. He cannot bring to mind the Master's name.

But it does not matter. The Master has decided to move on. He turns briskly on his heel and makes for the door.

Then come more tears. And an endless, terrible evening.

That night Joshua scarcely slept. When he did, he was pursued by Mr. Forsyth; when he lay awake he sobbed and wondered where his mother was, wondered if anyone would ever tell him.

The next morning at breakfast — tea, bread, margarine, small piece of cheese — Thomas came down the aisle, stopping at the table.

'All right then, Joshua,' he said. 'Don't get the wind up. Stay calm.'

What could it be? Was his mother dead?

'Mr. Forsyth wants ye.'

For what?

Joshua's fingers gripped the table's edge. If they hadn't he was sure he would have fallen down with shock.

'I've told you, lad, don't get the wind up,' Thomas told him. 'Come on.'

Joshua stood up, closing his eyes.

'This way,' Thomas said, helping him over the bench. 'I'll take ye to Mr. Forsyth's room.'

They walked together out of the hall with every eye still on them. Eyes wide with horror or wonder or perhaps just blankness. As they passed, other mouths gaped, other mouths grinned. As the two boys went through the doorway, the sound began to swell behind them.

'Ye mustn't get on the wrong side of'm,' Thomas warned Joshua. 'He's all right, ye know. But don't get on the wrong side of'm. Just do what he tells ye.'

'What's he want?' Joshua asked in a breathy voice. 'Am I goin' to be caned?'

It was the second time in a few hours he had thought of that. It was no comfort now to think that Mr. McKie hadn't wanted to cane him.

'I don't know,' Thomas said. 'But if he's angry don't answer back.'

'What's he want with me?'

'I don't know. But don't answer back,' Thomas told him again. 'Sticks and stones.'

Sticks and stones? Joshua had never heard the expression 'sticks and stones'. Was he going to use them on him? He thought now of Mr. McKie's cane, remembered women in the Bible being stoned. To death.

'What's he goin' to do?' His back prickled, felt chilled.

Thomas stopped, putting his hand gently on the younger boy's arm.

'It'll be all right. Don't worry now. I'm sure it'll be all right.'

By now they had crossed the flagged yard and entered the large building. Mr. Forsyth's office was at the end of a long shadowed corridor.

'Don't worry,' Thomas said again. 'It'll be all right.' He went to the door, 'I'll knock. When he says "Come in", you go in.'

Joshua watched the little figure stand hesitantly in front of Mr. Forsyth's door as if summoning up the courage to knock. Thomas gave two sharp raps. After a moment's pause they heard Mr. Forsyth's voice.

'Come in.'

'Go on in,' Thomas whispered, one hand on the door handle, the other pulling Joshua forward. The door opened and now from behind Thomas gave him the slightest push to urge him into the room.

Mr Forsyth's office was to Joshua very like Mr. McKie's. It seemed to him to be all dark brown. But it was neatly kept, kept in exactly the way a short, squat man like Mr. Forsyth might be expected to keep it. Joshua's more immediate concern was Mr. Forsyth, sitting bolt upright behind his desk. And in the room, on the other side of the desk, was a smartly dressed woman. But to Joshua the only person there was the Master and he gave him his full attention. As soon as he came into the room, the man's eyes had locked hard onto him, staring at him intently. Joshua felt his knee resume its twitching, his hands beginning to shake once more.

'Now, Slater,' Mr. Forsyth began, his eyes never wavering under their fierce black eyebrows, 'ye just arrived here yesterday.' He paused, looked at the woman seated next to where Joshua stood, and then returned his glance to the boy. 'This lady's come to take yer away,' he said.

Mr. Forsyth made no attempt to explain anything further.

'Have ye any of your belongings you've brought here?'

Who is she?

'Ye know, anything personal? Clothes? Anything like that?'

And where is she taking me?

'Well?'

The sharpness of the question brought him back to the present with a jolt.

'No, sir,' Joshua replied.

'Nothing at all?'

'No, sir.'

Next to him, the woman stirred in her seat.

'He'll want to know what's happenin',' she said firmly. She was obviously not afraid of Mr. Forsyth. Her voice told Joshua that.

'Right, right,' he snapped. 'I'm coming to that.'

He was irritated by something. He scowled at both the woman and Joshua in turn.

'It's been arranged for ye to go an' stay with Mrs. ...er?'

'Mrs. Weston,' she said. 'Mrs. Dolly Weston.'

As she spoke, Joshua looked at her. She was not an old woman. Mebbes about his mother's age. She was dressed very neatly and her coat and hat were much better quality than any his mother had been able to afford. She was wearing gloves as well. She smiled at Joshua.

'You're comin' with me,' she said, looking as she spoke at Mr. Forsyth as if daring him to contradict her. 'I'm goin' to take you back to my house. Ye'll be all right there.'

Mr. Forsyth gave a sniff as if he disapproved.

'Your mother's already been transferred out of this institution and into the general hospital next door,' he said. 'They'll have to decide what to do with her. It'll be up to them.'

'Is she all right?'

The question was blurted out and before there was any answer the boy asked yet again, 'Is she? Is she all right?'

After a pause, the Master and the strange woman answered simultaneously.

'I've no idea,' he said.

'I'm sure she is,' Mrs Weston said.

'Can I see her?'

Joshua had been asking this question since his arrival yesterday and as yet had not received a satisfactory answer from anyone.

'Ye'll have to ask over there,' Mr. Forsyth told him, nodding his head vaguely in the direction of the window behind him.

'I'll do me best when we get out of here,' Mrs. Weston said, leaning over to Joshua and pressing his arm. 'Soon's we get out of here we'll go to the hospital. Leave it to me.'

Behind his desk Mr. Forsyth sat, his mouth twitching impatiently.

'Are there any papers?' Mrs. Weston asked him. 'Ye know, papers to sign?'

Mr. Forsyth made no answer but dug down into one of the desk drawers and brought out a tattered form of some kind which he completed, his lips forming the letters as he wrote them. Eventually he handed it across to Mrs. Weston, pointing to where she had to put her signature. He dipped a wooden shafted pen into the ink bottle on his desk, drew it out and flicked it at the oblong of pink blotting paper in front of him. Satisfied that the pen was clean enough to write with, he handed it to Mrs. Weston without a word.

Only when she had written her name and handed back the form did the Master speak and even then it was no more than 'Right'.

And thus without further explanation and with no more formalities, Joshua's release was effected. Mr. Forsyth, his face set in anger at what he evidently regarded as a criticism of his regime, came round the desk to open the door. As Joshua and Mrs. Weston went out into the corridor, he bade them a gruff goodbye. The door shut quickly and firmly behind them.

For a moment Joshua hesitated, looking up at the woman in whose care he now was.

But who was she?

Mrs. Dolly Weston.

But who was Mrs. Dolly Weston?

Nobody had said.

She was smiling down at him.

'I used to know your mam,' she said, and as if that was explanation enough, she put her arm round him. 'Come on then,' she said. 'Best foot forward.'

And off they set down the grey corridor and out of the door at the far end. They walked across the now silent asphalt yard and through the iron gate. They followed a crumbling cement path in the direction of the hospital, that wonderful building that had so impressed Joshua the day before.

In the hospital building, they went into a small crowded office with two women at desks.

'I'd like to see Mrs. Alice Slater,' Mrs. Weston said. She had a very determined look on her face as if she expected a refusal and wanted it known that it would not work with her. 'Mrs. Alice Slater,' she repeated. 'She's just been transferred across from the workhouse this mornin'.'

'I'm afraid that won't be possible,' one of the women told her. 'They won't let ye in the wards this time of day.'

'Where's the matron?' Mrs. Weston demanded in that confident tone of voice that Joshua had heard in the Master's office.

After slowly wrenching the information out of the reluctant woman, Mrs. Weston pointed her finger at Joshua's chest.

'Wait here,' she said, before turning and marching off briskly down one of the corridors.

Within five minutes she was back.

Within another three minutes, Joshua and Mrs. Dolly Weston stood in front of Alice's bed.

Alice ... she registered little ... just a few fleeting memories now. The boy at the end of the bed ... a woman ... speaking ... smiling ... ceiling ... white ... shadows ... fading ... and Edwin.

Edwin?

Edwin?

She was sure ... Edwin ... and she remembered.

Alice had walked all the way to Newhaven to see him that day. And she had waited outside the boat builder's yard where he worked. They were supposed to be celebrating this week. He'd be out of his time by Friday, a fully fledged shipwright. Two days to go. And all she had to tell was bad news. Right out of the blue.

Edwin came out of the gates at half past five with a couple of other men. He hadn't noticed her, he was so busy talking to the others. It was one of his workmates who pointed her out, standing there outside the tobacconist's shop. He crossed over. She thought he'd be pleased to see her but his expression was serious, his mouth turned down.

Alice spoke first, didn't even say 'Hallo'. Just came straight out with it.

'I've lost my place,' she told him.

He wrinkled his brow, put his head on one side as if he didn't understand. After all, he'd always believed she was well thought of. Could stay as long as she liked. She was a hard working girl, reliable.

'The mistress says I can't stay,' she went on. Only then could she bring herself to tell him. 'I'm pregnant. Three months.'

She didn't know how he'd react. Had kept it back. But he had to know now.

'The housekeeper, she told the mistress she thought I was. She asked me this morning. I finish Friday.'

Alice had bent her head, the tears starting. She did not want Edwin to see her cry. He never had in three years.

Suddenly, she heard him laugh.

At her?

No. He put his hands on her shoulders, there, in full view, opposite the yard gates and in front of the tobacconist's.

And he shook his head and laughed some more.

'Right, then,' he said. 'And I'm out of my time on Friday. My apprenticeship over. So I'm getting the sack. They don't want me either. I'll be too expensive as a fully fledged skilled man.'

But Edwin was positive. He'd had to be. No parents ever. No home but an orphanage. He was determined now to face up to things. But then Alice had had the same background. But she was never positive.

'What we going to do?' she asked him. Great fat tears coursed down her cheeks, ran into the corners of her mouth.

'I know exactly what we'll do,' he said. 'You've got some money, a few pounds.'

It wasn't a question. He knew she had money. If anyone ever gave her a penny beyond her wages, she saved it.

'And so've I. I've got a bit tucked away,' he told her though she knew that already. He was a saver too. 'We're going to find work and we're going to get married.'

Some days later they took a train north, found lodgings in a sad, grey town where shipbuilding was thriving. When the boy was born they were the happiest couple ever.

And when Edwin fell off a gantry into a dry dock, Alice was left with a six months old baby. Absurd, but they had never bothered to marry, though it had sometimes worried her. But she had taken his name. She was proud to do that.

The chapel at least offered some consolation. After Edwin's death she'd started to attend. She would never go to the church again. After all, her mistress in Sussex had been the vicar's wife.

Lying there in the hospital bed, she ran through those scenes and episodes time after time. Remembered his hobnailed boots, the new ones, that they had handed over to her with the rest of his belongings.

'We think he slipped,' someone told her. 'The hob nails, ye know.'

His own fault, the bosses said. No compensation, madam.

But the boy at the end of the bed. Alice had no idea who he was.

Nor the woman.

Nor any idea where she now was.

His mother's eyes were open but Joshua could not tell if she knew who he was.

Only yesterday she had been talking to him. He had had tea and a slice of bread spread with condensed milk for his breakfast. She had sat there facing him, neither eating nor drinking. She had talked fast, never pausing, never asking anything, just talked on the usual subjects, the people in the street and how common they were; how she had let down everybody in the chapel over Billy Moffat; and Edwin, his father, except that when he was mentioned, she seemed to speak directly to him, as if he was there in the room with them. She had recited some verses from Leviticus and then she darted to Mr. Samways and how he had been so disappointed in her. And so it had gone on, as it had for weeks now, months really, the constant circling around the same few subjects, her voice rising and falling, cascades of tears occasionally interrupting what she was saying. Every morning he listened to her: sometimes she was like this in the evening. She was not very well, Joshua had known that. He wondered if a doctor could help her and if so, how he could get one. Would he have to pay? How would he arrange it even if he could afford it?

But that was yesterday and many other yesterdays.

Now, Joshua looked at his mother lying there, her face expressionless though she still looked beautiful. Even though she had not been well she was still beautiful. He glanced up the length of the ward. There were about thirty beds on each side. In most of them, the occupants were asleep. Nobody had visitors. Just his beautiful mother. He thought Mrs. Weston must be very important to be able to get them in to see her. He tried to talk to his mother. They both did. But she didn't answer. They couldn't tell if the frail figure lying in front of them was even aware of their being there.

'Say goodbye to your mam, Joshua,' Mrs. Weston said after ten minutes or so had passed with no sign of recognition from her.

Joshua stepped closer to the bed, bending over to kiss his mother on the cheek. As he did so, he put his hand hopefully in hers but felt no answering grip.

'We'll come and see ye again,' Mrs. Weston said, raising her voice as if that might attract the attention of the woman in the bed. 'We'll both come.' She nodded briskly in confirmation. 'He'll be well looked after, your boy. He's comin' home with me. So don't worry. You remember me, Alice, don't ye?'

Alice was motionless on the pillow, giving no sign that she understood what had been said.

'And they were goin' to change his school,' Mrs. Weston told her as a kind of afterthought. 'But he won't have to now. He'll go back to his old school.'

Back to his old school? Back to Michael and Jackie, Willy and Ernie? He had had no chance the day before to say goodbye to anybody at the school. He had just been called out and had never had any opportunity to speak to Mr. Pybus or any of the others. Apart from Mr. McKie, that is, and even then, Joshua thought, as he stared down at his mother's pale face, even then he had not really said goodbye to Mr. McKie. It had all been so hurried.

Now, with final half-hearted waves, almost apologetically, he and Mrs. Weston made their way down the length of the ward, past the rows of beds. When they reached the door Joshua looked back hurriedly, hoping that his mother might be sitting up and waving them off, that she'd made a sudden recovery. But at that distance he could scarcely make out her bed from that of her neighbours. Was that her thin arm stretched out over the counterpane? Or was he looking at the woman in the bed next to her? In any event, she was not sitting up and waving. The weight of despair which he had felt for most of the past twenty-four hours overpowered him and he stumbled closer to the woman with him. Gently she put her arm round his shoulders.

3

Mrs. Weston had been nice to him on the way back. Even on the tram, when he had been worried because he hadn't the fare to pay for himself — a matter which had not troubled him when he was with Mr. Newton the day before — she had laughed and shaken her head when he had begun to explain. He had, of course, fumbled in his pocket, pretending to look for a coin and he had been getting ready to tell her that he must have lost it. Perhaps he might even say that it had been taken by the boys in the workhouse. They had stolen it while he was sleeping, he might tell her. But then he thought of Thomas and the others who had talked to him and then he thought of the terrible Mr. Forsyth so that he could not bring himself to suggest that those boys were responsible for his having nothing.

But it was not necessary.

'Don't worry about that,' Mrs. Weston had laughed, seeing him ferreting about first in one pocket and then in another. 'I'll attend to it.'

She took off her gloves to rummage in her purse and for the first time Joshua noticed her hands. It was because she looked so grand, so well dressed, that he had not been prepared to see such workworn hands, the nails torn, the flesh almost raw and ingrained with the grime of hard work. His mother's hands were like that; he was used to seeing them like that. But this woman, with her very good clothes, and her very confident manner, like a real lady, ought not to have hands like that. Mrs. Weston saw him staring at them as she pulled her gloves on again.

'Oh, Joshua,' she said, shaking her head and smiling. 'I'm not a toff if that's what ye think. I work hard for me livin'. Cleanin'. Cleanin' folk's houses. Like your mam. And it's dirty work. Doesn't do your hands any good.'

The conductor came up the tram to collect their fares. Only when he had gone did she continue.

'But I've got a few nice clothes as ye can see. I put them on today because they help, do good clothes.'

Mrs. Weston rolled back the cuff of her glove and with her wrist crooked at an angle she cleared a circle on the steamed-up window. She looked out at the sad, depressing rows and rows of houses.

'Just because we come from round here doesn't mean we can't do our best for ourselves. And I'll tell ye this,' she said, peering closely into Joshua's face as if to emphasise what she was saying, 'they wouldn't't've been quite so helpful today, that old devil Forsyth and the folks in the hospital, if I'd gone in wearin' a shawl round me shoulders and me old work skirt. They'd've been difficult, I'll tell ye. They couldn't have stopped ye comin' out but they'd've been awkward. And there'd've been more fuss gettin' in to see your mam.'

Mrs. Weston folded her arms across her chest and nodded her head as if she was confirming the truth of what she had said.

'I keep me eyes open, ye know. If somebody I'm workin' for is throwin' clothes out, things they don't want any more, I offer to buy them, if I think I can do them up nice. I mean that. I do pay. Not much, mind, and I do get some bargains.' Mrs. Weston looked triumphant, happy. 'It doesn't take all that much to make things nice. I've got this coat and a jacket and some skirts and a couple of blouses that way.' She nudged him. 'As I say, it's no good bein' poor and lookin' poor.'

She looked out of the window, checking where they were.

'So there,' she announced. 'I'm tellin' ye.'

At that, she stood up as the tram approached the stop.

'Come on,' she said, grinning at Joshua. 'Let's get home.'

Wherever home was he wanted to be there. He felt so tired, so weak. But at least he did not feel as beaten as he had yesterday.

Dolly's house was in the street behind Joshua's. It was just like his house only hers was upstairs. Everybody always said it was a better class of street, the one Mrs. Weston lived in, even though the houses were exactly the same. Except that Mrs. Weston's had a glass door. Theirs did not. But in every other way, the two streets were indistinguishable. There was always the little bairns sitting on the pavement or in the gutter, playing their incomprehensible games. And the lasses tied their skippy ropes to the lamp posts and chanted their endless rhymes, their skirts tucked up into their knickers. For the lads it was endless games of football or cricket with whatever makeshift equipment they could find. If they got too noisy, if they threatened in their boisterousness to break windows with their ball or knock old folks down, they were chased off with shouts of, 'Go on, off ye get', or 'I'll skelp yer lugs if ye don't stop that.' There were always women at the doors, arms folded, with fresh news to exchange every day and their men, in or out of work, always just managed to find a copper or two for a pint or a skinful. It didn't differ from Joshua's street at all but it was always classed just that bit superior. You couldn't really say why, though.

To get into Dolly's house you came in off the street, through the front door and through the glass door with its blue glass panels in each corner. Other strips of red glass surrounded the central pane of frosted glass. When the front door was open and the sun shone in, the colours spilt onto the first treads of the stairway. Upstairs, to the right, was a room that Mrs. Weston always called the front room but which Joshua's mother in their house had always called the sitting room. Beyond was a kitchen and a scullery and there were two bedrooms. The backstairs led down to the yard, their own private yard, not a shared one like in some streets, and there was a coalhouse and a whitewashed lav and their own little wash house. In next door's yard, chickens scratched a living out of a small, black patch of earth.

To Joshua it seemed that Dolly's house was so much brighter than his own. The paintwork was not nearly bare in places; it was not even chipped and the sitting room and the front room had been papered. Even the kitchen and the bedrooms were smart because obviously they had been painted recently. And there was clean net on the windows of all the rooms. In the front room as he looked in, the green curtains looked very grand. And even the kitchen seemed smart. And the lino which in parts was scuffed and worn, looked as if it had been washed over that very morning. The fender with its brass rail and the oven and fireplace, the table with a new oilcloth, and chairs, all of them shone. Everything was neat and clean and orderly and still it was warm and homely.

'Take your coat off, Joshua,' Mrs. Weston said. 'I'll make a cup of tea.'

He hung his jacket on a hook on the back of the kitchen door while she went through to the scullery to fill the kettle. He stood by the table, his fingers on its edge, wondering if he should sit and where.

'Make yourself at home,' she called through to him.

Joshua's stomach churned. 'Home,' he thought. A lump came into his throat. Tears started in his eyes. 'Home' was him and his mother together.

Mrs. Weston came into the room, a heavy black kettle in her hand. She picked up the brass handled poker in her other hand and leaned into the fireplace, flattening the coals so that she could rest the kettle securely.

'There now,' she said, as much to herself as to Joshua. 'That won't take two shakes.'

She was smiling as she turned round from the fire.

'I expect you're ready for a cup,' she said.

He had never given it a thought. He had never understood why grown-ups seemed to think a cup of tea so important.

'Sit down,' she said, indicating a horsehair chair by the fire.

Joshua sat on the hard, shiny, black material feeling it scratch his hands and the back of his legs. Again a great wave of sadness swept over him. It was only partly because of his mother and thoughts of his own house. Partly what made him want to cry this time was the kind way this woman was treating him after all that had happened since the day before.

'Ye'll be all right here,' Mrs. Weston said, giving him another of her smiles. She looked pretty, he thought. Pretty and kind. 'Ye wouldn't want to be back in that place, would ye?'

She broke off suddenly as if thinking perhaps she had not said the right thing. For a moment she looked down at the floor.

'Ye can stay here as long as ye like, ye know,' she said, still not looking up at him. 'No need to worry. There's a nice bed for you.'

Joshua wriggled uncomfortably, partly because of the horsehair but mainly because he could not imagine being there for a long time, being there long enough to think it his normal home. Impossible. Would he be here next week, he asked himself. Or next month? He could not contemplate it. By then, things would be different. But how, he could not say. It was as if this woman, this Mrs. Weston, when she was offering him to stay as long as he liked, was saying his mother would not be home next week, next month even. And why should she want to look after him? Why? He had not had time to think very much about that question since they had met. There had been so many other questions. So much to ask and wonder about. Only now did he ask himself why she should want to take him into her home. He did not remember ever seeing her before. She had said she had known his mother but he did not know her. He knew some of the women in his own street even though his mother had never encouraged him to talk to them. But this woman, Mrs. Dolly Weston, was a total stranger. He had never seen her before, he was sure.

As if she read his thoughts she spoke up. 'Your mam and me got on well, ye know.' She bit her lower lip, hesitating. 'I was sorry she couldn't get work and that she wasn't well. When they took her ... When she went away yesterday mornin' ...'

Her gaze travelled beyond Joshua to a side table just behind him. Its surface reflected the shape of the window which gave on to the back yard below. On it was a photograph in a silver frame. A boy stood by a small table, his hand resting on a chair back. On the table was a plant of some kind, an aspidistra Joshua thought it might be, although he was not sure. The boy wore a jacket, buttoned up, with matching knickerbockers, woollen stockings, boots. He looked smart. He was tall, strong looking.

'My oldest brother,' she said. 'Henry. When he was a bit older than you.'

Henry looked about twelve, thirteen perhaps.

'He's passed on.'

Mrs. Weston had intertwined her fingers, was pressing them tightly against the back of her hands.

'He was in the fightin' at Loos.'

Joshua wondered what if anything he ought to say. Boys and girls at school had lost fathers, brothers, uncles. At Loos, Hooge, "Wipers", other places he couldn't remember. Quite a lot had been killed. He had seen lists of local men lost in battle. Pages in the newspaper were regularly filled with long lists of names and sometimes they had put these in behind the glass of a notice board outside the churches. In the chapel they always prayed for victory and for the men who were fighting. And for the dead ones. And their families. They kept a Roll of Honour in the chapel and brought it up to date every week.

Mrs. Weston stirred in her chair.

'I wouldn't've wanted him to end up in one of those places,' she said. She put her hand up to her mouth, leaving it there for some seconds before speaking again. 'I wouldn't've wanted that for any bairn.'

Joshua licked his lips, unable to think of anything to say in reply.

'He's dead now anyway,' she said. 'I had a letter saying he'd been buried.' She shook her head slowly and took a deep breath. 'I've another brother. That's Rob. That's him there,' and she waved her hand across towards a small chest in the corner of the room. There was another framed photograph there. A soldier, head and shoulders, in sepia. 'He's in the army as well. He's all right. At least, I think he is. I've heard nothing to the contrary. Least he wrote a month back. He was all right then.'

She took a handkerchief from her wrist.

'More than I can say for me husband.' She dabbed at her lips with the handkerchief. 'He's been missin' for months. Over a year.' She nodded over at a photograph on the mantelpiece. 'That's George,' she said. He was wearing a smart suit, a button hole in his lapel, and sitting on a rustic bench. Behind him stretched the forest, stiff on a painted backcloth. 'George Lawson Weston,' she smiled vaguely as if to herself. 'George Lawson Weston, to give him his Sunday name.'

'I once had a little boy of me own as well,' she went on. Suddenly she stood up and went over to the window, looking down into the cement yard, the roof of the little washhouse, the green doors of the lav and coalhouse, the zinc bath hanging on the wall. In the yard next door, the chickens still pecked away for grain. For an age, it seemed to Joshua, she stood there looking down and he felt a kind of mounting pressure in his chest, worrying that he ought to say something to her, to console her perhaps. After all, she had been kind to him. But before he made up his mind to speak, Mrs. Weston swung round, gave a sniff and a half reluctant smile.

'Anyway,' she said, pushing the handkerchief back, 'this won't get the bairn a new frock, will it, eh?' She laughed to herself and got up from the chair.

She walked over to the fire where the kettle was now boiling. She reached over and moved it on its bed of coals and then brought back her hand sharply to blow on it. 'Ye blighter, that was hot.' And she laughed. 'Serves me right at my age, thinkin' I'm fire-proof, eh?'

She seemed to have cheered up ever so quickly, Joshua thought, and he was pleased because if she was sad, he really would find it difficult to say anything.

'Won't take long now,' she said. 'Then we'll have ourselves a nice cup of tea.'

She seemed to have put her dead brother and the other one and her missing husband out of her mind. And there'd been a baby as well.

Later, after tea, after they had talked for ages about going to school next day and explaining to Mr. McKie about what had happened; about her father killed at the colliery twenty years earlier; and about his mam in hospital because, as Mrs. Weston explained, she believed it was right that painful though it was they should talk about such difficulties; and after they had ranged over all these and other matters, Mrs. Weston looked out at the sky. It was just beginning to get dark.

'The light's goin',' she said. 'Listen, now, we'll have a bite to eat shortly. But d'ye want to go over and get your belongin's?'

What belongings?

Well, ye know, a towel, a shirt, underclothes, vests. Anything like that. What about trousers? Another pair of boots? Anyway, whatever he had, he'd better bring over tonight. Tomorrow, she'd have to sort out what belonged to his mother and what to the landlord.

She handed him the keys which she had picked up at the hospital. And a box of matches, just in case there wasn't any in the house or in case he couldn't find them if there were.

'Don't be long now,' she called out to him from the door as he crossed the road.

It was odd going in to the house he had left only yesterday. Already he felt like a stranger. Usually when he got in the house

71

he shouted out something like, 'I'm here, mam,' or more likely, 'Are ye there, mam?' knowing always that she would be there.

But tonight, as soon as he put the key in the lock, he was aware of the difference. He could feel the emptiness after just a few hours.

He opened the front door. It was suddenly unfamiliar to him. Like a strange house. He took out the matches Mrs. Weston had given him and lit the gas mantle in the sitting room. Then he went through to the kitchen and lit the gas there too.

He glanced out of the kitchen window into the yard. After lingering there a while as though he was a stranger visiting it for the first time, he went back into the sitting room. He wondered if in the sideboard there were any of his 'belongings' and decided that there would be nothing there. He went through to his bedroom. The bed had been made. He didn't question this, just as he had not questioned the washed dishes and the general tidying-up, done by the woman next door, one of the neighbours Alice so despised. He opened the small chest of drawers in his room. There were two shirts, a combination suit, some socks, a heavy woollen vest, two other vests and he took these out and carried them into the kitchen, placing them in two piles on the table. He remembered that in the little cupboard in the scullery was a pair of sandshoes his mother had brought home with her from one of her jobs. The woman in the house had given them to her. Her son had grown out of them. They had fitted him a treat but his mother had not let him wear them. Not yet. He brought them out and placed them on the table by the piles of clothing. Nothing else, he was sure. All he wanted now was a bag to carry the things in. He went into his mother's room, lighting the gas there as well.

He did not bother to look in the drawer because only her things would be in there. He did not feel able to look at them knowing that such personal things would be upsetting. And why disturb them? She'd be home soon, wouldn't she? Wouldn't she? He went across to the cupboard in the corner of the room and holding the candle above his head, he leaned in. There wasn't much there apart from his mother's coat hanging from a hook on the back of the door. On the floor were two pairs of women's shoes, well worn down at the heels. There were two blankets folded up on the shelf. They used those in the depths of winter when it was really cold. Last winter had been terrible. Worst for years. They'd needed those blankets then. And there, right at the back of the cupboard, was just what he wanted, a strong leather shopping bag that would hold most of the clothing that he had put on the table. He would carry under his arm what would not go in the bag. When he pulled it, however, the bag was resistant. Something inside stopped it coming out of its corner easily and he had to step further into the cupboard to release it from a small spar of wood nailed to the wall.

Joshua was surprised at the weight of the bag. As soon as he released it, he looked inside. There was a small black lacquer box with a small padlock on the side. Attached to the hasp on a piece of string was the key.

Now without warning he was overcome by a deep sense of his own unhappiness. Once more the tears rolled down his cheeks. He wiped them away with the back of his hand. He sat down at the table, staring across it at the empty fireplace until once more he felt ready to pack his clothes. He'd have to get on with the job. Mrs. Weston would be wondering where he was.

He placed the box on the table and left it, preferring rather to pack his clothes in the bag first. He wondered about the box. Should he take it to Mrs. Weston's? It was not heavy. Curiously he was not as excited by it as perhaps he might have been. But then there had been enough excitement, too many surprises in the last day or so. His whole world had been turned upside down, inside out. And the box seemed so personal to his mother that only with an effort, when the clothes were in the bag, did he take the key and open it. The gas hissed in the background, the only noise in the house. Outside, the dark street was unusually silent.

He had not known what to expect. What should there be in a black lacquer box? What sorts of things did grown-ups keep locked away? Grown-up secrets? He supposed that like anyone else, grown-ups must have secrets. Perhaps Mr. Pybus had secrets and Mrs. Weston. And his mother and Mr. McKie and all of the other grown-ups he knew. But he could not believe them to be interesting secrets. Just bits of paper and sometimes, he knew, old and faded letters and dried flowers.

So that when the lid came open, he could scarcely believe what it was he saw.

Paper money. Silver coins.

How?

How had his mother saved so much? Or was it a mistake? Had the box just got there? But no, it was hidden there, deliberately hidden.

His head whirling — all this after such a day — he went over to the thin limp curtains and closed them in case any one passing by should see him. See it, more like. See the money in the black lacquer box.

So much. And he'd gone to the butcher, Saturday after Saturday, for cheap cuts; his boots were stuffed with cardboard; his mother was or had been in the workhouse. If he showed it to Mrs. Weston ... but what if the money had not been come by ... honestly? He played with the word. Honestly. Impossible to imagine his mother behaving dishonestly. But just supposing ...

He should count it. And then just as he reached into the box, closing his fingers around some of the coins, the gas flared. The whole room lit up in a clearer, brighter light and then came the splutter, the final pop. He was in complete darkness. Even the fading daylight gave no relief to the weight of dark which now enveloped him.

He had matches but no candle. He felt in his pockets looking for coppers for the gas. None. He had not expected to find any.

His mother usually kept a pile of coins on the mantelpiece for emergencies like this. At least she had done until lately but she was forgetful these days and two or three times in recent weeks they had been caught out just like this. But perhaps ...

He stood up from the table and stepped over the steel fender to get nearer to the mantelpiece, taking care not to break the ornaments, especially the china dogs which over the years had had a few narrow squeaks. Standing on tiptoe he felt along the mantelpiece, beyond the drawing pins which held the tasselled runner in place.

Twice he ran his fingers along but he found nothing.

And the questions went round and round. About the box, the money. He had never been aware of anything like that. She'd never mentioned it. And if he told somebody, not just Mrs. Weston but anybody, what if he wasn't believed? And his mother was in no position to say anything. Not at the moment.

Sudden footsteps in the street stopped at the door.

The door knob, turning, squeaked as it always did.

A lighter square of sky as the door opened.

A silhouetted figure.

'Are you all right in there? Ye've been so long. Is there not a light?'

As he answered and as Mrs. Weston fumbled in her purse, Joshua closed the lid of the box. He opened the knife drawer at the end of the table and slid the box in as quietly as he could.

'Ye should've come over it ye hadn't any coppers, man. Ye can't see to do anything in the dark, daft lad.'

By now Mrs. Weston had found some coins in her pocket and fumbled to put them in the gas meter. It was not difficult. The meter was in exactly the same place as in her house, by the front door.

She turned the knob and the coins fell. He felt Mrs. Weston brush past him in the dark, heard the box of matches rattle as she took them out of her bag. A match scraped on the side of the box and as it flared she raised it to the mantle. As the light came up they both blinked. Mrs. Weston smiled across at him.

'Well, then, if ye've got all ye need, go out and I'll bring these things.'

She was pointing down at a shirt and the sandshoes that had not gone into the bag. Joshua stood by the front door ready to leave. She was still waiting by the mantelpiece, the gas chain in her hand. The room dissolved once again into darkness.

'Tomorrow', Mrs. Weston was saying as she locked the front door, 'ye've got to go back to school and I'd better try an' sort things out with the landlord.'

But Joshua scarcely heard her. The money. He didn't dare say anything about it to her. Because if it was stolen ... he couldn't believe it could be; impossible, really, he knew, but supposing she thought it was, she might turn against his mother. And against him. He'd not say anything about it, he decided.

First chance tomorrow he'd have to come back into the house and get the box from the drawer. He'd have to hide it somewhere. Mebbes later he could ask his mother about it, get a proper explanation. There was one, he was sure.

Bars, cafes, restaurants, music halls, girls, women. The place was alive, hectic. There was a kind of frenzy here, some fellers going up to the Front, others going back on leave. You put together Australians, New Zealanders, Canadians, Indians, some Americans now, Welsh, Irish, Scots, English. You put that lot together in a port like Boulogne and you get what you expect. All sorts of fun and mayhem. They say that some of them going on leave never got nearer home than Boulogne. Set off with every intention of seeing mother, father, wife, children. Family men, they never made the ship but they had the best time of their lives, some of them. Spent fourteen, twenty-one days in a haze of alcohol, in a daze of loving or lust.

But Dexter did get on board. Went past the Provost Marshal's men waving his leave pass.

They never even looked at it.

Joshua came awake only slowly, vaguely aware of the softness of the bed, of the clean smell of the pillow. Once he opened his eyes but fell asleep again, conscious only for a moment or two that he was in some place new to him. When he woke fully, blinking through stuttering eyelids, he saw that the sun was shining onto the white counterpane. It was a diamond bright morning and the dust motes danced across the room, caught in the shaft of the sun. There was a light hint of frost on the black slate roofs and slow twists of smoke rose from the house chimneys. In the background, hooters from the factories and shipyards urged men to work.

'You're awake then.'

Only when he saw Mrs. Weston standing in the doorway did the events of the past two days come back to him. Shy and uncertain now he nodded his answer. She looked so cheerful, Mrs. Weston, not quite as old as his mother. Not young of course. He wasn't good at guessing ages but he knew his mother was thirty and he worked out what he thought Mrs. Weston's age might be from there. Twenty-eight? Something like that.

'Ye'll have to get up soon,' she told him.

Joshua made no reply but he sat up in bed.

'It's goin' to be a grand day,' she said encouragingly, trying in a way that was painfully obvious to keep his spirits up. Just as she had done all the day before right until bedtime.

Back to Mr. Pybus and the others, he thought. See them again.

At least that was something. Then he remembered the black lacquer box and its contents. He had to do something about that. It was not that which worried him. It was what it signified, what it meant about his mother, with all that money and keeping it a secret. What might it all lead to?

Mrs. Weston went over to open the curtains, still reassuring him about the weather. When she turned round Joshua had his head in his hands. He gave a great heaving sob.

'Go on, then. Have yourself a good cry,' she whispered, sitting on the edge of the bed and putting her arms around him. He pressed his face against her warm breasts.

'There now,' she said, patting him gently as she had done several times the day before. 'Ye'll be all right soon.'

She moved him away from her and with the crook of her finger under his chin she pushed up his face so that they were looking at each other.

'I promise ye, ye'll be safe here with me.'

Would he, he wondered. If she found out about the box; if it turned out that ... He eased himself even closer to her.

'I've told ye,' she murmured quietly, repeating what she had told him several times the day before, 'your mam was kind to me. When I was a young girl. I've not forgotten that.'

He liked to hear her say that, kept consoling himself that whatever happened she would not just tell him to go.

'That's better,' she murmured to him at last. 'Just a few tears, pet. Don't worry.' She gave a little giggle. 'I sometimes have a few tears meself. Next time I do, I'll come over and ye can give me a bit cuddle.'

Joshua drew away from her, drying his eyes with the back of his hand. He liked her; he liked this Mrs. Weston.

'I'll get up now,' he told her.

By the time she had given him breakfast — tea, bread and an egg from Mrs. Rimmer downstairs — he was ready to face the day.

'I've got to hurry,' Mrs. Weston said. 'Eight o'clock here. I've got to dash.'

She gave him a key.

'Ye know how to let yourself out?'

He did.

'I'd like to go back over the road,' he said to her, saying 'over the road' instead of 'home'. 'Can I?'

'I'll give ye the key,' Mrs. Weston said.

Later he let himself into his old house, went to the table drawer and took out the box. He was not at first sure where he ought to hide it. Taking it back to Mrs. Weston's, he kept it out of sight under his jacket. Only when he reached the house did he have a good idea. He went downstairs into the yard and opened the coal house. It was stacked with coal. He took off his jacket and rolled up his shirt sleeves. He clambered over the heap right to the back corner. The coals there would probably never be used. They would be constantly covered by new deliveries. He moved several pieces of coal, digging down with his hands, until he had a cavity about two feet deep. He placed the box in there and covered it up.

'I must be mad, interferin' like this,' Dolly told herself. What, she wondered, had she been thinking about, sticking her nose in like that.

She walked briskly from the tram stop towards the pier.

Daft as anything, she thought. Her mother had always told her not to jump in without thinking.

'Our Dolly,' she would say, 'ye give as much thought to what you're doin' as that cat of ours.'

Yet it was not true. She did not normally act without thinking. She was capable of planning, working things out in advance better than many. Better than most in fact. She had worked; she had saved her money; she had bought wisely. When George had been alive ... my God, she thought, that's how I think of him now. He's only missing and I say, when he was alive, and I wish, I sometimes wish ... and she cut off the thought before it prospered ... but when George was in work, and he had always been in work, good work, at a time when many had no work ... before he went into the army, he had made good money. And hadn't she managed it? He wasn't like some, keeping the money to himself on a Friday. Some of them came home drunk as lords on Fridays, scarcely a penny left to put on the table after they'd placed their bets, had their games of pitch 'n' toss against the pub wall, backed their horses and their dogs. How their wives coped she had no idea. But George used to come home, put his packet on the table and take out what little he needed. The rest went to her. Not great sums, of course, but properly managed. So no need to tell her she couldn't plan, think ahead, work out the consequences of what she was doing. Look at her house. Compare it with the others in the street.

She laughed to herself, pulling her coat round her as she crossed the road to the pier. It was quiet at half past eight in the morning. There were some of those strolling old men who never could keep away from the river and the sea, old sailors eyeing the waters on which they had spent their lives. But few others.

In the distance she saw Hector looking out at the rough grey waves, waiting in the usual place by the lighthouse.

Mad? she thought. I must be. First it's him and then a bairn. What have I taken two of them on for? And me down here on the pier, stuck out in the North Sea at this hour in the morning.

Hector waved, came walking towards her. You'd have taken him for a soldier just by the way he carried himself; the straight back; the crisp sure-footedness; the eyes steadfastly ahead as though he were led by distant trumpets. His light overcoat, his homburg, could not hide what he was, a real soldier. As he came closer he waved again and Dolly could tell even at that distance how he looked, the cheerful boyish expression, the kindliness of his eyes.

The first time, she thought, as he walked towards her ... the first time ... the day he'd come to Mrs. Waterstone's ... she had answered the door and let him in.

And what a mess she'd been, her hands covered in black lead. She'd never expected a caller and there she was on her knees rubbing away at the oven door, when the bell rang.

'I've come to see my sister,' he had said. 'I'm Mrs. Waterstone's brother,' he had added unnecessarily.

And Dolly had been conscious of her dirty hands and her bare arms. I'm a skivvy, she thought, but I wish I didn't look like one.

'Oh, right, sir,' she'd said, standing aside, feeling she wanted to wipe her hands on her apron and knowing that would make things worse. She stood aside at the open door, her hands flapping uselessly at her side and wondering if her face was smudged. She had stammered out how Mrs. Allen, the full-time daily, had been called away on family business and that she, Dolly, had been asked in just for the day.

'She hadn't a chance to get anybody else,' Dolly told him, explaining herself away as if she had no right to be there, as if she was unworthy and yet this was the work she usually did. Why in God's name was she like this with this feller?

'She'll be back later today,' Dolly had gone on explaining Mrs. Allen's absence further. 'She had a letter from Newcastle the first post and she had to go off. I'm sure she'll be here tomorrow.'

Hector had smiled as if it did not matter that his sister's regular woman should almost as you might say, desert her post.

'Mrs. Waterstone's all right,' Dolly had said, leading the way up to the bedroom. 'She's had a good night and she's had some tea and a bit toast. She seems quite canny this morning.'

At the top of the stairs they had paused outside the sick woman's bedroom.

'I shan't stay long,' Hector had said, almost as though excusing himself, as though his sister was in Dolly's care. 'It's all right to go straight in?'

Dolly had knocked at the door and peeped round it.

'Ye've got a visitor, madam,' she had said and then she had turned to Hector to let him know it was all right to go in. She had heard the faint cry of surprise from Mrs. Waterstone as the tall young man had gone into her room.

Later, when he came downstairs, he had walked along the passageway and through the kitchen, then beyond the scullery and had found her at the side of the house. She was emptying a bucket of dirty water down the drain. Again she had felt awkward, foolish, doing what she had done for years, awkward and foolish in front of him in his fine tweed suit, in his glossy brown brogues.

'I'm just temporary here,' she had explained. She felt the words tumble out of her mouth. 'I'm not usually here on Tuesdays. It's just circumstances. I'm here on Fridays. That's when I'm here normally.'

She had flushed, realising that she had already told him why she was here today.

'But you've been coming for a month or so,' Hector had said. 'My sister's pleased with you.'

And ungratefully she had thought, patronising bitch. She

never acts as if she's pleased. Dolly had crushed the thought. It was unkind. The woman was ill.

'I wouldn't've been here today,' Dolly went on to tell him, 'but a job I was goin' to got cancelled.'

Cancelled because the death of a son had been reported only a couple of days before. Killed in Mesopotamia. They had sent a message to Dolly asking her not to come this Tuesday. So she had been free when Mrs. Allen asked her.

'Just holding the fort, eh?'

Typical of Hector, holding the fort.

'I wasn't goin' anywhere.'

And that was the first time.

Damn it, she thought, watching Hector walking across to her, the long grey pier stretching behind him. He's wonderful and I love him. Damn it and blast it. As they came together he placed his hands on her shoulders and kissed her on the cheek.

'Well?' he asked her.

Dolly patted him affectionately on the forearm.

'I think so,' she answered as if she was not sure how to reply.

'Is the boy all right?'

'He's a bit upset. But he's gone to school.'

'Good.'

Hector slipped her arm in his and they strolled along the pier towards the lighthouse. Out here, already half a mile from the mainland, the breeze whipped up and Dolly pulled her collar round her ears.

'And his mother?'

She told him.

'I've got to thank you, Hector. It was kind of you.'

He gave a short laugh.

'I asked a favour on your behalf, that's all,' he said. 'No more. You've got the consequences of it.'

They walked on. Out at sea there were a few fishing smacks, a dredger. Beyond on the horizon there was a smudge of smoke. They could be German ships, she thought. They'd bombarded the coast before. Look at Hartlepool. But it did not worry her.

'Was your father surprised when you spoke to him?'

Hector looked down at her.

'Of course he was. You can't imagine my father not being surprised at a request like that.'

'But he wasn't angry with ye or anythin'?'

'He's not as bad as that,' Hector said, springing to his father's defence. 'He's not always flying into rages or being difficult. I've no idea why you have this idea about him.'

'Well, he treated Alice Slater badly,' she answered, a shade more sharply than she would have wished.

Hector stopped, took her hand out of the crook of his arm and faced her. He was serious, pained.

'Dolly, he wasn't unfair to Alice Slater. He was annoyed with her. Other people were annoyed too. They were disappointed. They blamed her for that business with the Moffat boy. Some of them might have taken it out on her but my father wouldn't.'

No? Dolly thought to herself. Well, it's natural to stand up for your father no matter who or what he is. But she knew his father for what he was. She had had a hard experience, a bitter experience. She'd never change her opinion of him.

'Of course he is strict in his views and sometimes a shade unreasonable. But I'm sure he has nothing to do with what happened to Mrs. Slater.'

He was pleading with her, wanting her to believe the best of his father, wanting her to believe the best of him.

'When I went to him yesterday,' Hector told her, his voice having about it an unaccustomed nervous pitch, 'when I told him what you had said about a former chapel member being taken off to the workhouse, he was concerned. Truly. Believe me.'

But she did not, could never bring herself to believe anything but the worst of Hector's father. She looked at Hector.

Why on earth have I got myself tied up with him, she wondered. Him of all people, that man's son. Funny world, she reflected. All the houses to go to and I end up at old Samway's daughter's house. She would never have gone there, would never have considered working for any of his lot. Not that she harboured any really strong feelings against them now. That was long over. But it would have been daft, especially after all these years, to become involved with any of them.

It was just a recommendation really. One job led to another and one day she had found herself being interviewed for a cleaning job by Mrs. Waterstone's regular daily. It wasn't too onerous, no yards or floors or stairs to scrub. But with the missus very ill, Mrs. Allen could not cope.

'She's very poorly, the missus,' Mrs. Allen had told her. 'And she's lost her husband and there's no children.'

And never any mention of the name Samways until her third or fourth week. Too late then. She had not known Mrs. Waterstone previously and her father came only infrequently to see her and then only in the evenings. Dolly never saw him. I need never see him, she had reassured herself.

But she did meet Hector.

'He's been badly wounded,' Mrs. Allen had informed Dolly that first time, that Tuesday, when she got back from Newcastle. 'He's been in France and it was touch and go for a bit. His lung, ye know.' He was getting better, Mrs. Allen had said. He was hoping to get back on active service, she was sure.

And perhaps it might have ended there. But it did not.

'I told my father it was Mrs. Slater,' Hector was saying. 'He said straightaway he'd see she was transferred from the workhouse to the hospital. He'd pull strings. As soon as she's better ...'

'She's never goin' to be better,' Dolly snapped, cutting across his optimistic assurances.

'Well, at least you got the boy out quickly enough and that's good.'

Hector was looking at her, his expression taut and expectant, seeking her approval for what he had managed to persuade his father to do. He was eager, like a small boy hoping for praise.

And Dolly, seeing this, sighed and put her arm in his once more. Now she could taste the tang of sea salt on her lips.

'Yes,' she said at last as though she had been thinking his last remark over carefully. 'Joshua's out. I'm goin' to try to keep him. I said I would and I will.'

Hector shook his head.

'You are a funny girl,' he told her. 'You scarcely know them. You once knew her but you've not been in much contact with her since you came back here. It's illogical.'

'What's logic got to do with it? Anyway, we did some jobs together a few months back. So I did see her. So what's logic got to do with it?'

'A lot.'

'How?'

She was making to withdraw her hand from his arm again but he prevented it, placing his hand firmly on hers.

'Simply this. You can't pass a street corner at half past eight in the morning and see some poor sick woman being carted off to the workhouse and decide quite out of the blue to do some kind of rescue act.'

'Wasn't like that.'

Dolly tightened her lips, looking straight ahead.

'It was exactly like that. And I wonder,' Hector appeared to muse, 'what you would have done to help them if you hadn't known me, if you hadn't been coming to meet me.'

Of course, she had no idea what she would have done. Nothing probably. Just stood aside and felt sorry most likely. She realised that one reason why she had done something was precisely because she knew Hector. He could speak to his father, could try to get something done that way. If Hector could persuade him to do something about the poor woman then she knew it would be done quickly. She wondered now if old Samways did not feel some prick of guilt about Alice's deterioration. After all she knew about the business with the boy preacher even if she herself never went to chapel now. Or church for that matter.

'Doesn't he worry about you not goin' to chapel?' she asked out of the blue.

'My father?'

They had never spoken of this before. Dolly had always kept away from this area, from old Samways, from chapel.

'You used to go to chapel,' she said.

'Yes, but before the war. Till I joined up.'

He was reluctant to talk about it, she could see that.

'Don't you go on church parades? In the army?'

'Yes.'

'Well, then,' she said with what seemed a faint smile of success, 'ye could just as easily go to chapel.'

Hector glanced over the wall towards the harbour and then across towards the shipyards with their huge derricks outlined against a leaden sky. He did not answer her. But she was not to be diverted.

'I mean for form's sake, ye could go, couldn't ye? While you're at home.'

He grunted, though it was difficult to tell whether that was to signify agreement or disagreement.

'Well?' Dolly asked, pursuing the subject. 'You could go. And it would please your father.' ·

As if she cared about chapel or about pleasing the old man.

'It would please him,' she repeated.

'Would it?'

Hector came to a sudden stop. His pleasant relaxed expression had disappeared.

'Dolly,' he said sadly, 'it may be that my army days are over. The Medical Board may just say thanks and goodbye, any day now.'

Hector had spoken to her very rarely about the Medical Board, what decision they might reach. In the ten weeks since they had met, he had referred to it perhaps two or three times and then only briefly. He felt well enough now after three months' leave and the wounds were less severe than had been thought. It was fifty-fifty. The Board might think an injury to the lung to be permanently damaging.

Did it show in his face, he wondered as they spoke. Did Dolly ever suspect how he really felt, his terror out there? If they ever told him he was unfit for active service, he would dance for joy. And he felt ashamed of himself.

Dolly thought he looked forlorn, like a child almost. She had never seen him in uniform but she knew just how he would look with his breeches and shining leather riding boots. He'd never talk about the fighting he had been in, and she never brought it up.

'If I'm home permanently and I start chapel going now they'll expect me to continue.'

And what if George comes back? What about that? If he had never gone, this would never have happened. No need for him to have gone. Not a married man. The army didn't want men with wives in 1915. And he'd been doing so well. But, no, all of a sudden, out of the blue, he'd volunteered.

'I've got to go, love,' he'd said. Simple as that. 'I've got to go.'

As she thought of it she was furious with him. With herself. Now, as she looked at Hector, she was furious with him as well.

They had reached the end of the pier and stood leaning on the wall. Hector took Dolly's small fist in his, occasionally kissing it as they looked out to sea.

'I'll stay up here if the army doesn't want me.'

She had not wanted him to say that. When she had first met him, just those ten weeks earlier, he had spoken of working in London after the war.

'Well, that's up to you.'

She tried to inject an offhand note into her voice.

'You're free to do what you want,' she told him.

'Am I?'

And then she had to blurt out the question. Simply had to, the question she had never before dared to ask him. Out it came, loaded with guilt and bitterness.

'And what if George comes back?'

She knew Hector had no reply to that. She had thought of it so often, knew that he too must have weighed it up. But never before had it been voiced.

Hector looked at the top of the cement wall where they were leaning. He scratched at it inconsequentially for a moment and then shook his head wearily.

Dolly shook her head too, sighed and nudged him, smiling reluctantly.

'Hey. Come on. I've got to get to work. I'm not a lady of leisure. I've got a couple of hours' cleanin' to do. Then I've got other things to do.' She squeezed his arm, 'I'm not like some, ye know.' She was putting the best face on it that she could.

It was not so difficult as Joshua had imagined to explain to Mr. McKie that he would not be leaving the school. Mrs. Weston had written him a note explaining what had occurred and Mr. McKie had only raised his eyebrows and said, 'Right, fine.'

In class nobody even asked what had happened to him because children were often taken out of school unexpectedly for one emergency or another. Only Mr. Pybus seemed slightly surprised but Joshua thought he was pleased to see him.

When he went back to the house at dinner time Mrs. Weston had a bowl of soup waiting for him. He had not been used to that the last few months: his mother, especially in recent weeks, often forgot what the time was and as often as not there had been nothing for him.

Mrs. Weston had little time to spare. She had to go out to work at one o'clock. Another cleaning stint. But she had already been to see the landlord of Joshua's house and found out that the rent was paid up to the end of the week. Most of the furniture belonged to the landlord: there was only a few personal bits and pieces to bring over, so little in fact that she would have no difficulty in storing them even in her small house.

'The Lamb' was in a side street just off Berwick Market, and even at ten o'clock in the morning it was full. They'd said there were beer shortages back in Blighty. Well, there was no shortage here. Only after a couple of minutes did the barman glance in Dexter's direction, seeing the tall soldier waiting his turn patiently.

'Bugger me!'

Guthrie was drawing a pint for a market trader and his arm froze. The last drops dribbled into the glass and he placed it only half full on the counter in front of him.

'What the bloody hell, Dexter? What you doin' here?'

Dexter grinned, waved over the head of another customer in front of him.

Guthrie had reached under the bar for a stick and now he came hobbling round, deserting his customer.

'What you doin' in London?'

He placed his stick on one of the small tables and seized the soldier by the shoulders.

'Sight for sore eyes.'

'Ye always said I should call in.'

'I did. But I never thought ye would. I thought you always took time off in France. All them mademoiselles. Changed your mind now, have ye?' Guthrie's eyes shone with pleasure and he laughed as he spoke. 'Gettin' too hot for ye, Dexter? The lasses, I mean.'

Dexter nodded.

'Somethin' like that,' he said. He put his kit bag on a leather bench and went over to the bar whilst Guthrie picked up his stick and made his way painfully back to his place behind the counter.

'See this feller?' Guthrie announced to his other customers. He jerked a thumb in Dexter's direction. 'See him? This is Rob Dexter. Hadn't been for him I'd've lost more than this.' He pointed down at his foot. 'Thanks to him I'm here today.'

The customers had heard the story before. Guthrie on the wire, his foot just a bloody mess. Then up comes the corporal. Snip, snip, he goes. And off comes Guthrie. But then a sniper starts up...

'That's enough,' Dexter said, shaking his head. He wanted no reminders.

'Too true, it was enough. More than enough if ye ask me,' Guthrie said, laughing loudly.

Dexter reached across the bar for the beer that Guthrie had drawn for him. He didn't want to remember. He was getting away from it. At least, he hoped he was.

The talk continued. For three or four hours as new customers came in none of them was left in ignorance of the fact that there was a hero in the bar. Rob Dexter, Military Medal, Guthrie's saviour. Not till three o'clock was there a lull. Outside the barrows trundled, cars hooted and made their slow way up the crowded street; the traders called their wares. But at last 'The Lamb' was quiet.

'Well, now,' Guthrie said, picking his teeth with a match stick, ' you've been a bit quiet about your plans.'

He pushed a packet of 'Black Cat' across to Dexter who shook his head, fumbled in his pocket for his pipe.

Guthrie was peering closely into Dexter's face.

'I know you, Dexter. Ye've a scheme on, haven't ye?'

Dexter's face was noncommittal. Only the tremor of his hands betrayed any anxiety.

'I know what it is,' Guthrie said at last. 'You're not smart enough to fool me.' He grinned sourly at Dexter. 'I'm not a kid, ye know,' he said. 'Ye've skipped, haven't ye?'

Guthrie stood up straight, folding his arms and studying Dexter. The smile had left his face. He understood the seriousness of the younger man's position.

'Come to your old sergeant, eh? Bit of advice? That it?'

Dexter nodded.

'I'm not sure about the next step.'

'Stay here for a bit. Get yerself sorted. Work things out. Go careful or they'll have ye.'

Dexter told him about the wad of leave passes he had collected.

'Good for the time bein'. I'll say that. Ye can stay here. I can give ye a job in here. Say ye're discharged.'

His pay book wasn't up to date, Dexter told him. He hadn't the company stamp. He'd have to be careful then, Guthrie warned him. Hope that if anyone pulled him up they'd be satisfied with his leave pass and a bloody good story.

They drank some more. To the platoon, to the regiment, poor buggers, but most of all to themselves.

'We've done our bit, Dexter,' Guthrie said. 'We have. There's no doubt about that. We've done our bit. Trust me. Your old sergeant knows these things.'

Dexter stared at an empty glass, played with it on the table top, not ashamed that Guthrie was watching his shaking fingers.

'What's me chances? Keepin' out of sight in London?' he asked.

'Pretty good if ye behave yerself, keep out of trouble,' Guthrie said at last.

He looked steadily at the corporal.

'If ye go up home ye've less chance. I'll tell ye that for nowt. Go up there and your chances halve. Less, mebbes. Don't go up there. Those small places, you're too well known. London, well, there's every chance.'

Dexter rattled the glass some more on the table top.

'I know the risks,' he said.

'Do ye?'

'Aye. It'll be ten years inside, mebbes. Or they'll ship me back into the line.'

'Wait a minute now,' Guthrie leaned across to his old companion, grasped him by the wrist. 'If you're caught, they'll ship ye back all right. But it mightn't be into the line.' He paused, staring hard at Dexter. 'They'll ship ye back and court martial ye in France.'

'Will they?'

'That's what they're doin' now. Ye can't be shot for desertion if you're tried here. They need you fellers back there. As examples. They can put ye agin a wall if they try ye in France.'

Guthrie sat back in his seat.

'Think on now,' he said. 'Better have another glass of somethin', eh?'

Good old Guthrie. Reliable old Guthrie. Tough as hell old Guthrie though no-one knew that in bed at night he still heard the dry crump and crunch of mortar fire; still felt the earth heave under him; still saw the oak tree, shriven of all its bark, shorn of every leaf, its colour bled away and way up in its highest remaining branches, the two bodies, neither with a shred of clothing so that there was no indication of whose sons might be suspended there, Tommy and Jack or Hans and Fritz.

4

It took him some weeks to become used to the rhythm of living with Mrs. Weston. His mother had worked hard, at least she had done until she became ill. But she had never worked such long hours as Mrs. Weston. Some days she left the house before seven; often she did not come back until six or seven in the evening. When she got in she would flop into the horsehair chair by the fire, puff out her cheeks and sigh, glance over at Joshua without a word and close her eyes. It was a kind of routine they worked up. Then, and only when he brought her a mug of tea — 'I hope ye haven't forgotten the sugar this time,' she always told him although he had only done that once — and she had taken her first sip, she would say what she always said, 'Just what the doctor ordered.'

And that was the signal for them to begin to exchange the day's gossip. Joshua looked forward to that. She was always so full of laughter and stories. Something funny or startling always seemed to happen to her or to somebody she knew or knew of. And she'd insist on Joshua telling her what Michael and Willy and the others had been up to in school, what Mr. Pybus and Mr. McKie had said and done. And then when she had drained her mug she would stand up and say something like, 'No rest for the wicked' and go into the scullery to get something ready for their supper. That mug of tea and their half hour's chatter seemed to revive her and she was ready for anything after that.

Some days, of course, it was rushed, this drinking, gossiping interlude. And so was the meal preparation. Some nights, there was a grabbed mug of tea and a slice of bread with sugar on it before they ran to the tram stop and took the long journey to the hospital where his mother still lay completely oblivious to them. For Joshua, these visits were grim. Only Mrs. Weston's constant chattering and joking made the journey to and from the hospital at all bearable.

On Tuesday evenings, Mrs. Weston went without fail to a house out beyond Claydon. It was strange to Joshua, who could not understand it. Mrs Waterstone, the owner of the house, had died but Mrs. Weston still went there.

'Just to keep the place up to scratch,' she told him. 'There's lots of sortin' to do. It's a big house, ye know.'

Other times she was asked to houses where some kind of special function was taking place. Once, for example, she had had to help serve at table at a dinner party at one of the mansions in The Village. It wasn't every cleaning woman who was asked to do that kind of work, Joshua knew, but Mrs. Weston was neat and graceful as well as sharp in her movements and he was sure she could do that kind of work easily.

'Ye should've seen me, Joshua,' she told him one night when she came back quite late. 'I'm sayin', "More soup, sir?" and the bloomin' soup's drippin' off me ladle onto his missus's best frock. Thank God nobody noticed.'

She had gone into screams of laughter over that. It wasn't like her to be so careless but she could tell a joke against herself. That night after she'd been working since early morning, she ought to have been totally exhausted, especially as she'd had to walk home after washing up. But it was her cheerfulness which buoyed her. She had enjoyed that dinner party and her rare carelessness so much that the next morning she told Joshua about it twice more.

Another day, when she had just got in and was having her mug of tea, a neighbour called in to ask if she could help out at the theatre.

'Do a turn, d'ye mean?' she asked with a straight face. 'D'ye want me to do me fan dance?'

Joshua blushed. He wasn't totally certain about fan dancing, what it required, but he knew it was daring. More than daring, in fact: it was rude.

But all she had to do was to go down to the theatre and help during the interval, cleaning between the seats, emptying the ashtrays, picking up the orange peel and the monkey nut shells and the tab packets from the floor. They were short of staff; this neighbour thought Dolly might welcome the chance of a couple of bob. She did. She went down just before the interval, did her work, saw George Robey, and then after the second house was over, cleaned up more tab packets, orange peel and monkey nut shells. Joshua, sitting up in bed when she came in, saw Robey's act through eyes heavy with sleep.

Occasionally, through no fault of her own, she was free in a morning or an afternoon but if work unexpectedly presented itself she'd go off at five minutes' notice.

'It's money, son,' she would tell Joshua.

But he wasn't to think her greedy.

'It's not greed,' she'd say. 'But ye've got to look after yourself. Nobody else can be expected to do that for you. One day, you're on your own. Ye've got to look after yourself.

And as if that mightn't be clear enough she'd explain that there was the present to take care of as well. You couldn't feed yourself or keep yourself or your house looking decent if you had no money. She didn't begrudge anybody anything provided they worked.

But the best day, the most important day for Joshua, was when she announced that they were going on a picnic. He'd been there about a couple of months and this came as such a surprise.

'We're goin' to Claydon,' she said suddenly the night before. And the next morning, a Sunday, she was more than cheerful. It was supposed to be a treat for him but she was as excited as any child.

Joshua pointed at the water tower, half laughing at himself and at the same time hoping to prove that he no longer believed what his mother had told him when he was younger.

'She used to say the giant baked his bread there.'

He looked at Mrs. Weston and Lieutenant Samways to see how they had taken that. He hoped they didn't think he really believed it now. He wasn't a baby.

'The things they tell ye when you're little,' he said, shaking his head.

He was suddenly conscious, sitting there on the grass, that he had just mentioned his mother as if she belonged only to the past. Even though he saw her, every two or three days, lying in the same bed, her eyes showing no sign of recognition, never saying a word to them or to anybody, she was another part, a separate part, of his life. And uneasily, he wondered if he wanted her back now.

The visits ... he did not recognise her in the bed ... she was not like his mother any more ... she was more like a stranger ... he didn't now really want her, this stranger, coming back ... and he felt weak, giddy, guilty.

'And my mother used to say that's where he ground his flour,' Mrs. Weston said. Her nose was wrinkled against the sun and she was shading her eyes with her hand.

They looked, all three of them, at the deserted stone mill just below the crest of the rise.

The Lieutenant, leaning back on one elbow, shifted his glance and looked seriously at Joshua hand.

'And isn't it all true?' he asked, his eyes wide open, innocent like a child's, a young child's. For a moment Joshua was uncertain. Did he, could he, believe in giants? Only when Mrs. Weston laughed, pushing the Lieutenant's shoulder with the flat of her hand, could Joshua be sure.

It was strange really, Mrs. Weston knowing the Lieutenant. When he had been introduced to him an hour or so earlier, when he heard the name Samways, he had been alarmed. He had thought at once of Mr. Samways at the chapel. His mother had been frightened of him and so was Joshua. They had seen him nearly every week in life until several months ago, after the Billy Moffat business. But the Lieutenant was different, not at all like his father. He'd been friendly to him straightaway, had joked with him as he was doing now about giants. And he obviously liked Mrs. Weston.

This was just about the nicest occasion he could remember. The sun was warm for the first time in months, the best kind of late spring day. When Mrs. Weston had suggested a picnic the night before he had been delighted. She'd had some eggs from Mrs. Rimmer downstairs. She already had some flour and she had baked some scones. They had bought a bottle of lemonade and they had packed everything in a carrier bag.

And now they were really out of town up here, out in the country, though you could still make out the priory and the houses on the other side of the river; you could see the town hall and other important buildings, and the smoke from the riverside factories, working even though it was Sunday, stained the sky. And all around if you looked you would see villages, pit heads, the glancing light from the tops of trains. But the fields and folds of grey-green land seemed never ending, the horizons so distant from Claydon Hills.

They had met the Lieutenant at the tram terminus. Mrs. Weston had seemed nervous when they went up to him and Joshua was unsure, still was after an hour or so, whether they were expected to meet him there. She had said nothing to Joshua about anybody else coming to the picnic, though on the tram he thought she was unusually quiet. Then when they got out at the terminus there he was, just standing there.

'This is Mr. Hector Samways,' she had said, appearing to Joshua not to be her usual confident self. After a pause, as if she was trying to recollect the information, she said, 'He is a lieutenant in the army.'

The Lieutenant had held out his hand.

'You know Mr. Samways' father, at the chapel,' Mrs. Weston had gone on, jabbering the words out as though she was glad to be rid of them. Her face was flushed and she had seemed to run out of words, seemed to be waiting for Joshua to cry out angrily at the mention of Mr. Samways.

'I'm not as bad tempered as he is,' the Lieutenant had said and as he spoke he turned his head away from the boy to give Mrs. Weston the benefit of what he was saying. But he was smiling as he spoke. 'I'm quite tame,' he added.

'Mr. Samways is on leave from the army,' Mrs. Weston said, talking rather as if she was addressing total strangers. As if to mock her, the Lieutenant sprang to attention.

'And he's a bit of a hero,' she said. 'He's won a medal.'

It almost seemed that she was scrabbling round to find good points about him, so that Joshua might like him.

'Have ye got it with ye?' Joshua asked him. 'Have ye got your medal with ye?'

The Lieutenant was sorry. He had left it at home.

But that was enough for Joshua.

And the ice was broken. And all the way to Claydon Hills, the Lieutenant had talked, more to Joshua than to Mrs. Weston.

The Lieutenant offered to carry the bag but he had not insisted and Joshua had held on to it right to the point they were at now, where they had put the Lieutenant's macintosh down and sat at its corners with the eggs and the scones and the lemonade bottle in the middle.

They had eaten their picnic and the Lieutenant told jokes and made fun of Mrs. Weston and she had laughed and blushed. Then Joshua had decided to go up the hill.

After he had been across to the top of the hill, by the grey-white stone wall, and gazed out to sea for ten minutes or so, Joshua came back to where Mrs. Weston and the Lieutenant were sitting. They had scarcely moved all afternoon and now they were engaged in a quiet conversation.

'No worse a life than any other, soldiering,' the Lieutenant was saying to her as he lay in the meadow, his jacket folded neatly under his head. 'There are discomforts but lots of jobs have their discomforts.'

Mrs. Weston, sitting upright and running her hands under her thighs as if to ensure that her dress gave no sign of forwardness, smiled at Joshua as if she was glad to see him back.

'For instance,' the Lieutenant went on, sucking at a blade of grass, 'your work is as hard as soldiering. Don't worry, I've seen you at work.'

Before she could reply, he had sat up and seized both of her hands and although she tried to pull them away, his grip was too strong. Now her face was pink with embarrassment and she turned to Joshua who was just sitting down beside them. It was as though she feared he would disapprove of such behaviour. She pulled her hands more roughly than she needed to release them from the Lieutenant's grasp.

'I'm not going to hurt them,' he laughed. 'But look at them.'

She looked at her hands. Joshua looked at them too. They were like his mother's for just like his mother, Mrs. Weston had started work at thirteen. Though not at the same house. Not even in the same part of the country. But kitchen maids both of them. Lowest of the low in large residences. These days Mrs. Weston cleaned a day here, half a day there. Different houses nearly every day. His mother did the same, when she was well. Every day of the week they had both somewhere to go, somewhere to clean. Most days they blackleaded other people's stoves and grates, washed front paths, whitened steps, polished door brasses, swilled stone flagged larders, scrubbed kitchen benches. They made beds, polished chairs, tables, sideboards. And now sitting on Claydon Hills Joshua looked at Mrs. Weston's fingers, at the cracked skin, the immoveable grime and grease. In winter she would have chilblains. His mother always did.

'Go on,' the Lieutenant, still with a smile in his voice, urged her. 'Look at them.'

No different from any other woman's hands, Joshua thought. Only when she went out, she wore gloves usually. He'd noticed that. He'd noticed it the first time he saw her in Mr. Forsyth's office.

'I don't want to talk about that, Hector,' Mrs. Weston said, her tone unusually high pitched and irritable. 'Don't spoil it.'

For a moment Joshua wondered about George whom he had never met but about whom Mrs. Weston sometimes spoke. Private George Lawson Weston. Missing. Believed killed. Mrs. Weston could not understand him. He had volunteered.

Now the Lieutenant's voice was quieter.

'I'm sorry,' he said gently. 'You should be proud of those hands. They're like your campaign medals.'

Campaigns. Mr. Pybus was always on about campaigns. This campaign, that campaign. Campaign in France. Campaign in Italy. In Palestine, Serbia, Gallipoli. Will I ever be on some kind of campaign? Like George Lawson Weston? And the Lieutenant.

'... people have all got their value. You mustn't think signs of work are anything to be ashamed of ...'

Was the Lieutenant really a hero? He was nice and kind and quite jolly. But a hero? He had a medal so he must be brave. But he didn't look like one. He was a bit thin and fair for a hero. His moustache was light coloured not a ferocious black one. Sometimes Mr. Pybus put up pictures of heroes, stuck them on the wall with drawing pins. Sir Lancelot. Sir Bedivere. The Knights of King Arthur. And the explorer Scott. He had shown them pictures in books of some old Greeks and Trojans. Achilles. Hector. People like that. But this Hector did not look like the Hector in the book. He, the old Greek one, was strong and dark and fierce looking. He carried a short sword and a round shield. On his breastplate and those things on his legs, there were designs, fruit, angels' heads, arrows. This Hector was not like that. Not fierce. He could not imagine the old Hector sitting up and reaching out to tousle a woman's hair the way this one in front of him was doing.

'D'ye know about Hector in the Trojan War?' Joshua asked suddenly.

And the Lieutenant looked up from Mrs. Weston's hands, halfsmiling and nodding.

'He got killed.' Joshua informed them. 'They tied his body to a chariot and pulled it round the walls of Troy.'

He waited for a response, but neither of the others spoke.

'It was cruel, wasn't it?' he asked when it was obvious they had nothing to say.

'Yes, it was,' the Lieutenant conceded.

Dolly was inspecting the palms of her hands and did not look up. For a moment they all three sat in silence.

'Can I go up to have another look over the wall?' Joshua asked. He liked them, Mrs. Weston and the Lieutenant. He liked them very much but they were content just to sit there and talk. But they didn't seem interested in Hector the Trojan. 'I just want to see if there's any ships.'

And Mrs. Weston, turning to him, her eyes shining, laughed and squeezed his hand.

'Course ye can,' she said.

Suddenly Joshua thought he had never seen her look as she did now. Usually she looked his mother's age but now she appeared to be young, like a girl almost. She was pleased, excited.

'Go on,' she said to him. 'You go up there and have a look. Let us know if there's any ships.'

When he got to the wall he turned to see if they would wave. Or if they had forgotten him. He had wondered as he climbed up the slope if they were so occupied talking to each other that they would forget him. He had been unable to make himself look back just in case he would see that they had put him out of their minds. They might never think about him, never turn in his direction. So as he walked up the grassy incline, he had kept his eyes on the wall ahead. For five minutes, since leaving them, he had never risked a backward look in their direction. But once he reached the wall, placing his hands on its rough texture, still cool despite the sun, he took in at one quick glance the grey sea, its rough white caps, and then breathed in deeply before swinging round and seeing them sitting down there, quite small, in the distance. They were looking up at him. And they waved to him, both of them, Mrs. Weston and the Lieutenant, for quite a long time. And he wanted to laugh and cry out with joy. But he just waved back.

At the afternoon's end as they made their way back down the stony track to the tram terminus, they were, all three of them, a little lightheaded with happiness. For the last half hour they had laughed so much. The Lieutenant had put himself out to be especially funny and Joshua had for much of the time tried to join in and match the Lieutenant's wit. But it was Mrs. Weston who had seized the day, who transformed it with her happiness.

Now, on the way home, it took little to set her off into explosions of laughter. Joshua had never seen her so obviously happy. She would be one minute clinging to the Lieutenant's arm, gazing up at him fondly and the next she would burst into quite helpless giggles, at first pulling herself away and then just as randomly moving closer to him, resting her forehead on his shoulder whilst he smiled over her head, winking at Joshua.

'You're quite the jolliest girl I know,' the Lieutenant said to her. As he said that he wore his serious look.

Mrs. Weston reached to her ear, and took a strand of hair between her fingers. She stretched it across her upper lip and grinned across at Joshua.

'Oh ho,' she said and her eyes sparkled. 'I say, quite the jolliest girl you know. Is that really so, old bean?'

The Lieutenant was not prepared for that. He looked at her, uncertain of her. Was she making fun of him?

Of course she was.

But Mrs. Weston released the strand of hair and now she was smiling at him understanding his confusion.

'And you're quite the nicest lad I know,' she told him.

The Lieutenant took her by the hand.

'I meant what I said,' he told her.

Mrs. Weston closed her eyes, leaned closer into his shoulder, smiling quietly to herself.

'And I meant what I said,' she murmured, 'every blinkin' word.'

Then she pulled herself free of the Lieutenant, tears of sheer happiness almost blinding her. She staggered over to where Joshua walked at the lane's edge. She gathered him in her arms.

'I love you,' she crooned in his ear and she kissed him hard on each cheek. And she was serious now: she meant what she was saying. 'You're a lovely lad.'

It was a special moment. Joshua had never before felt like this about Mrs. Weston. To him she had seemed just like any other grown-up; after all, she was not much younger than his mother. Yet today, she seemed more like an older sister.

Always after that moment he felt that way about her although he never made any mention of it. Though he would always, when speaking to her, continue to call her 'Mrs. Weston', in his head and in his heart she would be forever 'Dolly'.

Joshua heard the knocking long before he got out of bed. Whoever it was knocked twice and he heard Dolly calling out as she went downstairs, 'Hold on, man, hold on. It's not the end of the world.' He heard her open the glass door and then heard the tussle with the bolt, the key in the lock. When the door opened with a kind of rushing, sticking sound, he heard her say something like, 'Oh! Oh! What's this then?'

And then a sudden silence fell.

He began to wonder if whoever it was that knocked had gone away quickly because there was no more conversation. It was almost as if she had been spirited away too because he didn't hear her voice any more. Then he made out the sound of the door closing quietly and he heard her trudging upstairs.

When he went through for his breakfast, she was sitting at the table, a cup of tea in front of her. She was unusually still. He was used to seeing her bustling about, talking as she went, nineteen to the dozen. Sometimes he wondered if she talked so much just for his benefit, to cheer him up. He was half sure that this was the case. His mother talked a lot as well ... used to, he reminded himself, she used to talk a lot before she lay in that bed staring at nothing, speaking to no-one but that was a different kind of talking. Dolly was usually full of jokes about people, about the funny things they did, the funny things she had done or heard about, not just in the distant past, not just when she was a little girl, but last week, yesterday even. And usually she went on chattering as she banked up the fire or tidied round or got ready to go out on one of her cleaning jobs. But today, she just sat there. When he went in she smiled at him in a quiet sort of way. She got up and poured his tea and gave him a slice of bread.

'There's some jam if ye like. Or drippin',' she told him.

She sounded so strained.

Briefly he wondered if everything was all right. Something was seriously wrong, that much he could see. Was it his mother? Or had Dolly been thinking that he'd been there long enough? Mebbes, he thought, she hadn't bargained for him being there so long. Oh yes, she'd said to him that first morning that she would look after him. But people sometimes changed, he knew that. What if she didn't want him staying on? He remembered the picnic only a week ago, how he had gone up the slope to the wall. When he looked back, they had waved to him. But what if that was the Lieutenant's doing? And on the way back, she'd hugged and kissed him. And he remembered what she'd said then about loving him. A lovely lad, she'd called him. But what if she hadn't meant it? What if the Lieutenant had not been there? What if for all these weeks she had been regretting taking him in and had been hiding her feelings? And anyway, they hadn't ever really discussed how long he would stay there. Sometimes, he had wanted to ask, come straight out with it. Because now, he liked being with her, in her home. But he would have liked to know, without any doubt, how long she would keep him. It was on the tip of his tongue sometimes, the questions, 'Are ye sick of me? Do ye want me to go?'

Should he ask her now, this morning?

And if she said, 'Yes. I think it's time ye went,' what would he do? Where would he go? The bread in his mouth formed into a ball of paste; no matter how much he chewed it he could not swallow it. It just went round and round in his mouth, just as the questions circulated in his mind.

Dolly came in from the scullery.

'I think I should tell ye,' she said — she was wringing a tea cloth tightly in her hands — 'I've had a telegram.'

Me mam? A telegram from me mam? About her?

'The War Office. They've confirmed it. About George. He's not missin' any longer.'

Wasn't about his mother. Nor about him.

'He's dead. They've said so. Officially.'

Not about him. She was not silent this morning because she was angry about him or sick of him. He felt relieved, glad, and he swallowed the bread in his mouth.

'I'm very sorry, Mrs. Weston,' he said. He wondered if he ought to say she should be proud of him, the way Mr. Pybus said they should be proud of the dead. But the words didn't come.

When he came in for his dinner, Dolly had made a special effort. Usually she was out and she left him a piece of bread and something to put on it and there was usually a small kettle on the fire ready to be boiled. But today there was a tablecloth — one of her mother's, she said; her mother had given it to her when she got married — and the knife blades and the forks and spoons were shining. And she was there, not out at work.

As he came in, she was taking a pot pie out of its cloth. There was not much meat in it but it beat sandwiches any day.

'It's no good bein' miserable, is it?' she asked him. 'Especially when things are bad.'

It was a sort of joke but he did not know if he should laugh.

'Have ye not been to work?' It was obvious that she had not but Joshua felt he ought to ask.

She shook her head.

'No. I didn't go. I sent a message to let them know. Then, of course, I had the whole mornin'. So I set to.' She nodded at the table. 'Not often you're treated like royalty,' she said.

Treated like royalty. She must like him. There was no doubt now. She didn't want to be rid of him.

Now he wanted to say something kind to her, to show her how much he loved her.

'Ye look nice today,' he said. 'Really nice.'

Of course she was always smart. She was always neat, made the best of herself. But he thought it would cheer her up if he told her how smart she looked.

Dolly smiled at him.

'It's this skirt,' she said. She was wearing a tan skirt and an eau-de-nil blouse, buttoned at the collar. 'Ye've not seen it before. Nice colour, isn't it?' She looked down fondly at her lap, fingering the material.

Joshua nodded. Really he had not realised that it was new, that he had not seen it before.

'It's not new,' Dolly said as if she could read his thoughts. 'It was one of Mrs. Waterstone's. Hector ... Mr. Samways ... he said I could have it.' She looked at Joshua shyly, perhaps wondering how much she ought to tell him.

She put the pot pie on the table and took a knife out of the table drawer.

'We were clearing out her wardrobe last week,' she said at last. 'Mr. Samways and me.' She was beginning to look sorry that she had begun the explanation. 'I didn't ask him for it,' she blurted out. 'There was lots of nice things, dresses, costumes, shoes. Lots of things. But I asked for nothin'.'

Dolly swallowed hard. This was difficult for her.

'He said it would suit me and I could have it if I wanted. But I insisted on payin' for it. I gave'm two shillin's. I've never had anythin' else from there.'

Joshua, confused by her obvious embarrassment, said nothing. He simply waited, watched her cutting into the pot pie, dividing it, keeping her head down so that he could not easily see her face. She put down the knife on the side of the plate.

'I go up to the house every Tuesday night,' she said as though impelled to go on. She drew a deep breath. 'Keeping the place straight. There's a lot of straightening up to do. It's a big house. Mrs. Allen's left now that Mrs. Waterstone's passed away.' As she looked up at Joshua her cheeks were burning red.

'It's nothin' bad, goin' there,' she told him, almost pleading. Joshua was sure it was nothing bad. Not with her and the Lieutenant. They were good people. How could she think he would believe it something bad?

She threw her head forward, covering her face with her hands. For some seconds, her shoulders shook uncontrollably and then, just as suddenly, she put her hands down, clasping the table edge tightly. Her face was wet with tears and it was drawn, almost haggard.

'I did love George, ye know. Truly,' she sobbed as though Joshua needed to be persuaded.

He looked down at the table, wishing now that he was back at school.

'He never should've gone. I asked him not to,' Dolly said, more to herself than to Joshua. 'I didn't want George to go.'

Some days later, a week or so, Dolly had a letter. It came with the half past four delivery: Joshua had seen the postie on his way from school.

'It's from his C.O.,' she told him. 'The letter. It's from George's C.O.' Her voice was flat and the words sounded tired.

She reached over and passed the letter to Joshua.

George was dead, the C.O. wrote. Or rather, Private Weston was how he referred to him. The C.O. could confirm it now. He was very sad for Mrs. Weston. They had found some proof that her husband was dead but did not say what it was. He had been laid to rest in a place that neither Joshua nor Mrs. Weston could pronounce but it was a proper cemetery. Private Weston had been a brave soldier, very popular with his comrades, a man they could all rely on. He had died in a noble cause. If Mrs. Weston had any problems she had only to write and the C.O. would do his best to help her. Finally he said the regiment was proud of her husband. And so was Great Britain.

'He's a hero,' Joshua told her. 'I think that's really good. He was brave and people liked him.'

He hoped that would cheer her up.

But in the night he thought he heard her weeping but he could not be sure.

The following day, the Saturday, she woke him quite early.

'Will ye do me a favour?' she asked as she leaned over the bed. Her face was drawn, tired looking, but she was smiling at him as he opened his eyes. As he struggled up, rubbing away the sleep with his fingers, she put her arm around him.

'You're goin' to do me a kindness, eh?'

'Aye. Of course.'

'Up ye get then.'

As he was dressing, she sat on the edge of his bed, telling him what it was she wanted.

'I meet him there sometimes,' she said. 'On the pier. Before I go to work. He's always there.'

In answer to Joshua's puzzled glance, she said, 'He just likes lookin' at the sea. He's always liked it, goin' on the pier.

It was not so much that he was surprised that the Lieutenant should go to the pier, but he had not known about their meetings there. She had never said. That was probably why she went out very early some days. Seemed strange, going all that way.

'Just for a bit walk,' she said, as if she read his thoughts. 'We have a stroll along the pier before anybody's about. It's quiet and nice there.'

She put her hand in the table drawer.

'I've got a note for him,' Dolly said, holding up an envelope. He recognised her laboriously printed capitals. 'Will ye take it to him? I just didn't think I could go today.'

She looked out of the window. It was a cold, grey day. Not much fun for the downstairs hens still gloomily scratching their way in the back yard.

'He knows about George,' she said abstractedly. 'About the telegram.' She fiddled about with the curtains. 'I've just popped in this letter from his C.O. I think he'd like to see it.'

Of course he would. One hero would want to know the fortunes of another. Heroes didn't always have to be alive: but they were always heroes. Only a week or two ago Mr. Pybus had told them about Beowulf's last struggle.

Against the morning's chill he pulled his cap down hard and wrapped his muffler round his ears. Daft in the summer having to do this.

Dolly fussed around him this morning, straightening his cap, pulling down his muffler from his ears, saying, with a smile, that it wasn't that cold. She handed him threepence although the return fare was only a penny for him. She stood at the front door, seeing him off, standing there till he reached the corner.

He ran to the tram stop. Funny, he hadn't run for ages. It didn't seem so. Not a real run. Like the night he had run with Billy Moffat. He often thought about that night, wondered about

Billy, hoped he might see him again because after that one time in hospital he had never seen him again. He would not like Billy to think that he had not wanted to see him. It was just that they had not been allowed to, his mother and him. And now, as he trotted through the chill air of that early August morning, through the searching bite of the North Sea air, his thoughts flickered to his mother, lying there in her hospital bed. And the black lacquer box, hidden in the coal house. He never liked to think of that, the money, how ever his mother had come by it, so much of it, why it should be kept locked away like that.

On the tram he tried to think of other things, of Mr. Pybus, the holidays from school, and the Lieutenant, but thoughts of his mother and the black lacquer box kept returning. Always there, in the back of his mind, was the fear that Dolly might come across the box. She would not light the fire at this time of year, cold though it was. But supposing she did? And just supposing, unlikely though it was, she took her bucket of coal from that far corner of the coalhouse. If she dug down deeply enough, her coal shovel might just seek out the box. And then what? He shivered at the thought of what might happen and felt guilty, thinking how much he now worried about what his mother might have done, how all that money had been come by.

It was no brighter, no warmer, when he reached the pier. It was quiet. He had never been there before at this time of day. Later it would be crowded. It usually was on Saturdays. Every Saturday and Sunday there were crowds parading up and down the pier and along the wind-swept, sand-strewn promenade. Now, as he looked down its length, at its cold cement, its old grey stone flanks, its rusted iron gates, the grizzled tops of its high walls, it was deserted, unwelcoming.

On one side of the wall, the water, where river met sea, was cold, steel grey, choppy. There was little life on it this morning, but further upstream he could see great tankers, a warship, the funnels of a huge troopship, the derricks in motion and he heard the clamour of the shipyards, already busy at this hour of the day.

Over the wall on the other side were the long flat sands and the low grass-topped cliffs, deserted and still. He had been there many a time with his mother. On her good days, they had taken off their boots and socks, hanging them round their necks and she had raised her skirt almost to her knees. Together they had plodged along the water's edge. Once a sudden gust of wind had surprised them and it had blown his mother's hat away along the beach. They had raced after it, a couple of hundred yards or more, and even then, when Joshua had caught up with it, the breeze caused it to skip away from his grasp three or four times. They had laughed about that, he remembered, just as they had laughed the time that an extra large wave had drenched both of them.

And he had come here with Dolly three times, and once the Lieutenant had joined them. But today, at this hour, he could see only a young boy walking a dog in the far distance and a little nearer a man stood at the water's edge, backing away from time to time as the sluggish waves of low tide lapped up the beach. It was not the Lieutenant, Joshua noted with disappointment.

The Lieutenant. He thought of him by that name now, even though he always called him Mr. Samways. Sometimes he used to think about old Mr. Samways at the chapel. It had taken quite a while to get used to the idea of a young Mr. Samways. Joshua would have liked to call him Hector. Just as he would have liked to call Dolly by her first name to her face. But they had never told him to. So it was Mrs. Weston and Mr. Samways. But even so, they were friendly towards him, made jokes, told him things. They liked him, he was sure.

'Joshua?'

It was the Lieutenant, standing next to him. He had not heard his approach.

'Good morning, Mr. Samways.'

The Lieutenant was puzzled: he was frowning with his head on one side as though he was going to ask a question, a strand of pale hair fell across his brow, and he flicked it back with a toss of his head. Joshua held out the envelope.

'Mrs. Weston's sent this.'

The Lieutenant took the letter, made a stiff sounding remark about the unexpected cold for the time of year. As he took it out of the envelope, Joshua recognised the letter which had come from France the day before. As he read it the Lieutenant shook his head. He took a long time with it even though it was only a short letter. Then he took a deep breath as he returned it to the envelope.

'I'm very sorry,' he said. 'Really I am. I'm very, very sorry.'

Joshua took the envelope from the Lieutenant's outstretched hand and put it in his pocket very carefully. It was too important a letter just to fold up and thrust away out of sight.

'Is Mrs. Weston all right?'

'I think so.'

Joshua wondered if he could mention that she had been crying in the night. Perhaps he should.

'She was cryin' in the night,' he confided, 'but not all the time.'

He observed the Lieutenant closely. He did not wish to give the impression that Dolly was too upset because that in turn might disturb him. He did not want the Lieutenant to be upset because he liked him. On the other hand he did not want the Lieutenant to think that Dolly was unfeeling. It seemed to Joshua that there must be some proper balance of grief. He hoped he had conveyed this.

'Well,' the Lieutenant said. 'I'm truly sorry to hear the news. Naturally. I hope that she will be pleased with the C.O.'s letter. Find it comforting.'

Joshua nodded. He had thought the C.O.'s letter was really good.

'I hope you'll let her know that.'

'I will. I'll tell her what ye said.'

They had begun to walk back towards the town. The wind off the sea this hardgrey morning pushed them from behind.

'You're going back now?' the Lieutenant asked.

'Yes. I said I wouldn't be long.'

The conversation was difficult between them. Perhaps it was only when Dolly was there that it flowed freely. Joshua had never been alone with the Lieutenant before and he felt that the silences that fell between them were his fault.

'Why don't ye come back to the house?' he asked out of nowhere, trying to block a silence.

'To Mrs. Weston's?'

'Yes. Why don't ye come?'

The Lieutenant laughed quietly, shrugging his broad shoulders.

'It's a bit difficult.'

'Is it?'

'Just a bit.'

Another silence. But very short this time. More a brief pause but pronounced enough to encourage Joshua to ask another question.

'Does she come to your house?'

It was unnecessary to ask. He knew she didn't. She would have said.

'No, she doesn't.'

The Lieutenant seemed amused rather than angry. As he asked the questions, Joshua would not have been surprised at some show of irritation. It was not his business after all and he really would not have been surprised if the Lieutenant had rounded on him. 'What's it to do with you?' he might have said. 'It's none of your business. Such impertinence.' But he didn't and though his replies were short, it was easy to tell that he was in no way put out.

'Why do you want to know?' the Lieutenant asked, quite casually.

'It's just, ye know, that day we went to Claydon. On the picnic. Ye met us at the tram terminus. And that other time, when we came down here. We met ye here.'

He instanced the other two occasions when they had met.

'You didn't call for us. And we didn't call for you.'

'I see.'

'And Mrs. Weston comes down here sometimes early in the morning. It's a long way.'

'You think I'm not worth it?'

'Oh, no. It's not that.'

Now he was concerned that the Lieutenant had misunderstood him, that he did not realise that he liked him, admired him, was glad when they were together, the three of them.

'No,' he repeated. There was a note of appeal in his voice. 'You're worthy, right enough. It's not that.'

'Sure?'

And now the Lieutenant was smiling down at him, his eyes alive with amusement.

'Yes, I'm sure. It's just that it seems a long way for her to come. It would be nearer if she came to your house. Or if you came to ours. It's nearer The Village than comin' all the way down here.'

As he spoke he realised the way in which he had referred to Dolly's house as 'ours'. Even as he spoke the word he recognised what he was saying.

'I see what you mean,' the Lieutenant told him. 'It's just a bit inconvenient.'

They walked a few yards in silence.

'She's a tough girl,' the Lieutenant said suddenly.

Girl. That sounded odd. Girl. She was nearly his mother's age.

Ahead of them, a hundred yards or so, the tram came to a halt. The conductor walked round to speak to the driver. One of them took the pole and raised it to the overhead lines.

'I'd better get a move on or I'll miss it,' Joshua said.

'There'll be another.'

'No. I'd better get back.'

On the tram he wondered if he should have dashed off so soon. The Lieutenant seemed to want to go on talking.

Dolly said little when Joshua reported back to her what the Lieutenant had said. He did not mention to her anything about the questions he had put to the Lieutenant about not calling for her. He did not even tell her that the Lieutenant had called her 'a tough girl'. He could not get his mouth round the word 'girl', talking about someone her age.

Down on the seafront, Hector's thoughts turned back to Dolly. He would marry her when the war was over. If he lived.

His mind moved to the boy. Last time they had met, Joshua had told him about the Romans, or was it the Spartans? Hector wasn't sure; how their mothers had told them to come back with their shields or on them. His mind shifted. One morning, seven or eight months ago, he remembered the whistles, the shouted orders ... he was just up the ladder and over the top ... a seventeen year old signaller and a forty-five year old infantry man following him ... and another time there was a night exercise ... seven of them picking their way back through the wire ... then, the heart-chilling star shells lit them up ... so many night exercises, so many letters to next of kin. He placed his hands on the rough sea wall and closed his eyes.

Joshua had saved the question. At least, once or twice when he had first arrived at Dolly's he had asked it, and each time she had reassured him.

'She'll be all right, pet. Don't worry.'

That's the sort of answer she had given him and after that he hadn't asked again, scarcely daring to in case what she told him was different, as though she might give an answer that he did not want to hear, that he could not bear to hear.

So he had saved the question. But today, he wanted to ask it again. But not now as they walked down the long flagged corridor which echoed their footsteps and Dolly saying, as she always did, how nice the nurses were, trying to cheer him up in this dismal place.

But once they were outside, once they had walked down the long pathway to the porter's lodge and beyond into the street, he would ask her once again.

'D'ye think she's goin' to get better?' he would say.

Because today, the question needed to be asked.

Because today, it had dawned on him as he stood at the end of the bed that every time he went to see her his mother's expression was slightly different, her cheek might be more pressed into the pillow, her eyelids slightly more or slightly less open, her lips just touching or just apart. Her body might be at a different angle, imperceptibly so, her head nearer the top of the bed or a knee ever so much more close to the bed's edge.

Yet though he noted these changes he never saw the most minimal movement when he was there. It was almost as if to spite him, as if when he was not there, she moved around as she liked, probably even talked. It wasn't so. It couldn't be. But it was not how he wanted her. If each time he came she was exactly the same he could have borne it. Or if when he came she altered her position as he stood there, watching her from the foot of the bed, he could have put up with that. But it was as if what life she had she kept for when he was absent. All his mother presented him with were different attitudes of death.

That was how he thought of her now.

As if she was dead.

And when he came to ask the question, which he felt he had to ask, he wondered if he wanted Dolly to answer, something like, 'It won't be long now. I'm afraid she's not long for this world.'

But when they passed the porter's lodge and walked along the road outside, he found he could not ask.

A great fat tear rolled down his cheek.

Dolly leaned over him.

'Don't worry, pet,' she said. 'Don't worry.'

5

Since coming back after the summer holiday things had felt different. Mebbes because he was properly settled at Dolly's now. At first he'd never imagined it possible. He thought about that day he'd first arrived there and they'd talked. He hadn't been able to think of his mother being away for a week even, yet now it was months and being with Dolly now was his normal life. He could scarcely think of any other existence. His memory of living with his mother, how it had been, was fading. Or when he thought of it these days, it seemed strange.

But at least the classroom smelt the same. It did this morning when he came in. There was the same smell of children in old clothes, the same smell of old wooden desks, of chalk, of wooden pen shafts with nibbled ends. The big ink bottle, standing in its usual place on the broad window ledge, was reassuringly permanent.

Joshua had sat next to Michael Lawrence for the last two years. He was a yellow-haired boy with strong fists and thick fingers, scarred from working with his father's fishing nets. Michael and Joshua winked at each other before turning to concentrate on Mr. Pybus, standing in front of the blackboard waiting for silence.

'Ye've all got your speeches ready?'

Mr. Pybus rubbed his hands expectantly and twitched his moustache. He had brought out another map. This one he had had from 'The Sketch' and it showed the whole Front, the whole line of trenches all the way from Belgium to Switzerland. He had made his own little flags, coloured them appropriately according to the nations involved. He had stuck these into the map to show the dispositions of the different armies and now his map was on the board, pinned there. The British Empire map which had seen such service last term was rolled up in a corner and he might perhaps return to that later in the year. But today it was the talks entitled

'The Western Front'. Even those boys and girls who had lost fathers and brothers ought to feel glad to give such a talk, Mr. Pybus had assured the class. It would prove that English boys and girls had the ability to stick it out no matter what the odds, that English boys and girls had the spirit of sacrifice.

'Now, who's going to be first?' Mr. Pybus asked.

Not me, Joshua prayed. He had no wish to stand up in front of everybody. There were other matters on his mind. Going to see his mother. At first he had been worried and just hoped that one day her eyes would light up and she would speak to him. Often he wondered what it was he would like her to say. And he hoped it wouldn't be verses or anything about the people in the street or Mr. Samways. Especially Mr. Samways because he was the Lieutenant's father and he liked the Lieutenant very much and it would embarrass him if she started talking about his father. But what did he want her to talk about? Mebbes she could explain the box at least. But he couldn't really think about anything he would really like her to say. And ... he hated to admit it ... going to see her ... she was like a stranger now.

A girl called Lizzie Ricks was telling them about the brave soldiers. They lived in trenches and sang songs like 'It's a long way to Tipperary'. She sang the chorus for them.

Mercer Charlton told them about his uncle. It was his mam's only brother and he was sixteen and a half when he joined the army. He had lied about his age but he would not have gone if he hadn't lost his job in the chemical works. Somebody asked Mercer why his uncle had lost his job but Mercer didn't know. Anyway, his uncle had lost an arm and was home again. But he was proud to have been at the Front. No, he didn't have a job. No, he wasn't eighteen yet.

Mr. Pybus was very satisfied with the way in which the first two pupils had spoken out. Just the way he had told them to. They had stood up straight, hands by their sides, heads up, nicely balanced. And their gestures were very good, Mr. Pybus told them. When Lizzie had said 'British soldiers' she had cast her left arm away from in front of her and held it out to the side and when Mercer had said his uncle was proud to have served his country, he had placed his right hand on his heart.

'That's the secret of making a speech,' Mr. Pybus said. 'That's the way to make it tell. Good posture, good gestures.'

There was more about the heroics of brothers, cousins, uncles, fathers. There was gas and mortars, rats in trenches. Messines, Cambrai, Bethune, "Wipers", the Somme, all fell from the pupils' lips.

Through the partition Joshua heard the infants reciting a verse from the Bible. The same verse, seven, eight, nine times. Outside it was early autumn. His mother lay there ...

'Questions, now?' Mr. Pybus asked.

So he had escaped. He had had nothing new to say. He would have had to repeat what he had heard from the others. No point in that really. And he could've told them about a real hero, about the Lieutenant with his medal. But the Lieutenant was his friend. The Lieutenant was not for sharing. And neither was George Lawson Weston, though he didn't know much about him.

'Come on, now. It's been very interesting. Questions.'

Mr. Pybus was peering round, his finger pointing along the back of the room, the middle area, the sides, the front.

'Come on, now,' he encouraged. 'Come on. Questions.'

... In the hospital, the last time he had seen his mother ... two days ago ... they had stood there ... Dolly and him. Dolly had had a heavy day, working at a house on the other side of town but she had got the tea, got everything ready, cleared away and he had helped her and then they'd had to catch the tram, changing at the market ... and like every other time, three, four times, every week, she lay there, less beautiful now ... at least, he didn't see her beauty any more ... just lay there and there was no recognition in her eyes ... didn't speak ... never recognised either of them, never a word to them, never moved ... he hated the visits ... they worried him.

'Joshua Slater. Come on now. Let's have a question.'

Mr. Pybus flicked his moustache impatiently.

... didn't want her to speak to him ... didn't want her to break all these weeks of silence now ... ever.

'Joshua.'

A question.

A question?

There was nothing he wanted to know. Over the months Mr. Pybus had told him all he wanted to know. Today, Lizzie, Mercer Charlton and the others had told him more.

He shook his head.

'Now, come along, lad.'

Mr. Pybus looked at him quizzically, his head on one side, his hands on his hips.

'Yes, you. You. Joshua Slater.'

His mouth was dry. Words, phrases, disjointed, ran round his head.

'The Germans ...' he began.

He knew they were cruel, that they had murdered innocent people, women and babies, but at the same time they lived in trenches only a hundred or two hundred yards away from our soldiers.

Something the Lieutenant had said. He did not often talk about the trenches or the war. But once he had said something about how it was just as hard for them, on their side.

'... do they get trench foot?'

It was a desperate question. But somebody's uncle or father had had trench foot.

Mr. Pybus nodded.

'Of course they do.'

He seemed pleased to confirm it. He explained to the class the condition known as 'trench foot.'

'They have it bad as well,' Mr. Pybus said. 'It's not just our soldiers. So don't worry. They're not getting away with it. They're not in luxury in the trenches. Don't you worry about that.'

Mr. Pybus shook his head vigorously. It would be outrageous, he was saying, if only our lads suffered out there. Let the Germans stand up to their knees in mud and water, let them lose their arms and feet.

'Yes, they get trench feet and all the rest of it,' he concluded, half smiling at Joshua. 'It's as bad in their trenches as in ours. Worse in fact.'

Now why did he say it, Joshua would ask himself later. When he came to think about it, it had not been planned that way; you sometimes plan what you're going to say or not going to say. But this time the words just came out. Again, something the Lieutenant had said that day on Claydon Hills, the time he had told Dolly about her hands. He had said that the Germans looked no different, acted no differently from our soldiers. They put up with the same hardships.

It was that conversation which must have stuck in Joshua's mind, that which had led to the question and then to what he said next.

'They must be brave then,' he said to Mr. Pybus.

And worse, he said, 'They must be as brave as our soldiers.'

His tongue was suddenly too large, seemed to stick to the roof of his mouth, his left leg began to jerk and he wondered if it could be seen and his heart pounded violently. Could it be heard, he wondered. The whole class, every lad and lass in it, was looking at him. On his bench, the others stirred, leaning forward, craning to see him. He felt Michael next to him stiffen in his seat, heard him breathe in fiercely.

Then all the rustling movement that had followed his remark had suddenly stilled. Every back straightened, every eye was on Mr. Pybus who looked as if he had been struck in the face.

'Never in my life have I heard a remark like that,' he said. His voice was more sad than anything. 'That's a dreadful thing to say after all the sacrifices being made for you.'

Mr. Pybus looked down at Joshua.

'Never heard anything like that,' he repeated. 'All our brave men and there's the children of some of them in this very room and you have the audacity to say that.'

There was a heavy silence, impenetrable almost. No-one moved. It was as if they were overcome by disgust. That anybody in this room should talk that way about our side and compare them with the enemy. It was a disgrace.

'Traitor.'

Only a whisper. Only once. But everyone could hear it and Joshua blushed. What right had he to say things like that? He wondered what had possessed him. It was like the most awful swear words. And he had no father or brother or uncle or anybody in his family at the Front. What right had he to say that kind of thing?

'Least said, soonest mended,' Mr. Pybus told them, mumbling the words. His face was drawn, sad: he had been betrayed. His lesson was ruined. In silence he took out the flags from the map and placed them carefully in a flat tin box which had once held cigarettes. He took the map down from the board with deliberation, putting thick elastic bands around it and then placed it in the corner. Every one of Mr. Pybus' movements spoke of personal disappointment.

'We'll do dictation now,' he said, going to the shelf where their copy books were stacked. He was so deeply hurt.

At four o'clock, when he reached the gate, Willy and four or five others were waiting for him.

'Give'm a good hidin',' one of the girls shouted as she passed by them.

'Aye, a bloody good hidin'. Serve'm right,' someone else shouted in agreement.

'Haway with us,' Willy said and Joshua was gripped by the other boys.

'Haway,' Willy repeated, leading the way along the wall, not the usual way home. They were taking him round the back, away from the houses, over to where rank grass and a few stunted bushes grew, to the traditional place where scores were settled.

As Joshua was led away he heard other shouts, questions follow them.

'Chase them little 'uns off,' Willy snarled and two of the boys left them to disperse a group of questioning infants.

'Gan on. Get away,' Joshua heard them shout. 'Gan on or we'll be after ye .'

There were more shouts but they were from further off, boys and girls standing in groups. But as Willy and his party made their way across the grass towards the bushes they were lost to view.

'Ye're a bloody traitor.'

Willy pushed his face close to Joshua's.

'D'ye hear what I say? A traitor.'

Joshua shook his head. Somehow he did not wish to deny in words what they said. It would only support the idea that he was a traitor, defending himself. So he said nothing even when Willy grasped the front of his jersey.

'Ye're a traitor,' Willy said again, pushing and tugging at the jersey. 'What ye a traitor for?'

Joshua lurched forward, prodded from behind by one of the others.

'Ye'd better answer or ye'll be in some more trouble. What ye a traitor for? Why are ye on the Germans' side?'

'Ye'd better say,' came a voice from behind.

Joshua swallowed hard. What was all this about?

'Me mam's in hospital.'

The words came out involuntarily. He did not want them to think he was a traitor. He did not want them to hit him.

'She's been in hospital for weeks.'

Perhaps that would change their minds. Make them understand. For a moment he thought they had for they were all suddenly silent.

'Come on,' Willy said at last shaking him to and fro. 'Are ye daft or something?'

'I'm not ...' Joshua began, unable to finish.

'Eh?'

'What's he say?'

A pause.

'What'd he say?'

Willy laughed, staring him straight in the eye.

'What'd ye say?' he demanded. 'Ye're like a bloody foreigner, you.'

'Bloody foreigner.'

'Traitor.'

Is that how it seemed?

'Bloody foreigner.'

'Joshewah.'

'Joshewah, foreignah.'

'What's the idea?' Willy was shouting now, shaking him by the shoulder with one hand and still, with the other hand, pulling the front of his jersey. 'Ye're a traitor. Ye're on the Germans' side.'

One of the boys behind Joshua laughed.

Another had found a length of twine lying by the wall and he had twisted it into a succession of thick loops. He slashed it across the back of Joshua's legs.

When Willy went sprawling suddenly backwards, when the blood spurted from his nose, when he lay there looking upwards with a surprised expression, Joshua hoped that would be the end of it. Hoped. Knew differently. And raised his fists to the others.

119

'Sod.'

'Bugger.'

'Bloody bugger.'

'Shitearse,' Willy snarled, struggling up and looking at the others. 'Get that shitearse.'

And on the ground now, all of them. Struggling. Arms flailing. Fists punching chests, forearms, faces, air. Nearly away there. Joshua wriggling free somehow, until Willy comes landing on top, giving him a punch on the side of the head. Someone sitting on his legs now. Another on his chest. A couple, Willy and Jackie Udall, struggling to keep his hands and arms in check and sitting with their knees pressing hard down on each forearm.

His shoes came off first. He saw one flung into a patch of grass behind him. He didn't see where the other one went. Willy tugged at his trouser bottoms.

'Wait a minute.' It was the Hogg lad speaking. 'Wait on,' he said, rummaging around to unfasten Joshua's buckle belt.

And down came his trousers, over his thighs, knees, legs, feet and Joshua all the while struggling, wriggling, gasping angrily, trying not to show himself afraid.

The trousers went over to the left somewhere.

Then his stockings went.

'Get his jersey off,' Willy panted.

They tried to pull it up over his neck but they couldn't and finally, puffing and pushing their hair away from their foreheads with the backs of their hands, they stood over him while he sat there, looking not at them but at his bare, bruised legs.

'Ye'll get this again, ye know that?' Willy told him. 'Ye're a traitor, that's what you are.'

'Ye're on the Germans' side.'

'Ye want them to win.'

When Willy bent over him, Joshua could see the blood trickling from his nose, could see that his lip was swollen. A slow gob of spit fell, landing on Joshua's shoulder. And the next gob went on his chin and neck. Again he felt the twine cut across his legs.

And then they were away, sauntering off, looking back, shouting at him, raising their fists. Before they went out of sight, across the road, some of them called out, 'Traitor.'

He sat up, thinking at first not about what had just happened but that only ten minutes before they had all been saying the afternoon dismissal prayer with Mr. Pybus. He looked down at his shoeless feet, at his knees, his white thighs. He took the spittle off his chin and neck with the back of his hand and satisfied with this, pulled a handful of grass and cleaned his face all over, his hands now shaking.

Had he really said something so terrible? It had just slipped out. He didn't really think the Germans could be as brave as Englishmen, knew that they couldn't be. For a start, there were more Germans than Englishmen. Mr. Pybus had told them so. And they were more warlike. They liked going to war, liked fighting, so it wasn't so hard for them as it was for Englishmen who liked, Mr. Pybus had said, peaceful pursuits. But when we were roused, we were lions. Brave like lions.

Joshua looked around. His trousers were lying in the middle of a huge clump of nettles. How would he ever reach them? He walked to the edge of the nettles. What if he couldn't get them? Would he have to go back? It was too much, too awful to think about. He hung his head down and more tears rolled down his cheeks.

'Joshua.'

The first time he heard his name called he took no notice. It did not register. Only on the second calling did he look around to see Dolly standing there. She looked pale, anxious, but she tried one of her usual smiles. It seemed an age that she stood there, in her tan skirt and her brown shoes, ever so much smarter than his mother ever was. She walked over to where he stood, him in his shirt tails down to his knees and his rumpled jersey with blood — not his — on the collar.

'I asked some bairns where ye were. I wanted to meet ye at school,' Dolly said, speaking very fast. 'I was a bit late but they said ye'd come over here.'

Joshua ran a finger under his nose and looked over at the nettlebed.

'Just a minute,' she said. She looked around. 'Give me a hand.' She pointed in the grass near her. There was a plank just visible. 'Come on,' she told him, placing her hand on his shoulder. 'Unless ye don't want to. Mebbes ye think ye can walk home like that.'

The same old Dolly smiling down at him.

Together they picked up the plank and carried it to the edge of the nettles.

'Right, then. One, two, three,' and together they swung the plank towards the trousers. There was a path now, narrow enough, but if he was careful, he need not be stung. He teetered along its length, at first holding on to Dolly's outstretched arm but then, for the last three or four feet, he was on his own, balancing, reaching down slowly to pluck the trousers out. Then, gingerly, he turned round and made his way back along the plank.

By the time he had his trousers on, Dolly had found his shoes and stockings. He sat in the grass, struggling to put them on.

'What was that about?' she asked him.

He shook his head, too ashamed to tell her.

Eventually she reached down and pulled him up. He stood there, nearly up to her shoulders and with her hand she brushed his hair into place. Then she took out her handkerchief and licked the end of it and rubbed a smear of blood — not his, he told her — from his cheek. At last, satisfied, she stood back to judge his appearance.

'Ye'll be wondering what I'm doing here,' she said though really he had not wondered, had taken it as perfectly normal for Dolly or any grown-up for that matter to turn up anywhere, totally unannounced.

'I've got some bad news,' she told him and her face was white. 'It's bad, Joshua.' She fiddled with his collar, straightening it. 'Your mam died in the hospital this afternoon. At half past one.'

Joshua drew away from her and looked around just to make sure he hadn't lost anything from his pockets, hadn't forgotten anything. He looked back at the nettlebed and at where the grass had been trampled down, where they had struggled only minutes earlier. He didn't think anything was missing.

And he didn't want to think about what Dolly had said. He went on looking at the ground. No. Nothing missing, he was sure.

Joshua came up the back stairs as quietly as he could. He did not want to waken her this early. Usually, always in fact, she was up before him, tidying round the house, getting things straight, getting herself ready for work, sometimes even doing a bit of baking so that she was up usually mebbes an hour or more before he stirred. But not this morning. The sun had scarcely risen and it was chilly. He had had to scrabble round in the dark of the coal house and the box, when finally he came upon it, had shifted its position. If it had gone on moving at that rate, he reckoned, Dolly would have been as likely as not to rake it out into the coal bucket in a week or so, once she started fires again.

Now with the box under one arm and his other hand on the rail, he mounted the stairs slowly on tip toe. Only when he reached the second last step from the top did he see her standing there as if she was waiting for him. She was wearing her overcoat and from her knees down he could see the white cotton nightdress which fell to her ankles.

'I thought somebody'd broken in,' she said. 'You're lucky ye didn't get a wallop with this.'

She was brandishing the poker and smiling down at him.

'Anyway, what ye doin' up this time of a mornin', eh? What's possessed you?'

He didn't answer, just shrugged.

'By, I don't know.' she went on as if talking to herself. 'Ye might as well not go to bed at all at this rate.' And half chiding him in this inconsequential manner, she led the way back through to the kitchen. Now she was filling the kettle, telling him that there was no point in her going back to bed, she would never sleep. Would he like a cup of tea, she asked him or was he going back to bed after successfully ruining her sleep. She expected he would go and sleep away until it was time for school. But he wouldn't let a poor old body like her have her beauty sleep.

The words fell round him, did not work their way into his consciousness. He looked down at his hands and arms, at his knees.

'Where have ye been?' she asked him but this time there was no mock exasperation in her voice now, no jolly irritation. She wanted to know. His silence had provoked her.

'Ye've been in the coal house,' she told him. 'What ye been doin' there? What a mess. Look at ye. Look at those hands. And your knees.'

He made no reply but she followed his eyes across to the horsehair chair, the box set foursquare in the middle of the seat.

She seemed not to have noticed him carrying it when he came up the stairs.

'What's that?' she frowned. 'Is it yours?'

Not exactly. It was not exactly his.

'It's me mam's.'

'Your mam's?'

'I found it in the house.'

Dolly's frown was deeper than ever.

'Ye've been to the house? This morning?'

She could not understand it. Another family had moved into his old house months ago, after Alice had gone into hospital.

Joshua shook his head, swallowed. Somehow this would have to be explained. He had been thinking about it, off and on, since he had first come here. He had tried hard not to think about it. But since yesterday's news, since he had heard of his mother's death, he knew that it had to be resolved.

'I've had it in the coal house.'

'Ye've had it where?'

Not that he needed to repeat what he had said for she had heard him well enough.

'In the coal house?' she asked before he had had time to answer the first question. 'In the coal house? When did ye put it there?'

And he told her.

'But why?'

And he explained why.

Dolly picked the box up.

'Ye've got the key?' she asked.

He took it out of his pocket and held it out to her.

'Beats me,' she said to herself, putting the key into the lock. She gave him another look and tutted and lifted the lid.

And there it was, such a sum as he had never seen before, note after note, coins. He flushed, felt sick, dizzy.

Dolly had poured the contents of the box onto the table and now she was counting it. When she finished, she sighed.

'Well, what d'ye make of it?'

Joshua stared at the floor. He had tried for months to make something of it, to explain it.

'Sit down,' she said to him quietly. 'Ye've no idea about it, eh?'

Again, looking down now at his boots, he shook his head. He felt unable to look her in the face.

'D'ye know how much there is?'

'No.'

The word came out scarcely audible.

'Ye don't, eh?'

'No.'

And this time his voice was even less distinct than before.

'Well, there's just over fifteen pounds,' she said.

Over fifteen pounds. Such a sum. He had thought it was large.

'And shall I tell ye how it got here?'

Miserably Joshua nodded his head.

'When your mam and me went on jobs she used to talk a lot about things. About you. And your dad. And oh, lots of things.'

He remembered her going out to work in those days before the cleaning jobs finished. He remembered in summer a wide brimmed straw hat, in winter a cloth hat with bits of tulle gathered on it. And always the same grey overcoat, the same leather bag in which she carried her pinny and her indoor shoes.

'She said a lot of things,' Dolly was telling him. She reached over, took Joshua by the hand, drew him to her, and then put her arms round him.

'Your mam had no man to help her. Nobody there after your father's accident. She did it all herself. She knew she had to save. What if she fell ill? What if you fell ill? And she told me about the black lacquer box. Funny that, eh? She even told me about that box. I completely forgot about it. Was years ago she first told me about that box.'

She tightened her grip on Joshua's shoulders.

'She had to save. It was no hardship to her, of course. She'd always saved. When her and your father came to live here, she'd had money saved up in that box. She'd used it right from bein' a little girl. She told me that.'

... hadn't stolen it ... hadn't kept it from him ... hadn't done wrong ... and when she had lain in that bed, silent, unseeing, he had thought ... had blamed ... hated ... her ...

'Is it not really a lot?'

Well, it was fifteen pounds, she conceded. Wasn't chicken feed. But really, it wasn't all that much. Some people earned as much as that in a month. But it wasn't to be sniffed at.

'Ye'd better put it away,' Dolly advised him. 'But not in that blessed coal house.'

She sent him back to bed for an hour. When he got up for his breakfast, he told her he had been thinking about the money.

'I've had an idea,' he told her. 'It is my money, isn't it?'

Joshua would always remember the black plumes, the black horses, the glass-sided hearse. It was a real funeral. And he was proud to be part of it, the author of it really. And relieved too. He had thought bad things of his mother. Mebbes this was a way to say sorry. Even if it was out of her hearing. In front, the undertaker in his top hat walked as if it was his affair, as if the occasion had been created specially for him, as if Alice in the coffin was only secondary and it was himself on display, with his shiny horse-drawn hearse. It was only a short walk from the undertaker's to the cemetery and Joshua was glad of that. Other funerals he had seen, there was a long line of mourners. But here, there was only Dolly and him and a straggle of those half-known neighbours who in her lifetime Alice, in her mistrust, had held at bay. They had collected for a wreath — pennies, sixpences, shillings — though it was impossible to know if this was out of genuine respect or simply custom.

The cemetery was located amid wide roads with plane trees where behind high hedges lurked sedate detached houses. On the left was the park, the bowling green, the cricket ground and at the next turn the broad highway with the tramway in the middle leading way out to the terminus where, weeks before, he had first met the Lieutenant. Joshua looked up at Dolly in her tall wide-brimmed black velvet hat with its heavy veil. She looked sombre yet so beautiful in her long black coat and black shoes with their tiny brass buckles.

His mother had never worn anything quite so eye catching but this was Dolly and she was different.

Dolly had accepted the veil as a present from Joshua; he had insisted, wanted to give her more but she had refused. 'No, a little present. That's kind. That's enough,' she said. And for himself, wisely, out of what was left, he had bought a pair of good hobnail boots.

The whole morning had passed in a haze of chatter. She had never ceased talking about the weather, her clothes, how much time before they would have to set off, which jersey Joshua was wearing, how she had let a few neighbours know what was on. She was always talkative but he had rarely heard her so talkative as that morning, from the moment when he had got up and gone to the kitchen until the very moment, after the long tram ride, when they arrived at the undertaker's.

And then it was so quickly over. What had happened at the graveside was lost on him. It went in a haze, a blur. He was home, or at least what he had so quickly come to regard as home, and the few women — not a man there — who had come to the burial had had their tea and boiled ham sandwiches, their home-made sausage rolls and their maid-of-honour tarts. She had made an effort, Dolly. She'd been all over for the sausage meat and the extra flour she'd needed. The visitors had not stayed long, perhaps because Dolly had provided neither port nor sherry but they all in turn came to kiss Joshua. 'Ye'll be all right, hinny,' or 'God bless ye, pet,' they had said as they placed their dry lips on his cheek, as they had pressed their wrinkled flesh to his, bringing their old ladies' smell to him.

And now only Dolly and Joshua were left in the room, in the late afternoon light.

'Don't forget,' she said. 'Your mam was a nice, decent woman. A good woman.' He was glad she had said that. He just wished he had been nice and decent to her in her last weeks, wished he had felt right about her.

Guthrie had shown Dexter the paper just out of interest as he did every week when the paper came.

'I never bother, man,' Dexter told him. 'The North East Clarion is of no interest to me.'

How Guthrie could retain any interest in it, after all these years away from home, Dexter could not understand.

These days the main interest in the papers seemed to be the lists. Column after column, name after name of local lads under headings like 'Killed in Action', 'Wounded in Action'; 'Taken Prisoner'; 'Gallantry Awards', 'Missing'; and 'Missing, Confirmed Dead'. And today, scanning the names reluctantly, fearful always of what he might see, whose name might be recorded, it was as if some agency focused his unwilling eye on the heading 'Missing, Confirmed Dead'. And out of all of the names, his eye lit on one.

'Private George Lawson Weston', he read. It gave his number and unit. George. It could only be him. Must be.

He wondered about Dolly, wondered how she was taking it.

'I really ought to go and see her,' he told Guthrie.

'D'ye really think ye should?' Guthrie sucked on the end of a match stick, moved an ash tray round on the bar top, with the tips of his fingers.

'I mean,' he said, concentrating more on the ash tray than on Dexter or so it might have seemed, 'you're known up there. Plenty of people up there know ye.'

Dexter fumbled in his pocket and brought out a packet of cigarettes.

'Aye. I don't know many people there now. I've not been back to the town for years. Except a few days when me mother died. Most lads my age are away anyway. Or dead.'

Guthrie was not convinced.

'Just the off chance, ye know. If somebody claps eyes on ye, it'll be curtains. There's lads ye've been in France with. Some of them'll be back. On leave. Discharged even.'

Dexter had opened the cigarette packet and had taken one for himself. He offered the packet to Guthrie.

'I'll only be there a few days. See our Dolly, see if there's anything she needs.'

'Mightn't be him, ye know,' Guthrie said. 'No good running off up there and findin' it's not her man that's dead.'

'It's him all right. There'll not be all that many George Lawson Weston's "Missing, Confirmed Dead". It's George all right. He's been missin' months. She wrote to me about it.'

And he ought to go up. Feller's sister loses her man and there's nobody else for her to turn to. It's a wicked old world for women on their own. And he'd been thinking, these past weeks, he ought to make a move. Wasn't fair on Guthrie.

'If they pick ye up, ye'll get it hot and strong. They'll not court martial ye here.'

How often Guthrie had reminded him of that.

'They'll ship ye back to France and bloody stick ye up agin a wall.'

Little Ernie Grayson, they put him in a hand cart.

'You're just the sort of feller they'll want to make an example of. Even heroes, they'll say, even heroes, and experienced fellers, if they break the rules, they've had it.'

Guthrie had gone over this again and again, but this time Dexter was adamant.

He'd go up, see Dolly, spend a few days there, just to see if she was all right, then he'd be off.

'Off where?'

'Thought I might try Ireland.'

Guthrie pondered that one.

'Don't see why not,' he said eventually. 'I know some fellers have managed that way out. By Holyhead.'

Dexter drew a pint for himself, another for Guthrie.

'Worth a try, eh?' he said. 'After I've been north. An' if they get me, they can't frighten me more than puttin' me back in the line.'

'Well, look,' Guthrie said, 'if ye've made up your mind, so be it. But hang on for a few weeks. Give me time to get make some arrangements. I know just the lad. Old Dickie O'Hara, he'll help ye.'

6

At the end of school these days, Joshua was either first out and away as fast as he could or he hung around till the others had gone. He didn't think they would try to take him on again. He thought that in spite of the fact that they had managed to take his trousers off, he'd given a good enough account of himself, bloodying Willy's nose and giving some of the others one or two punches into the bargain. And he wondered, though he couldn't be sure, if because they knew his mother had died, they wouldn't just forget about it.

On the Friday, he asked Mr. Pybus if he could do anything once school was over. Mr. Pybus was looking at some of their copybooks and ticking them or crossing them in red and writing remarks in his small neat hand. He was a bit distant with Joshua these days but he had talked to him after his mother died and had said several kind things.

'Yes,' he said. 'Ye can clean the board.'

There was a rag that you ran under the tap because unless you used water, you couldn't get all the chalk off. That meant a wait for the wet blackboard to dry before going over it with another rag to get rid of any chalk that remained.

'While you're waiting,' Mr. Pybus told him, 'ye can fill the ink wells.'

Joshua took the glass bottle — there was no need to mix any fresh powder — and went to each desk, filling each ink well carefully, ensuring that there was no wastage, no drops on the desk tops. Not that the desk tops were not stained with ink: that was not the point. The point was that there should be no waste. Mr. Pybus hated waste. He was constantly telling them, 'Waste not, want not'. And sometimes when he said that, Joshua looked around at the other boys and girls. Some of them wanted decent clothes; others decent food; many wanted both. Joshua knew that. Were they all wasteful, he used to wonder.

'That'll do now,' Mr. Pybus said, when he indicated that he had finished.

When Joshua got to the door, Mr. Pybus called out, 'Thank you' and 'Good afternoon'.

It was well after four now. There would be no one outside now. The lads he was concerned about, Willy and the others, didn't hang around. They all sold papers. Joshua had only once asked his mother if he could be a paper lad but she wouldn't hear of it. Tell anyone you sold papers in the streets at night and they would think you were really poor. He thought of them now, with their heavy bags slung at their sides, yelling 'Clarion, Clarion' at the top of their voices, running the streets in their bare feet. He wouldn't have liked to do that. If he had sold papers he would have worn his new boots. But he knew that Willy's feet were hard and calloused, used to concrete and cobble, to uncertain flagstones, to melting tar in summer and wet autumn surfaces. As he walked down the corridor and out into the playground, his mind was full of Willy and the others. So full, that he started when he heard a voice behind him when he went through the gate.

'Hey, Joshua.'

It was Freddy Forster, smaller than him, a little younger, wearing spectacles, his jersey and pants and stockings and boots better than anybody else's in the class. A bit of an outcast really; he seemed cleverer, quieter than anyone else. Out of place, you might say, though he was not unpopular. It was just no-one took much notice of him.

'I've been waitin' of ye,' Freddy said.

'Waitin' of me?'

Joshua could not believe it. They had been in the same class for three years. They knew each other, of course they did. But they scarcely ever talked to each other. Nobody talked very much to Freddy.

'What d'ye want?' Joshua asked him. He felt rather uncertain. Was there a catch in this? What on earth could Freddy Forster want? He had never waited for him after school before.

'Ye know the other day?' Freddy began. 'Ye know. When ye said what ye said about the Germans.'

Don't say Freddy was upset about it as well. Don't say Freddy was going to try to knock him down. Freddy wouldn't have a chance.

131

'What about it?'

A nervous grimace came to Freddy's lips. He looked a little embarrassed, almost as if he had regretted starting the conversation.

'Well, not everybody agreed with ye.'

If he was going to try to start something, it was a bit late. And he just wouldn't have a chance. But he hadn't taken his specs off. Not yet. When he takes his specs off, Joshua thought, I'll know he means business. But he would be able to manage Freddy easily enough.

'I know ye had a bit bother with Willy and them. I know they hit ye.'

'I hit them as well,' Joshua answered. If there was a story going round, let it be the full story. 'I didn't just stand there and let them hit me. I gave as good as I got.' He hoped that Freddy understood that.

Freddy reached up and took off his wire-framed spectacles.

And without a word, resettled them on his nose.

'I know ye did. I know about that. I think they were rotten to do what they did.'

Joshua nodded. He didn't want to go into that, didn't want to talk about losing his trousers.

'Anyway, the point is,' Freddy said, adjusting his spectacles, wrinkling his nose as he did so, just to get their balance right, 'the point is that I think ye were brave to stand up to them.'

Joshua didn't blush. He wanted to smile, to laugh aloud with pride when he heard Freddy say that but he knew he shouldn't do so and he kept a straight face. But he was brave. At least, somebody thought he was.

'More than that, I think it was brave of ye to say what ye did about the Germans.'

That part of it was best forgotten. It hadn't seemed especially brave to say that. Perhaps what he had been struggling to say was that if the Germans weren't brave, our soldiers lost some of their own bravery. He wanted worthy opponents for Mr. Pybus' English heroes. If the Germans were cowards, where was the glory in fighting them?

'I've got a confession to make,' Freddy was saying. He had lowered his voice. The embarrassed look had gone. Now he looked simply ashamed.

'I haven't told anybody about it,' he said. He swallowed hard, fidgeted with the cuffs of his jersey. 'Me granda's a German. And me grandma.' He swallowed hard. 'Nobody else in school knows. I couldn't tell anybody because I thought they mightn't like me.'

'I'm sorry,' was all Joshua could think of.

'It's all right. They're not bad or anything like that.' Freddy was desperately seeking for words. There was more to tell. 'Ye know about them nuns?'

Joshua shook his head.

'Nuns?'

'Aye. Ye know. They said that they'd killed some nuns and tortured them.'

Joshua had not heard that.

'They are supposed to have tortured them in the places they live in. In the nunneries. The Germans.'

Freddy was shaking his head as though to cast the very idea of what he had said out of his mind.

'Me granda and me grandma, they say they didn't do it. They say they wouldn't. Not the Germans. They think it's the French. They said the French might've done that but I don't think so. They're on our side.'

They crossed the main road in silence, each of them thinking about the cruelty of the Germans.

'They're good people, me granda and grandma,' Freddy resumed. 'They'd like to see you.'

See him? Two Germans? Wanted to see him? Freddy's grandparents were Germans.

'Where'd they live?'

'Here, man. They live in the town.'

Here? Living here with us? And could you just go and meet Germans when there was a war on? Weren't they enemies? He didn't think he'd like to meet any Germans. Not now. Not ever perhaps. Wasn't Freddy asking him to be a traitor? Mebbes even speaking to Freddy was being a traitor although he hadn't known Freddy was a German. Or a part of a German.

'Your dad ...' Joshua began.

'He's in the army.'

Was it possible, Joshua wondered. He had to ask.

'Which one?'

'Which army? Why, man, what d'ye expect? Ours. The English one'

He had not known what to expect.

'I don't think I can go and see your granda and grandma.'

It had taken some getting out. He didn't want to hurt Freddy with his neat appearance and his specs. He was a nice enough little lad.

'Ye can't?'

He couldn't be nasty to a lad who'd told him he was brave but it was difficult what he was asking him to do.

'I don't see how.'

'Ye don't see how? Why, man, they're here. They're not in Germany.'

'Aye, ye don't know what I mean.'

Joshua could not bring himself to look the other lad in the face.

'I can't go and meet Germans. Not when there's a war on.'

Freddy's brow furrowed.

'But plenty of people do,' he said. 'There's plenty see them. They go to their cafe. Doesn't stop them. They have a cafe in the town. Their customers see them.'

Joshua was not persuaded.

'What they called?'

'Forster.'

Joshua frowned. He knew some other Forsters. There was a family of that name two doors away from the house he used to live in.

'That's English,' he said. 'They've got an English name.'

'Of course. It's my name. But it's German as well,' Freddy told him. 'It's just the same in German.'

They had reached the cross roads. Joshua had to go straight over. Freddy, he knew, turned left here.

'Will ye not go to see them?'

He wished he hadn't been asked. He didn't want to disappoint Freddy. He'd never had any bother with him.

'I'm sorry. I can't.'

A car went past. A couple of workmen on bicycles were approaching. In the distance he saw a tram set off from the stop.

On the other side a heavy lorry rumbled by. Half way down the other side Rington's green van made a stately progress with the man up on the box, his whip in his hand, poised over the horse's back.

'Really, I'm sorry.'

There was a gap in the traffic as the cyclists went past.

'I can't go and see them,' Joshua shouted over his shoulder as he ran across the road. When he got to the pavement on the other side he glanced back. Freddy had not moved. He was just staring over at Joshua.

'I can't go and see them,' Joshua repeated, this time to himself.

It was one of those nights, the kind when you know you are loved and when you know you love. It was one of those nights when you can confide in each other, tell each other things that at other times you might have difficulty in saying. They could hear the bairns outside, in the street and in the back lane. Autumn games, evening games; Jack Shine Yer Light, Knocky Nine Doors, Tiggy, British Bulldog, Statues. Over all came the sharp call of a mother. The noise the young ones were making went on. The same woman's voice came again, louder this time, more strident, more angry. 'If you are not in here in two minutes, our Norman ...'

Dolly and Joshua had sat down each side of the empty kitchen grate – it was too warm yet for a fire – and Joshua had told her about Freddy.

'I don't know why he wants me to go there,' he had complained. 'I'd only get into worse trouble if people found out I was visitin' Germans.'

Even when Dolly had pointed out that Freddy's grandparents had lived in the town for years, he was still reluctant to go to see them.

'They're still Germans, but,' he had said. 'They're still our enemies.'

'Not Freddy Forster's folks. They're not enemies.'

Even so, they had had their windows broken on more than one occasion. Dolly had even heard someone say, 'Serves them right, bloody Germans'. Once upon a time, she told Joshua, it had

135

been quite a treat to go to the Augusta Tea Room in Zetland Lane just behind Prince George Street, but now she imagined they had very little trade.

'I do feel sorry for them,' she said.

'I'm still not goin',' Joshua told her, remembering what Mr. Pybus so often told them about England's enemies. 'I just couldn't bring meself to go to see them.'

'Well,' Dolly had smiled across at him. 'Things aren't easy to work out always. You'll have to decide for yourself. Nobody can force ye to go there.'

He was glad when she said that. For a time he had thought she was trying to persuade him to visit the old couple.

And then they had gone on to speak of other things. As the dusk fell, Joshua, scarcely able now to make out Dolly's features in the unlit room, began to talk of his mother, to speak about the last months of her life before she went into hospital. He realised now she had been ill. And then it came out, what he had kept to himself, what he had never wished to say, what he had wanted to remain his secret.

But it just came out, the admission.

'Before she died, I didn't like her.'

Another even stronger word had flickered in his mind, had almost reached his tongue, but he couldn't bring himself to use it.

He told Dolly how, when they had visited the hospital, he had always wished the visits over, how he had longed to be away from that mute, unseeing woman lying there.

And he wondered now if he was bad, if it was the worst sin of all, not liking his mother, not liking a helpless sick woman. Not liking. Hating. He kept pushing the word away.

And Dolly, as she always did, stretched out her hand to him, soothing him, with her soft, wise words. And he believed what it was that she told him and was comforted.

Then it was her turn. Only she told her story with gasps and giggles and nudges. She told him about the Lieutenant. About the first time they had met at Mrs. Waterstone's.

'I might never have met him but for that off-chance. I just went there to fill in. If I hadn't done that I'm sure I'd never have met him. There wouldn't've been a chance now because she's passed on, poor soul.'

She had paused there.

'Perhaps it would've been just as well if we hadn't met.'

Joshua was taken aback.

'Why? D'ye not like'm?'

Her remark had surprised him. He hoped she did like the Lieutenant. He did. Tremendously. It would be dreadful to find out if now she did not like him.

Again she did not answer immediately. Instead she stood up.

'It's dark in here,' she said. 'I'll put some light on.'

She found the matches on the mantelpiece and lit the gas. As she made her way back to her chair, she spoke.

'Course I like him.'

'Why did ye say what ye did then?'

She plumped up a cushion before she sat down.

'Just one of those daft things people say, I suppose.'

Now she was smiling across at him.

'Course I like him,' she repeated. 'Ye don't think I'd waste me time, do ye?'

'Are ye goin' to marry him?'

Her jaw dropped and she opened her eyes very wide.

'That I don't know,' she told him. 'And it's none of your business.'

But she was not angry; she was only pretending, he could tell. And he could tell that she liked talking about the Lieutenant. At least, if he asked the right questions.

'When did ye meet the second time?' was a right question to ask.

Well, she told him, they might not have given each other a second thought but for the Saturday evening in Prince George Street. It was early still, just on the point of dusk. And there were crowds out on such a fine mild winter day, people all the way from the market and down the whole long mile and a half to the pier head. Such a noise there was, such a bustle, such gangs of girls arming each other along, such numbers of families, mothers, fathers, bairns, such mobs of fellers, soldiers most of them, such laughter. And the soldiers and the girls laughed loudest of all.

And Dolly Weston, who did not then know if she was or was not a widow, stood at the tram stop outside Gildhorn's Emporium and wished she was younger than her late twenties, wished she was single and as daft as the lasses parading up and down the street. She'd just been visiting a woman she had never seen for years, since well before the war, since long before she had met George.

At the tram stop, she carried with her the memory of Bella Urquhart's face, drawn, lined, with overwork, grief and worry.

'I'll manage,' Bella had told her. 'Good job there's no bairns.'

And she had looked at Dolly, not needing to say more about her husband, dead in Belgium, and the five infants, three girls, two boys, who had preceded him over the last six years.

Dolly had clenched her hands together, her body shivering suddenly. It wasn't that it was cold, but she had wanted to get home, away from the street, away from all this laughter. The tram was waiting over at the far side of the market place, the driver and the conductor standing outside smoking their pipes. Dolly had known that if she went for it the tram would set off before she reached it and she would be stranded between two stops. She had stayed put, thoughts of Bella Urquhart chasing each other.

It was more a shriek of triumph than anything else from a trio of lasses, their arms linked. They had just passed by her and now from them came this piercing scream but it was the triumph in it that made it so arresting.

'They broke into a run,' Dolly told Joshua. 'One of them, the lass in the middle, she was holdin' her hat in one hand. Her other hand she had stretched out in front of her, towards a feller comin' towards her.'

They were shouting something, she couldn't say what, at the man, just a jabber of words and a pointing of fingers, starting first at the man as he came towards them and then when he passed by, they called out, stuck their fingers towards his retreating back.

As for the man he did not look at them. He never broke step, just gave a slight shrug of the shoulders in his heavy brown overcoat and pulled his homburg down more firmly over his eyes.

'Was it him? Was it the Lieutenant?' Joshua asked her.

'It was. And then, just as he passed by he happened to look in my direction. He walked on a few steps and then he stopped and looked back.'

'Mrs. Weston,' the Lieutenant had said, raising his hat and walking back to the tram stop. 'I thought I recognised you.'

Dolly had no idea how to answer. Even if there had not been that minor fracas, she would have been surprised to be greeted in that way by Lieutenant Samways, a man she had met only once. But this evening, there, with the girls no more than fifty yards away, she wondered if she ought to delay him. It must have been embarrassing for him. Or it should have been, she thought, but he was quite calm as if nothing had happened. Even so, other people were staring at him. Bound to be after what happened. One or two even shouted remarks at him.

'I should wear my uniform,' he had said. 'They don't like young men like me not in uniform.'

He opened his gloved hand. There was a white feather lying in it.

'What did he think of that?'

Dolly smiled. 'What d'ye think? You know him. He never gave it a second thought.'

'Did he bring ye home?'

'Certainly not,' Dolly replied. 'He saw me onto the tram and said goodnight. He raised his hat as I passed by him further down the street.'

And on the Monday he had visited his sister.

'I was a bit embarrassed,' she explained to Joshua. 'As usual I was up to me elbows in muck. The outside sink was blocked and ye can imagine what I was like.'

And Mrs. Allen had never suspected that whenever he called after that he stopped to speak to the cleaning woman. Mrs. Waterstone never gave them a thought. How could she? Her brother and a skivvy. Neither mistress nor Mrs. Allen knew that one morning the Lieutenant had waylaid his sister's cleaning lady on her way to work and that from then on, two or three mornings a week, they met and walked the cold, grey length of the stone pier. And no-one would suspect that now, every Tuesday, Dolly met the Lieutenant in the empty house.

'So that was it,' Dolly told him with a sniff. 'And that's quite enough for tonight.'

Outside there was still the laughter of the menfolk, the shrill shouts of children and over all a mother's voice, 'Do you hear me? Do you hear what I say? If you are not back here in two minutes ...'

On his last evening Guthrie gave him a name and an address, scribbled on a dog-eared post card.

'He's a good lad,' his ex-sergeant reassured Dexter. 'You look'm up. Tell'm it's me that's sent ye. Dickie O'Hara'll look after ye if ye tell him I sent ye.'

Guthrie had patted Dexter's shoulder as if to give him courage.

'When your lass is settled down, don't hang around. Give yourself no more than two or three weeks up there or some bugger'll start askin' questions. What's that feller on leave so long for? Ye know what they're like. No need for me to tell ye.'

Guthrie had paused, stared at Dexter, almost daring him to reject his advice.

'You get yourself out of there as soon's ye can. Take the train down to Birkenhead. Dickie'll see ye right.'

At Kings Cross, away from Guthrie, he felt more alone, more vulnerable than he had done in months. More alone, more vulnerable than he'd sometimes felt in France even. There were patrols of military police all over the station, picking up soldiers, inspecting their papers. Not that his papers wouldn't stand scrutiny. Unless they looked closely at his pay book and saw when he was last paid. He'd make up a story of course. He couldn't forge the unit's stamp, that was the trouble. But the leave pass was all right; he'd plenty of those still and that's the one that counted.

He was more confident of his papers than he was of his face and hands. He was conscious of them these days, how at odd times the cheek would twitch. They might wonder about that. And they might wonder about his fingers, how they sometimes shook. Daft if they picked him up on that, because if his cheek twitched or his fingers shook, it wouldn't be because he was frightened of the military police. He'd been twitching and shaking like this for months. He'd twitched and shaken when they'd given him his medal but nobody had said, 'You've had enough of this lad. You'd better go home.' He'd had to make that decision himself.

It was Joshua who spotted him first. They had just turned the corner at the top of the street, Dolly and him, and straightaway Joshua picked out the figure a couple of hundred yards beyond them.

'Somebody at the door.'

Dolly narrowed her eyes, peering the length of the street. There was quite a lot of folk about but she couldn't be certain if somebody was at her door.

'I need a pair of glasses,' she said. 'Are ye sure?'

Yes, he was sure. No doubt. He could make out, even in this fading evening light, Mrs. Rimmer's whitened front step. And he was beyond that, whoever he was. But he wasn't as far down as the bottom corner. Of course, he might be at the Charltons, but Joshua did not think so.

'I'm sure he's at our house.'

He was comfortable now, saying 'our house'. He did not even notice when he used it.

Dolly reached over, put her arm round Joshua's shoulders and increased her pace. But she wasn't all that certain, he could tell. She was hanging on to him, almost relying on him. That's how it seemed. She was suddenly nervous, pent up, holding her breath as she stepped out down the pavement.

The man at the door — they could see now that it was a man, tallish — swung round to face them. Now they could see a kit bag at his feet, a rifle slung across his shoulder.

Only when they were within feet of each other did the soldier make a tentative move, stretching out his arms. Only then did Joshua hear Dolly's intake of breath. Only then did he feel her hand stiffen on his shoulder.

'I knew it was you,' Dolly breathed, her voice both hesitant and happy.

The soldier laughed aloud, threw his arms around her, the rifle on his sling jerking and slipping down to his elbow. The kit bag, which had rested against his leg, slumped across the pavement.

Dolly was overjoyed, Joshua could see that. She was speaking to him so softly now, quietly, talking against his cheek. She gave a series of sobs, some little uncertain laughs, buried her head in the collar of his greatcoat. Finally she drew herself away, running a finger first under one eye and then the other, rubbing the tears into her cheeks.

And was this George after all? Joshua noticed the heavy dark eyebrows, the pronounced cheekbones, the hawk-like nose. Could it be him? Was he really not dead? Had the telegram and the letter from the C.O. been mistakes? They had even put his name in the papers, in the list of names of those who had been killed. And he should feel happy because Dolly was happy, that much was clear. And as he stood there, on the fringe of their joy, he just wondered about the Lieutenant. Was it the end now as far as he was concerned? Would he not meet the Lieutenant again? Because he liked him very much. Dolly wouldn't be able to see him again. Neither of them would see him any more, he was sure. Why, he asked himself, did George have to come back to spoil things? Although he ought to be pleased, he told himself, that the man had escaped death. And he'd been a good soldier. The letter from the C.O. confirmed that.

'This is Joshua,' Dolly was saying, looking at the soldier through her tears, gripping his hand, squeezing it.

The soldier hitched his rifle back onto his shoulder, nodded, unsure of who he might be talking to.

'This is my brother, Rob Dexter,' Dolly explained. It seemed so formal, calling him that, by his full name.

Not George. And not Henry, the one in the photograph, the one killed at Loos. This was Rob, the head and shoulders in the sepia photograph, the one who didn't look like his sister. She had blue eyes to his brown; he had dark hair to her fair. Joshua remembered what she had said about him.

'By, he was a live wire,' she'd told him. 'Always carryin' on, laughin' and jokin'. Always out for a good time. A bit rowdy, he was. But never nasty. A decent lad really.' She had shaken her head at the memory of him.

And now they bustled into the house, Dolly talking away as fast as she could, questions and statements tumbling out and no-one else with any chance to get a word in.

'... did ye have any bother findin' this house?'

'... have ye been waitin' long?'

'... have ye had anything to eat?'

'... ye'll be tired after all that travellin'.'

Dolly talking.

Rob put his kitbag and rifle out of the way in the front room, hung up his greatcoat, loosened his tunic and went to sit at the kitchen table, while Dolly bustled around, making tea, looking in the larder for something for a sandwich, still talking — '... never expectin' anybody this time of night. I'll get a nice bit meat tomorrow if I can' — still asking questions. Joshua sat on the cracket, staring up at the man in front of him, now unwinding his puttees and easing off his heavy army boots.

'Three weeks,' Rob was saying in answer to one of his sister's questions. 'I'll be goin' ... I'll be goin' back after three weeks.'

He paused with only one boot off, his fingers on the laces of the other.

'I'm sorry about George.'

He looked shamefaced, awkward as he spoke. He must have seen scores of dead men, must even have joked about death, dying and the dead. Yet, still when he mentioned George, the words came out in a tumble.

'I never met'm but I know he was good to you.'

Dolly, standing by the table, seemed for a moment at a loss for words. She shrugged her shoulders.

'Yes. He was good to me. There was never a better man.'

Never a better man. Never? Joshua wondered.

'He was always kind and thoughtful,' she went on. 'Just a waste, isn't it?'

Rob had turned back to his laces and loosened them. As he eased the boot off his heel, he shook his head.

'It's a waste all right.'

'I didn't think ye'd have heard,' Dolly said. 'He wasn't with your lot. How did ye know?'

'Saw it in the papers the other day.'

'Did ye?'

'My old sergeant has them sent every week. He's been down in London for years and they still send him 'The Clarion'. I saw it there.'

'In London?'

For a moment, the confusion showed on Rob's face.

'No,' he said, frowning as he spoke. 'This feller, he has them sent out. But his home's in London.'

Dolly was satisfied with the explanation.

'I suppose I'd better explain this 'un away,' she said, indicating Joshua. 'I'm afraid I'm stuck with him now.'

She pulled a face.

'Trust me to end up with a lad like that.'

And he didn't mind now that she spoke of him in that way, wasn't worried that she mightn't want him. Sometimes the feeling came over him that she might be tired of him but it was rare enough. Tonight, he knew she was only funning.

And she explained, with very little drama, with fewer extravagances than was usual with her storytelling, how Joshua came to be with her.

'I used to know his mam years ago,' was all she said by way of explanation.

She made no mention at all of the Samways.

'By the way,' she said, as her story came to an end, tapping Joshua on the forehead. 'Ye've just lost your bed. Ye'll be sleeping in the front room tonight. I'll make ye a bed up there and put a bit fire on.'

Everything seemed wonderful, sleeping in the front room with a mattress on the floor. Soldiers did that. And they slept round camp fires.

Joshua had been up first. Not that sleeping on the couch in the front room was uncomfortable but he had not seen Rob in daylight. He wanted to see how different the soldier looked when he was not in last night's gaslight. Or how much the same. Just wanted to see him again, imagining him in France, seeing him there ... So that Joshua, up even before Dolly this morning, took the milk jug from the shelf in the scullery and when he heard the milkman's call, ran down the back stairs and into the lane where two or three women were already queuing at the front and their children patting the horse, smoothing its velvet muzzle. If they behaved, these children, they might get a ride on the float. Sometimes the milkman could be persuaded, a man who spent his days ladling out milk from a big metal churn and telling bairns all over the town that he could only take one of them at a time. No wonder he was always late at the end of his round. But now it was early, the sun crawling reluctantly back behind heavy clouds and the first hint of wind promising rain later.

'I hear ye've got comp'ny,' Mrs. Rimmer from downstairs said as she and Joshua stood together holding their jugs. 'I could hear ye all laughin' last night.'

She wasn't nosy. She wasn't interfering. Just being neighbourly.

'Is her husband come back?' she asked, her eyes wide open in anticipation, dying for Joshua to tell her. Was Mr. Weston back from the war? Had he not been killed? She couldn't quite bring herself to ask such direct questions. 'I saw a soldier at your front door last night. I was just goin' to open the door to him and tell'm ye were out, but then ye came down the street, you and Mrs. Weston.'

Mrs. Rimmer, good hearted soul. She would've asked him in. How she wanted it to be Dolly's husband. It would make a happy ending. After a hard old life, she still looked forward to happy endings.

Before Joshua could reply to her question, she asked him again, 'Is it him then, her husband come back?'

Joshua shook his head.

'Her brother, Mr. Rob Dexter.'

'Her brother, eh? Oh, well.'

'He's been in France.'

'Has he now? Ee well, she'll be so pleased to see him.'

She smiled down at Joshua.

'Now, listen,' she said. 'When you go back upstairs you tell Mrs. Weston I've got a chicken for her. I'll kill it fresh for her.'

As Joshua held out his jug, he heard Mrs. Rimmer talking across his head to the milkman, heard her telling him all about Dolly and Rob as if she was well in the know. The milkman was laughing, made a joke, grinned at Joshua. But he had no thoughts now save of Mrs. Rimmer's promised chicken. He knew those chickens, saw them every day as he looked down from the kitchen and scullery windows. They pecked their way round Mrs. Rimmer's back yard and he always knew when she came out to feed them with a few handfuls of grain and bread crusts because then they squawked and fluttered off the ground an inch or two in their excitement. There was only a dozen or so and she locked them at night inside her washhouse. Joshua knew them all. Everyone of them was familiar to him. There was one, black as coal, a couple of absolutely white ones, and the rest were various shades of brown. But every one Joshua knew.

'Don't forget now what I've told ye about the chicken,' Mrs. Rimmer was saying as he stepped away from the float. 'I'll bring it up in ten minutes or so. It'll be lovely and fresh.'

Joshua muttered his thanks, hoping that it would not be the black one. That was the one he liked best of all. But when Mrs. Rimmer came up with her gift just a few minutes later it was no real consolation to him to note that it was one of the brown ones.

'Oh, lovely,' Dolly said, delighted that she would be able to give Rob a decent meal, or as decent as food shortages permitted. And for her reward, Mrs. Rimmer was allowed to meet Rob coming into the kitchen ready for breakfast.

'Why, hinny,' Mrs. Rimmer told him after a few minutes' talk, 'ye're a bonny fine lad and deserve more than she'll give ye for your breakfast.'

And at that she scampered downstairs and came back up again, all in the space of a minute, with a couple of brown eggs in her hand.

'I bet ye cannot get them in France,' she said. 'Or if ye can, they won't be as tasty as these.'

And she promised him at least one egg a day whilst he was on leave.

'As long as they're layin', hinny,' she told him. 'They're not all layin' now but as long as I've got one, you'll have it. Ye deserve it.'

And she would have been disappointed if he had refused her.

'No, no,' she insisted when Rob assured her he had enough food in France, that he had never starved there, that food wasn't the problem.

'It's harder here,' he said. 'Ye've got less to eat in England than the lads in the trenches.'

But she would not have it.

'No,' she said firmly, 'you're goin' to have one of these eggs. They'll build ye up. Ye look as if ye needed buildin' up.'

And that was where matters stood when Mrs. Rimmer left them half an hour later.

The rest of the day flashed by even though the heavy rain confined them to the house. In the morning, while Dolly plucked the chicken, cooked and cleaned round and chattered, Rob and

Joshua played card games. Dolly was happy with snap and whist, but she was alarmed at pontoon and brag.

'Ye're never teachin' him to play those games,' she said, her tone horrified.

Rob smiled across at her.

'He's got to learn.'

'Not gamblin',' she replied. 'The bairn doesn't need to learn to gamble.'

'We're only playin' for matchsticks,' Rob had explained and Dolly had accepted that grudgingly. Every now and then she would look across at them as if to make sure that coins had not been substituted for matches.

But the chicken was a success.

After they had finished, Dolly collected the bones together. 'Nice bit broth for later. For supper.'

When Joshua had smiled at the prospect, she reminded him of how he had first received Mrs. Rimmer's gift.

'Doesn't take you long to change your mind,' she told him, mock seriously. And they had all laughed.

In the afternoon, Dolly had taken some of the books out of the cupboard.

'These were our father's,' she reminded Rob.

She laid Robin Hood, Arabian Nights and a poetry book on the table.

'I don't know what he could've wanted with a poetry book,' Dolly said, shaking her head. 'Anyway, let's have a read of this.'

So the long afternoon passed in a world of magic and genies and cunning and escapes from the Sheriff of Nottingham. Rob read some of the stories aloud and Dolly read others. They all looked at the pictures, each with its tissue paper protecting Caliphs and sailors and Maid Marian and the men in green.

A wonderful afternoon.

And an evening of songs followed even though Dolly had no piano.

'We were goin' to get a one,' she explained more than once. 'That was high on our list and I think, in fact I know, if there'd been no war, we would've had a one in 1914.'

If there had been no war George and Dolly would still have been in Carlisle. Successful probably. With a piano.

And Joshua would have been ... well, not here, he reminded himself.

The songs went on and on, there were so many they knew, every blessed word. Some of them were comic and Rob was best at these and others were sad and plaintive and Dolly's sweet voice was just right for such songs.

'I know she likes me, I know she likes me,
Because she says so ...'

They sang together, the three of them, till supper time.

'... She is my lily and my rose.'

And, as the last note died away, Dolly's last sweet lingering note, Rob squeezed her arm.
'Now what about a drop of that broth?' he asked her.

Perhaps in apology, the next day, the Sunday, was perfect, cloudless, warm. But in the early afternoon as they sat on the tram, heading for the terminus, Joshua felt uncomfortable. The Lieutenant had never been mentioned and that had not till now troubled Joshua. But here, on the tram, making for the very spot where they had first met, going with their picnic things to the place where they had been so happy so long ago it seemed, where Dolly had put her arms round him and told him she loved him, Joshua's uncertainty grew.
'What's up with you, long face?' Rob asked him, breaking off a conversation with his sister. 'Look at him. What a long face. What's up?'
Joshua could not meet Rob's eye and kept his gaze down at the boots and puttees opposite.
'Come on,' Rob urged him in his cheerful voice. 'What's up?'
Joshua glanced across at Dolly. She was smiling at him. Now she reached over and gripped his hand.
'There's nothin' wrong is there?'
Joshua shook his head, unable momentarily to speak, wondering if it was being loyal to the Lieutenant to come to this place for a picnic and not tell him. Was it right to come here to

enjoy themselves in what Joshua had come to regard as the Lieutenant's special place?

'Anyway,' Dolly said, releasing her grip and sitting back in her seat, 'you were askin' me somethin' else.'

She had turned to her brother. Perhaps she had guessed why Joshua was so unexpectedly quiet.

'What was it you were sayin'?' she asked Rob.

And they passed the afternoon sitting on the grass, dry in the warm sun of late autumn after the rain of the previous day, and looking at the giant's castle and at the mill and the grey stone wall just as they had done with the Lieutenant. Except that Rob turned cartwheels and somersaults and wrestled with Joshua. Except that Rob took a sorbo-rubber ball out of his pocket and they played French Cricket with a tree branch and Dolly was worst of all at it and kept getting her knees and legs rattled by the ball.

Ginger beer, an egg each — Mrs. Rimmer had come up trumps when she heard about the picnic — but no bread this time because the shops were short of flour.

On the way back to the terminus Dolly had walked between them, her arms linked through theirs.

Joshua was unsure which picnic he had best enjoyed. He desperately hoped that no-one would ever ask him.

7

The pier. A bright morning, a nice morning. Warm even at this early hour.

'You always seem to be the bearer of bad tidings, Joshua.' The Lieutenant, smart as always, today in a brown-checked sports jacket, shook his head wearily, holding the note in his hand. 'So her brother's come, eh?' he mused. 'Aren't I good enough to meet him?'

How to answer this? Of course, the Lieutenant was good enough to meet him. He was good enough to meet anyone. And Rob was good enough to meet the Lieutenant too. He had no doubt about that.

'Well, tell her I'll be patient and look forward to seeing her in three weeks or so.' The Lieutenant was smiling in his easy way. He wasn't too upset, then.

'He doesn't know about ye,' Joshua confided. 'She hasn't told him about ye.'

It seemed strange, this secrecy, at least to Joshua it did.

But the Lieutenant saw some point in it.

'Well, you know, people are funny. She's just been told recently about her husband.' He drew on his pipe. 'People are funny,' he repeated.

Yes, they were. No doubt about that.

Mrs. Weston, Dolly, she was funny for a start, not telling her brother about the Lieutenant. And telling Joshua not to mention the Lieutenant to Rob as well. Why not? There was nothing wrong with the Lieutenant. In fact, there was a lot right with him. So Dolly was funny. And so was the Lieutenant, taking it all so calmly. He would not see her for three weeks. It was an age to wait. Yet he did not seem very worried.

People were funny, all right. Even so, Joshua was glad that he did not have to confess that they had been on a picnic to Claydon the day before. It still didn't seem right to him. And he said nothing about going to the theatre with Rob and Dolly. He didn't want the Lieutenant to think they were enjoying themselves too much without him.

Right from the moment the electric lights dimmed ... No. Before that.

Right from the moment when Rob went to the box office to buy the tickets and Dolly and Joshua waited for him at the bottom of the stairway — red carpet, gold handrail — watching the crowds coming in. Right from then, with the man in the black bow tie shaking hands with some, nodding and smiling at others; with the feller in the peaked cap and gold buttoned uniform going out to greet some very posh people; right from that moment Joshua was in a new world.

Here there were smiling women waiting to show you to your place and Rob bought a programme from one of them. He made a joke with her and they both laughed and so did Dolly. From high up, in a red velvet seat, with the golden ashtray at his knees — 'among the best in the house,' Dolly had whispered to him proudly — he could look across at the boxes, families there, sharing opera glasses, or he could look down at the crowd in the stalls and the pit below, so far off, shrouded beneath their great veil of cigarette smoke, he could scarcely make out their features.

There was an orchestra. They came in ten minutes or so before the start, sitting below the huge curtain of blue velvet with the usual trimmings of gold. And the laughter and the chatter and the music travelled up and across to the magical figures on the walls; figures — the naked tops of women mainly but here and there some muscular giant seemed to be responsible for holding up the whole roof of the place.

'He's a Scottie, Harry Lauder,' Rob told him, blowing out a stream of smoke from his pipe. 'Cigarettes are for down there,' he'd said, pointing at the stalls. 'Pipes are for up here, among the toffs.'

'Aye, and here,' Dolly said, pointing halfway down the programme, 'look here. That's a ... well, he's like a magician. I can't say the word.'

And Rob reached over Joshua and took the programme from her.

'Aye. He does card tricks, things like that,' he explained. 'Prestidigitateur ... that's what he's called.'

Dolly giggled.

They all did.

'I've never been able to pronounce that,' she said, pulling a face.

No, long before the lights dimmed — all those electric lamps — it was a wonderland. The Imperial Theatre. His first visit to such a place. Rob had said, on his second night, when they came back from the picnic, 'I'll take ye to a show tomorrow. To the Imperial.'

And so he did. To the Imperial. Like a great temple outside and inside like a royal palace.

And there then, high up, Joshua, Dolly and Rob sat in seats among the best in the house.

After the lights dimmed, a hush fell and the orchestra went at it hot and strong with old favourites and some modern ones. Then it was a troupe of girls dancing and whistles and shouts from the fellers. And there followed a succession of jugglers, acrobats, tightrope walkers, a ventriloquist, a conjuror and in no time — though it was a time jam-packed with an endless variety of wonders — it was the interval.

They clapped, they cheered, Rob and Dolly reached over Joshua in the middle and told each other how good it was and then they told Joshua how good it was and then they asked each other what they thought of it.

'I'm just goin' to stretch me legs,' Rob said, standing up, laughing.

'Seats are a bit cramped, aren't they?' Dolly said but then added, perhaps fearing Rob would think she was ungrateful to him, 'but they're all right for me. Plenty room for me.'

'And for me,' Joshua added. 'I've plenty room an' all.'

'Just a bit tight for big fellers like you,' Dolly told her brother. 'Aye, go an' have a bit stretch of your legs.'

Several rows below them another soldier had stood up. The way he stood and bent two or three times at the knees suggested that he was also finding the seats cramped. He turned to each side from the waist as though loosening up his body, vaguely smiling as he did so, showing a set of large, badly formed teeth. Then, as he made to struggle past his neighbours, he looked up the banked rows of people sitting above him. And as often happens, his eye settled on someone who called his attention, another soldier standing up, a dozen rows behind.

And Rob glanced down at him, his eyes suddenly wary. He drew in his breath sharply and stared at the soldier in khaki down below.

'Listen,' he said, bending over to speak to his sister. 'I'll have to go. I feel rotten.'

It was such a sudden change. Only seconds before he had been cheerful, chattering away about the performance. Now, his face was drawn and his pale cheek twitched.

'Nothin' to worry about,' he was saying. 'I'll be all right.'

Already he was edging his way past the people sitting next to him, still reassuring Dolly as he went, calling across to her.

'It's me back. Bit o' back pain. Nowt to concern yourself with. You stay. Enjoy yourselves.'

And he was out of the end of the row, walking briskly enough up the staircase towards the exit, but with his head down, his shoulders hunched.

'What's up with him, Mrs. Weston?'

Dolly was frowning, shaking her head.

'I didn't know he had back trouble.' She watched him disappear at the top of the stairs, wondering.

The rest of the performance was wonderful and Harry Lauder with his outsize Glengarry and his crooked walking stick was given as much applause before he even started as some of them got at the end of their acts. Of course, he'd recently lost his son in France.

'Are ye enjoyin' it?' Joshua whispered to Dolly three or four times in the second half.

'Yes,' she nodded each time, smiling straight ahead, but really Joshua knew that Rob's sudden departure had spoiled it for her. He was disappointed because he knew how much she had looked forward to the show, how excited she had been when Rob had said that he would take them.

Walking home, Joshua felt just that shade uneasy, just a touch guilty, because although he was sorry for Dolly and, of course, for Rob, he had still had one of the most marvellous

153

occasions of his life. He had never before seen such colour, heard such sound. When they had all sung together, all the audience, singing about Roses in Picardy, about Home Fires, about Charlie Chaplin and a dozen other songs, how he had loved it. That was the best part, singing together. It was the songs and the music, the jokes, the tricks, the skills, that occupied him as they went home, not the disappointment that he ought to have felt for Dolly and Rob.

For the next few days, Rob could not go out.

'I've had it off and on for a few months, this bother with me back,' he told them. 'It's nowt to get upset about.'

But Dolly was upset. She insisted that he lie down in the afternoons but always with a couple of hot bricks in a flannelette blanket on his back.

'There. Is that better?' she would ask him.

And Rob would say, 'I wish ye'd stop your fussin', woman.'

He was very irritable even when there was no call. It was unfair on Dolly. She so wanted Rob to enjoy himself but at the slightest hint of illness she was a fusser. Thank God, she didn't believe in goose grease on brown paper when you had a cold. She'd given Joshua onion gruel for that. But for backs such as Rob's she knew exactly what to do. She sent Joshua down to the chemist the day after the visit to the theatre. He brought back with him medicated turpentine, aniseed and balsam of sulphur, twopennorth of each. She mixed them with sugar and gave it to her brother by the teaspoon, day after day.

'By God, lass,' he would shout, 'ye'll poison me with that stuff.'

But Dolly was determined.

'Get it down ye,' she would say.

But other another exciting event loomed on Joshua's horizon now.

The parade. It was going to be some parade. It was in all the papers; there were notices in shop windows; there were posters on walls. Some parade this was going to be.

'Is he goin' to be well enough to go to the parade?' he kept asking.

'I'm sure he will,' Dolly had said at first. But then she was not so certain. If this went on he would scarcely get outdoors before his leave was up. Over a week went by and he never left the house.

'Won't ye be goin'?' Joshua asked him on the Thursday night, two days before the parade. 'Will ye not be better?'

Rob sighed, looked away from Joshua.

'We'll see,' he said. 'We'll see. It all depends.'

Dolly, bustling about the kitchen, dusting here, polishing there, stopped and looked up at him.

'Depends on what?'

Rob shook his head impatiently.

'I've told ye,' he snapped. 'We'll see. Let it rest at that.'

He was trying to light his pipe. Suddenly the match box seemed to have a life of its own, jumping up from his fingers. All the matches spilled on the floor and as Rob bent to pick them up, Joshua could not help noticing how much his fingers shook.

'Sometimes ye can't put a name to a face,' Diggle was saying.

Or a face to a name.

Or a name or a face to a situation.

But the soldier did not take the argument as far as that.

All he said to the barman at 'The Eagle' was, 'Sometimes ye can't put a name to a face.'

Then he had shaken his head and bared his ugly teeth. Suddenly he looked angry and his voice came out husky.

'But straightaway this feller's name came to me.'

The barman went on polishing his glass. He wished there were a few more in, a bit more activity, then he would not have to stand and listen to Diggle going on, repeating himself, about this other soldier he had seen at The Imperial the other night. He didn't wish Diggle back in the trenches but he did wish him away from here.

'I was lookin' straight up at him. Blow me down, I thought, I'm sure you're Dexter.'

The barman knew what was coming next.

'Thing is,' Diggle told him for the third or fourth time that day, 'I heard he was dead.'

Course, Diggle was a good customer when he was home. And he had been an even better one before the war. And if he came back ... well.

'But ye weren't sure,' the barman prompted him, forcing himself to speak, to show interest. 'Pity ye couldn't've catched him.'

'Tried to, man,' Diggle said somewhat indignantly as if it was being suggested he had been half-hearted in following Dexter. 'Tried to but he was up an' away. Didn't come back.'

The barman took up another glass and stuck his cleaning towel in it.

'Mebbes ye could've made a mistake, like. Ye said ye'd seen him only once afore,' he said hoping that his customer would not be too affronted this time. Diggle pondered what he had said, sucked at his prominent front teeth.

'Mebbes. But I really couldn't forget the circumstances when we met.'

'What sort of circumstances?' the barman asked, at last showing a genuine interest. He had not heard this part of the story.

Diggle ran his hand across his forehead. For a moment the barman thought he was going to burst into tears. Surely not. Diggle wasn't the sort to do that.

'Just special like. I'd been chosen for a particular job. This feller, seems he'd volunteered. I've never forgot that. Volunteerin' for a job like that.'

And no matter how much the barman prodded him, Diggle would say no more. Just at the interesting bit. A job like what?

It was to be a grand parade, Mr. Pybus had told them. There would be bands and columns of old soldiers from the Boer War; the scouts and guides would be there and the Boys Brigade; there was going to be a large contingent of soldiers from the barracks, but best of all, it was to be 'B' Battalion on their last outing before being shipped off to France.

'Next month this time, these lads'll be in the thick of the fighting,' Mr. Pybus had said. 'For us. For us and our families.'

They had spent the Friday afternoon cutting out squares of paper and colouring them red, white and blue. Once Mr. Pybus was satisfied that the lines were straight and the colouring even, he handed them eighteen-inch sticks. And glue.

'Let them dry nice,' he warned them once the flags were glued. They were placed on the window ledge until the end of the afternoon and then, after the prayer, Mr. Pybus allowed them to take them home. 'Give them a good send-off tomorrow. Wave your flags and give them a cheer. They're fighting for us, for the right. They're brave lads, all of them, so give them some encouragement.'

'It's for tomorrow,' Joshua told Rob when he got home.

He was proud of the flag not just because it was as Mr. Pybus had said, a symbol of truth, honour and justice, but because he had made it; the glue was even and had not squeezed out onto the colour as it had with some of the other pupils' efforts. Alfie Mason's flag had come apart as soon as he got into the street outside the school building and others did not look as if they would stand up to any vigorous waving the next day. But Joshua was sure that his would.

When he reached home he had run up the back stairs. He just hoped that Rob would be better.

'Will ye not come?' Joshua asked, standing close to Rob's chair.

'Are ye not goin' with him?' Dolly asked. 'Ye said ye would. And it'll take ye out of yourself.'

Rob glanced across at her without moving his head.

'Ye know that I'll not go,' Dolly went on. 'Ye can understand why. I cannot abide bands and marchin', all that sort of thing. I couldn't stand it. But he'd like to go with ye. Won't ye take him?'

Dolly persuasive as ever but wondering at the same time how anybody could even contemplate waving off men going to die.

'All right,' Rob said, smiling ruefully at each of them in turn. 'But there'll be somethin' reciprocal from you.'

For the first time in days Rob allowed himself a smile as he stared at Joshua.

Reciprocal?

Joshua looked puzzled.

'Look, I'll go to the parade,' Rob explained, 'even though I don't want to. And you'll do somethin' you don't want to do.'

'Somethin' I don't want to do?'

'That's right.'

'But what?'

'Wait'n' see.'

'Oh, what is it?' Joshua was in an agony of expectation.

But Rob would not tell him.

'That's the price ye pay,' he said. 'Waitin' and seein'.'

The next day Rob looked smart in the navy blue suit. He had refused to wear uniform. 'Let's have a bit of a change,' he had said. He and Dolly had searched through the cupboard in her bedroom, sorting through George's civilian clothes. He tried on the suit.

'Fits well,' Rob announced, smoothing the front of the jacket and looking down at the sharp crease in the trousers. He seemed to be back to his normal self, much more cheerful, as if all that had oppressed him in the previous days had been lifted from him.

'He only wore it three or four times,' Dolly answered. 'He saved up for it. Said if he was goin' to be successful in business he would have to look the part.'

Rob pulled at the jacket sleeves.

'All right, eh?'

Dolly smiled, perhaps a little sadly.

'Yes. Fine. Suits you.'

Only Joshua was a shade disappointed. Why wouldn't Rob wear his uniform? He was smart in his uniform. People might think he was a coward wearing an ordinary suit. Remember what happened to the Lieutenant.

But time was pressing. It had taken Rob so long to get ready. They needed to be there by half past two to get a good place, he was sure. It was too far to walk and the trams would be packed. He was certain that everyone would want to see the soldiers. Hadn't Mr. Pybus said so? Even on ordinary Saturdays it was a struggle to get on a tram. Joshua wished Rob would stop admiring himself. And Dolly was just as bad. Worse in fact, because she had made Rob change the first of George's shirts he had tried on.

'This is nicer,' she had said, offering him a shirt with a blue stripe, 'with that suit.' Then he had to struggle a second time with the celluloid collar.

Now Rob would try the bowler. 'Might as well look a toff,' he said. He looked at himself in the mirror, testing it at various angles.

'No,' he said at last. 'A dutt's not right on me. I don't look right in a gaffer's hat.'

He placed the bowler on the chair beside the table.

'That's better,' he said when Dolly offered him the cloth cap. Rob was still adjusting the cap when the knock came at the front door. Dolly was fussing around, her head first on this side, then the other, judging how he looked.

'You get it, Joshua,' she said.

More time wasted, he thought, as he went downstairs. We'll never make it. We'll never get through the crowds, never see anything. And when he opened the door he could not believe his eyes.

Billy Moffat.

Billy, possibly a touch taller than he had been a few months ago, but still looking awkward, high shouldered, cheerful.

'Mr. Samways told me you were here,' he said. 'Remember me?' And he grinned.

Remember Billy Moffat? Remember him? Never forget him. Never. Ever.

'I'm staying with Mr. Samways,' Billy said, not waiting for Joshua to speak. 'To make up for last time.'

Then he coloured as if conscious that he had said the wrong thing. But he didn't hesitate, just went on talking. His preaching experience had given him enough confidence.

'I'm staying a few days. Doing a couple of services and lots of meetings. Then I'm off home Friday night after the social. My father's coming for me on Friday.' He stopped a moment, his grin broadening. 'I've had special permission to stay off school for this. Good, eh?'

And Joshua had hardly spoken. 'Aye, it's good,' he said. 'Would ye like to come in?' he asked.

Then as they climbed the stairs Joshua turned to Billy.

'Do ye mind not talkin' too much about Mr. Samways?' he whispered, looking earnestly at Billy. 'It's a bit awkward.'

Billy was puzzled.

'Up there you mean?' He pointed his thumb to the top of the stairs. 'The woman in the house? Not talk about him to her? '

'Aye. If ye don't mind. And her brother as well. If ye would just not say much about either of the Samways. If they ask where you're stayin'.'

Dolly's voice reached them on the stairs.

'Who is it, Joshua?'

She was walking from the kitchen to the stair head.

'It's Billy,' Joshua shouted. He tried to keep the excitement out of his voice. 'It's Billy Moffat.'

'Bring him up then,' she called down.

Joshua was in turmoil as they went up the last stairs and into the kitchen. Of course he was delighted to see Billy though he tried not to show it too much. Last time he had liked him so much and look what had happened.

'Well,' Billy said hesitantly after the introductions. 'I was wondering if you'd be going to the parade.'

'Good,' Dolly tried to appear enthusiastic. 'Exactly where these two are goin'.'

How could she bring herself to say this, she wondered. Just because Joshua was excited. Why didn't she tell him what she really thought.

'And where ye stayin'?' Rob asked, more out of politeness than interest.

'With Mr. Samways,' Billy replied without hesitation. 'I'm doing some services there and he's invited me to stay.'

Dolly's eyes met Joshua's and then they flickered across to Rob, but his expression did not change. 'We're goin' to be late,' Joshua said. 'We'll have to hurry.'

He led the way to the front stairs and the others followed him.

Trouble, Dolly thought to herself. This is where it'll start. She'd made no mention of any of the Samways family to her brother. But now, somebody was going to say something. She knew it.

The parade started at the market, behind the Old Town Hall. Down by the 'Sir Robert Peel' and the road to the ferry, there was a thin sprinkling of folk. In the roadway itself Sergeants and Warrant Officers, Second Lieutenants and Majors, stood in groups or broke off from time to time to march up and down the straggled lines of troops as if to inspect them. At last they formed up with a Colonel to lead them and he was high above them on a huge chestnut stallion.

Then with a single beat of a brass drum they were off on their way to the station, to the tracks that would lead them by stages to the Front.

In the old days, two, three years ago, before the first Ypres, before Armentieres and Plug Street, the Somme and Paschendaele, they'd waved them off all right. The crowds then were ten, fifteen deep in places. You could scarcely move an arm to wave. There wasn't anybody who didn't call out encouragement to the passing columns. But today, there was a poor turn out. This wasn't the old professional army; these weren't Kitchener's volunteers today, these were reluctant conscripts and those who came to see them were sad and sullen, for they knew all about where these men were off to.

But as he waved his flag, still intact, still brightly coloured, Joshua saw only heroes. Mr. Pybus's words came to him as he watched the passing comrades.

'Truth, honour and justice — that's what they're fighting for. Every man-jack of them.'

'Man-jack' — he'd liked that.

'And when ye see them on Saturday, don't forget it.'

Truth, honour, justice — the words lodged in his mind until long after the last man-jack had marched past. It had been so grand, so exhilarating.

And the let-down, Rob saying, 'Cup of tea, then?'

After all that thrilling parade.

Billy was keen enough. He was back to earth. But for the moment Joshua wanted nothing to distract him from the memories of the heroes who had just passed him by.

Rob squeezed him by the arm.

'Come on now. Somethin' reciprocal now,' he muttered, his mouth down at Joshua's ear.

They left the market and made their way into Prince George Street with its exciting range of shops — one major store and two slightly smaller; a jeweller, a musical instrument and sheet music shop; medical supports; chemist; joke shop (false noses and moustaches, masks, itching powder, conjuring tricks — 'Deceive your friends with sleight of hand'); milliners and others. They cut down a narrow lane and found themselves in Zetland Lane. By contrast, this street, running parallel to but behind Prince George

Street was less impressive. Here was the Registrar of Births, Deaths and Marriages; the fire station; the offices of The North East Clarion; the police station and at the far end, on the corner, the grand sounding Augusta Tea Room, smaller than its name might suggest.

'Come on,' Rob said, grinning and winking at Billy. 'I've found just the place for you.' He was turned now to Joshua as he said 'you'.

He guided the boys across the road, a hand on the small of each back. For some curious reason, he felt calm for the first time in days.

'Wouldn't make his mind up,' Rob said, addressing Billy. 'Kept yammerin' on. "I don't want to go there to see them." Then he'd ask me, "D'ye think I should go?" When I tell'm to go, he says, "Oh, no. I don't think I will."'

Billy laughed over at Joshua but said nothing. Joshua, pale, uncertain, looked up at Rob and did not speak.

'Look. I've been to the parade. That's what I've done for you. You asked me. Now, we're goin' in here for tea. I'm not askin' you. I'm tellin' ye.'

There was no anger in Rob's voice as he spoke. Really, he was joking. Only there would be no refusing to go in, joke or no joke. Joshua understood that. And now he understood the meaning of 'reciprocal.'

The three of them stopped a moment outside. In the window, so that there could be no mistaking the shop's purpose, was a kettle, a plain white tea pot, cups, saucers and plates, all plain white. These all stood on a small table covered with a cloth so pure, crisp and white that it might have been laundered only minutes before. On the door was a tariff, printed in a neat hand. 'Tea, Cup 2d. Tea, Pot 4d. Bread, scones, jam when available'.

'So in we go,' Rob said.

Joshua could have wished the earth to open up and swallow him, regretting ever mentioning what Freddy Forster had said to him. When he had talked about it to Rob as he had done on three or four occasions, he had always explained away his unwillingness to go because they were Germans.

'What's that got to do with it?' Rob had asked him each time.

Joshua had had to swallow hard. Surely Rob of all people could understand. He had fought Germans. He knew what they were like, he knew they were the enemy.

'They're our enemies,' Joshua would say, but he should not have to explain this to Rob.

'Have they got guns?' Rob had asked him once. 'Are they likely to fire at us?'

Another time he had asked Joshua how many men they had and if the pavement was mined.

But he had never expected this, never thought Rob would bring him here, force him into the Forsters' cafe.

'I don't want to go in,' Joshua said, stiffening his body as though preparing to offer resistance.

'Suit yourself,' Rob told him. 'Me and Billy's goin' in. Aren't we? Are you goin' to wait outside?'

And Billy — Billy the sober, the wise, the clever — stood there, grinning like a clown, saying, 'Certainly we are. I feel like a cup of tea now.'

Rob opened the door, standing aside with a laughing half bow as the boys passed him. As they went in a tiny bell on the top of the door gave a shrill tinkle. Inside it was empty, not a customer, no-one serving from behind the mahogany counter, nothing in the cake display cabinet, though a small silver urn gurgled in the corner. Then from behind the counter an old man came through the bead-curtained doorway. He pointed to a table.

They serve you here, Joshua thought. They come and ask you what you want. He had never been in such a place before. He had been in a cafe only three times with his mother and once with Dolly. On these occasions they had bought their tea from the counter. But here it was different.

There were seven small round tables, each with its white tablecloth, crockery and small vase of dried flowers and ferns. At each table were three or four delicate chairs. It was the kind of place you might see drawn in a book or a magazine. Or you might sometimes see a photograph of a place like this on display somewhere.

And now, standing by them, helping them to their chairs, as if that was necessary, was the old man. He was smart, in a dark suit with a white shirt and tie. He was a kind-looking man as well with a white walrus moustache.

Could this old man, this kind-looking old man, be Freddy Forster's grandad? Could he be a German, a man looking like this?

He could. He was.

Because Rob asked him.

'Are you Mr. Forster?'

And when the old man told him that he was, Rob introduced Joshua.

'Ah,' Mr Forster man said. His face lit up and he held out his hands towards Joshua. 'You are that boy.'

And what was he supposed to do, Joshua wondered. He nodded his head but could not bring himself to speak.

'You are that boy,' Mr. Forster said again. 'Wait.' He moved towards the bead curtain. 'Hannah! Hannah! Here quick,' he called as though Rob and the boys were on the point of flight. 'Hannah! Come!'

The old man turned back to the table.

'She won't be a moment,' he said, as though apologizing for Hannah's slowness. 'She will be delighted ...'

The door to the street opened.

The bell rang shrilly.

They all looked up.

Three soldiers. Not drunk. But not sober. They seemed to fill the remaining space, to darken it with their presence.

'Out. You.'

The tallest of them scowled at Rob.

'Out. You.' he repeated more loudly, emphasising each word, jerking his thumb in the direction of the street behind him.

His two companions stood behind him, perhaps a little less sure of themselves.

'What's this?' Rob asked, not moving.

'This,' the tall soldier, now bunching his fist and waving it in front of Rob's face, 'this is goin' to bloody knock you off that chair if ye don't get out of here. That's what this is.'

Rob put up a hand, placatory.

'All right,' he said. 'No need to get rough. Let's take it quietly.'

As he spoke, one of the other soldiers, short, bow-legged, sporting the beginnings of a moustache, threw down a cup from one of the other tables. The third soldier, an older man, maybe thirty years of age, giggled and copied his mate and another cup was shattered.

'Out! Out!' the tall soldier shouted, pushing his coarse young face closer to Rob's. 'D'ye not understand?' he asked, his voice now taking on a plaintive tone. 'These is bloody Jerries in here. Fuckin' Boches.' He gestured over to where old Mr. Forster stood silent. Behind him, Hannah, his wife, short and stout, came through the curtains. She stopped, her mouth opening and shutting with no sound issuing forth.

'These is Jerries,' the tall soldier repeated slowly as if for the benefit of the two boys. 'They're our enemies.' He turned his head to stare angrily at the old man and then shifted his gaze to his wife.

Another cup and saucer were smashed. The old man still said nothing, simply stood unmoving. From Hannah, there came a whimper as she put her hand to her anguished mouth. Then, as though making an enormous effort to speak, she whispered, 'Not again. Please not again.'

'Have ye been here before?' Rob asked, standing up slowly from the table. Joshua thought how tall and strong he looked.

'No, we haven't,' the bow-legged soldier told him. 'But ye'd better scram out of here and fast.'

'Other people. Three times now.' The old woman was barely audible. 'We've been smashed up three times. But other people.'

Her accent was still strong whereas that of her husband had taken on the local tinge. He could scarcely be recognised as foreign-born.

'Please go,' Mr. Forster said, finding his voice at last. 'We don't deserve this. We have a son in the army.'

The oldest of the intruders moved across to the old man, grabbing him by the jacket.

'You bloody shut up, Jerry.'

The soldier's face was twisted with hatred.

Joshua looked up at Rob. Perhaps they ought to go. He felt the fear in his stomach and legs.

'These young lads'd better go before ye start anything,' Rob said, moving over to stand at Mr. Forster's side. 'Come on now.

Just calm yourselves down.' Even though he was tall, Rob looked quite slight facing the tall soldier.

'Calm ourselves down?'

It was the bow-legged soldier's turn to speak.

'Calm ourselves down? We're calm enough. We're off next week to fight these bastards, but we're startin' now. I'm calm enough, don't you worry. I know what I'm doin' and so do these.'

The other two nodded, adding similar comments.

'All right, then,' Rob said. 'But let's get these lads out of the way first.'

The soldiers let their hands hang at their sides, no longer tensed up, as if willing to wait until the boys had gone.

'And then ye'll want to set about this place, eh?' Rob asked them, his tone still quiet and reasonable. 'And you'll be longin' to upset this lady and gentleman. Is that it?'

But no reason, no appeal, was going to work, no matter how much Rob cared to phrase himself. As the boys reached the door, they heard one of the soldiers ask why Rob was not in uniform.

'Have ye managed to escape army service then?'

Had he the nerve Joshua might have shouted back that Rob had been in the army, was in the army, that he was a hero and had a medal to prove it. But he hadn't time enough to summon up the nerve.

'Quick!'

It was Billy, pushing him from behind.

'Quick! This way! Let's get out.'

It was Billy who squeezed past and led the way, running down the street, away from the Augusta Tea Room. As he left Joshua had a glimpse of a kind of tableau, of no-one moving or speaking. The soldiers, Rob, the old couple, were frozen in their attitudes. It was almost comforting, as if nothing really serious was about to occur.

As he followed into the street, it struck Joshua that Billy's hobnails still clattered on the cobbles. But then, so did Joshua's these days.

'Where we goin'?'

They had only run a few yards and already he was panting. It was an effort to get the question out. All those weeks ago, he remembered how Billy had panted. But Billy's shortage of breath then had had nothing to do with being frightened.

'Where we goin'?' Joshua shouted again.

'Follow me,' Billy shouted over his shoulder.

It was Billy who reached the police station first; Billy who led the way up the grey mildewed steps; Billy who pushed his way through the heavy double doors to the desk.

'There's a fight,' he said. 'They're breaking up the Augusta Tea Room.'

The sergeant eyed Billy closely. He had to weigh him up. He knew the lads round here, what they were like, daft as brushes. But this lad was all right. He could tell. He knew good lads from bad 'uns.

'The Augusta Tea Room?'

'Yes,' Billy said. 'Some soldiers.'

'Mr. Forster,' Joshua gasped, feeling he ought to make some contribution. 'And Mrs. Forster. She's his wife.'

'Right,' the sergeant said, coming round the desk and jamming on his helmet.

'There's three of them,' Billy said.

'Three soldiers,' Joshua put in.

The sergeant paused in midstride.

'Only three, eh? In that case I won't need no help, will I?'

As he walked out through the doors, he already had his truncheon out.

By the time they reached the tea rooms the soldiers had gone. And there was no sign of Mrs. Forster, but her husband was bent over Rob who was sitting at one of the tables and dabbing at his eye with a handkerchief. He was cut on the brow and his top lip was starting to swell. There were splashes of blood on his shirt and waistcoat. All around, the tables and chairs were overturned — two of the chairs were broken — and the floor was littered with broken crockery.

'What's up then?' the sergeant asked.

And Rob explained.

'And I'm very grateful to this gentleman,' Mr. Forster said as his wife bustled in with a bottle of iodine and some cotton wool. 'He was so brave.'

'And these two boys were brave,' his wife said. 'It shouldn't be right to frighten young boys in that way.'

Which made Joshua feel better about the whole matter.

The sergeant was almost on his way, pausing in the doorway, disappointed that he had missed such a promising fracas, satisfied that there was nothing here he could profitably do. Perhaps it was his huge figure which attracted the newcomer, small, balding, weasel-faced, who squeezed his way into the shop.

'Oscar Solly,' he announced himself. 'North East Clarion.'

He was just passing, he said, on his way to the office.

'Couldn't pass up a shindy at The Augusta Tea Room now, could I? In the same street as the office an' all.'

He had never been in before. Didn't use tea rooms much in his line of business. Still, shame it should be such a sad occasion when he did come in.

'Now who's this gentleman?' he asked sidling up to Rob.

'Forget it,' Rob said, dabbing his eye. Mrs. Forster had put on some iodine so that it smarted still. 'Come along, boys,' he said, hustling them to the door.

'Wait on, there,' Oscar said, bringing his notebook from an inside pocket. Suddenly he was genuinely interested. 'I think I know who we've got here.' He was peering closely into Billy's face. 'Aren't you the preacher lad? Ye are, aren't ye? You're young Moffat, aren't ye? Tommy Moffat?'

'Billy.'

'Come on, Billy,' Rob called from the door.

'What's your name, sir?' Oscar asked him, switching his attention once more to Rob who had his hand on the door handle.

'Doesn't matter.'

Rob was agitated, anxious to leave. Joshua could see that. It was probably because he had been in a fight.

'But it does,' Oscar was saying. 'It matters very much.'

'Not to me,' Rob told him, tugging the door open.

Oscar blew out his cheeks. He was used to this. People were often uncooperative.

'In that case,' he said, changing tack, 'what about a few words with young Billy here, eh? You're preachin' here, aren't ye?'

'I'll be a couple o' minutes,' Billy told them, looking over Oscar's shoulder. He was used to being taken seriously: he had been interviewed before. He faced Oscar. 'If you hurry up but I can't keep my friends waiting.'

'Couple of minutes is all I want,' Oscar smiled.

The Forsters stood amidst the debris, looking at their shattered life's work, wondering why the young man and the two lads were leaving so quickly and why the sergeant seemed oblivious to all that was going on around him. He had made no real attempt to confirm what had happened. Most likely he would have enjoyed a set-to with the soldiers; that was what being a policeman meant to him. When he was young, chucking-out time on Saturday nights had been the highlight of his week. It seemed to happen less these days. He was more often in the station on Saturday nights now. It was the young fellers who got to see the fun. But he wasn't over-keen on writing reports about things like this; little bit of damage here, soon be swept up. Bad luck on the old folks, mind, but he'd already sympathised with them.

'I'll keep me eyes open for them fellers,' he promised.

He nodded at Oscar talking at the pavement's edge to the young lad, vaguely wondering where the other lad had gone to and the chap with the bruised eye.

Not very interesting really.

Dolly had answered the door. Joshua had offered to go in reply to the knock but she was nearer.

'Come in,' Joshua heard her say.

There was a man's voice, then a woman's. Then a slow and heavy tread up the stairs.

'He'll not be long,' Dolly was saying as she walked back into the kitchen. 'Give them your seat, Joshua.' He got up from the horsehair chair and went over and sat on the cracket by the fender.

'I hope ye don't mind comin' in here but the front room's cold. I've no fire on in there,' Dolly said, pointing at the fire in the kitchen grate.

They were both dressed in grey, the man and the woman. Him, a little downtrodden sort of feller with a sad, drooping moustache and her a vinegary sort with a turned down mouth in a lined face. But they were smart as if they had made a special effort. The man's suit, old, shiny, looked as if it had been freshly pressed. His wife's jacket and skirt only added to the severity of her appearance as if they had been ironed and ironed so much that the very life had been taken out of them.

169

'Sit down,' Dolly invited them, gesturing towards the chairs. They sat down rather self-consciously as if, having arrived, they had no idea what to say next.

'Me brother'll be back soon,' Dolly reassured them and they gave quick little smiles. 'He's not going to be long.' A heavy silence fell in the room. Dolly cleared her throat, smiled again. Then Joshua looked at the window and Dolly followed his gaze and after only a couple of seconds, she raised her finger as she turned again to the visitors. Almost immediately there was the rattle of the key in the door and Rob came in the house. They heard him shutting the glass door and hanging his coat on the peg at the foot of the stairs.

'That'll be him,' Dolly said reassuringly. Joshua thought how smart Rob looked in his suit. In George's suit, he reminded himself. He really looked quite handsome, a proper masher, Dolly had said. In the three days since the fight his eye was almost back to normal.

'This lady and gentleman've come to see you, Rob,' Dolly said, almost before he had entered the room.

Immediately a guarded look crossed his face.

'Oh yes?'

Rob did not smile. Instead his eyes travelled across to where the two newcomers had risen from their seats.

'Mr. Dexter,' the man said. 'Ye'll find this very strange, I've no doubt, but I think ye knew my son.'

His wife looked down at her feet as though embarrassed.

Rob waited expectantly, his expression puzzled.

'Grayson. Ernest Grayson.'

'Grayson?'

For the moment he could not bring himself to remember any Grayson.

'In your regiment. Different battalion, but same lot.'

Little Ernie Grayson.

Rob's head swam as he thought of the last time he had seen him.

'We learnt some months ago that he'd been killed in action,' Mr. Grayson said.

Little Ernie Grayson. They took him to the quarry in a hand cart.

'We wondered if ye could tell us anythin',' the mother's words fluttered out faintly from her turned-down mouth. 'He wrote, ye know. Told us he'd met ye. That was just before he ...' Here she hesitated, '... before he went.'

Mr. Grayson put his hand on his wife's arm. It was such a gentle move, such a reassuring gesture for a man with a drooping moustache to give to a sour-faced woman with a turned-down mouth.

'Ye see, the thing is,' he said, 'we had this letter but we've no idea of anythin' really.'

'We can't picture him,' Mrs. Grayson put in.

Why missus, he couldn't have walked there. He was so drunk he couldn't put one foot in front of the other.

'We've memories of him here in the town. But the hard part is we've no idea of what he was like, how he got on ... when he was away ... in the army.'

He lay on his back in the cart, his eyes closed and a daft sort of grin on his tearstained face.

'I didn't know him very well,' Rob said, all the time wondering how they had known where to find him.

'When we saw the bit in the paper,' Mr. Grayson said, 'we thought it must be you. I mean, there can't be many Corporal Dexters from this town, can there? We put two and two together.'

'What bit in the paper?'

The Graysons looked at each other and then at Rob.

'Have ye not seen "The Clarion"?' she asked.

Rob shook his head, glanced at Dolly questioningly, then at Joshua.

Mr. Grayson was fumbling in the inside of his jacket. He brought out a crumpled piece of newspaper which he handed to Rob.

'"The Preacher Boy" by Oscar Solly'.

'What's this?' Rob asked frowning.

'Go on. Read it,' Mr. Grayson said and Dolly came to look over her brother's shoulder.

'It's about Billy,' Rob told her.

'And you,' Dolly said, pointing to a paragraph towards the bottom of the article. Rob took the paper from her.

There were four paragraphs in all but Rob concentrated on the one that Dolly showed him. "Billy was spending the afternoon with local hero Corporal Robert Dexter who won the Military Medal at Ypres and who is spending a well-earned leave with his sister, Mrs. Dolly Weston, at Horden Street in the town."

There was no mention of the fight at the Augusta Tea Room. That had been of no interest to Oscar Solly. He was more concerned with what he called "deep character studies" not cheap brawls.

'When we read it we wondered what to do. Then this morning my husband went to "The Clarion" office to see if he could see Mr. Solly.'

Mrs. Grayson glanced quickly at her husband and he took up the explanation.

'I didn't want to waste anybody's time. I asked him about which regiment ye were in. Unfortunately he didn't know. So we've come here on the off chance. But ye did know Ernest, didn't ye? You're the one he wrote about. Ye must be. We've nobody else we can ask.'

Ernest Grayson? Joshua thought about him. Obviously another hero. Dead. Died for his country. Mr. Pybus used sometimes to say something to the class in Latin. 'It is good to die for your country' is what it meant. The Romans used to say that to the legionnaires. Mr. Pybus used to say it to the boys and girls in the class.

'Well, then,' Rob said. He was biting his lower lip, thinking what to say as he sat in the horsehair armchair. The muscle in his cheek flickered faintly and he ran his finger around the inside of his stiff celluloid collar.

The Graysons sat patiently, their hands in their laps, waiting.

Dolly coughed slightly, rose from her chair with an apologetic half-smile and said she'd put the kettle on. She took it from the side of the grate and carried it through to the scullery. As she ran the tap, Rob scratched his chin, wondering where to begin, how to tell it.

'Yes,' he said. 'I saw him, your son. I saw Ernest before he was killed.'

The Graysons intent on every word made no movement, no sound.

172

'I met him one afternoon. We were out of the line. And he saw me. We were in a village about twenty miles back.'

They were respectable, timid, narrow. And they would never forget their son. They loved him. Always would.

'We had a drink, I remember.'

Mrs. Grayson's mouth was pursed.

'Not too much, I hope.'

Even in death, Ernest was not to be allowed to have forgotten that he was from a respectable home.

'No,' Rob told them. 'Just a couple. Special circumstances,' he added. 'We were under a bit of strain. Ye know, fightin'.'

Mrs. Grayson's severe look relaxed slightly as she acknowledged that perhaps in those special circumstances, Ernest might be allowed one drink. But no more than that. The restriction was etched in her face.

'He'd had a hard time, Mrs. Grayson.'

It was true. He had. Every day since he had joined the army had been tough. It was difficult to know who his worst enemies were. Those in his own company or the Germans. As they had sat in the bar — and as Ernie had couple after couple after couple, though there was no need for the Graysons to know that — Ernie had told Rob what it was like for him.

'I'm frightened,' he had admitted without shame. 'I'm frightened I'm goin' to get killed or maimed. Lose a limb. Me face. Me balls.'

And Rob had told him that was what they were all afraid of.

'You're not,' Little Ernie had told Rob. 'You've been decorated. You proved you're not frightened.'

And Rob had told him how frightened he was every day on whatever side of the wire he found himself.

'And the lads. They hate me,' Little Ernie had confided, ignoring Rob's admission. 'Ye know what they do?'

And he had told Rob every instance of minor cruelty to which he had been subjected, to which he was subjected every day. If it wasn't the Germans, it was the Geordies, his own people.

'We'll get out of it eventually,' Rob had reassured him. He had wondered about Ernie. He was harmless. He was everybody's victim. Both sides of the wire.

'I never will,' Little Ernie had wept into his wine. 'I'll never get away from here.'

They were almost the last words Rob heard for Little Ernie had sobbed himself to sleep at the table.

Rob had paid the bill, asked a couple of lads to look after Ernie. He'd had enough. He hoped he'd never meet him again.

He did. Though only once. A couple of months later.

'No. He was gettin' on grand, Mrs. Grayson,' Rob was telling Little Ernie's mother. 'I mean, it was hard goin' for all of us but he was keepin' goin'.'

It was Mr. Grayson who put the question.

'Did ye see him, ye know, when he got killed? Were ye there?'

And Rob wondered about his answer.

'Yes,' he replied at last. 'I was there. Went like a hero. And I can assure you, as God's my witness, he never felt a thing.'

'Like a hero?' Mr. Grayson's eyes glistened and he placed his hand over his wife's.

Like a hero, the words echoed, re-echoed in Joshua's mind.

8

He missed the Lieutenant.

Strange that, missing the Lieutenant. After all, he had seen him only rarely. But sometimes, in the evenings before Rob had come, when they sat in the kitchen facing each other, Dolly would talk about him. Sometimes she would even laugh about him, the way he talked, the kinds of words he used, the way he pronounced his words. And his little moustache, Dolly sometimes laughed about that. And he did not know the town or its people very well even though he had been born here, even though his family had always lived here, still did. But he had been away to school and then to some college or other. Then came the army.

'He's a fish out of water here,' she would laugh, shaking her head.

'Is his father like a fish out of water as well?'

When he had asked her that her face had changed. She'd tightened her lips and said nothing straightaway. Then all she said was that, No, his father was not like him. Joshua did not pursue the matter: it was plain enough to him that she didn't want to speak about the Lieutenant's father. But he would have liked her view. After all, Joshua knew old Mr. Samways. He'd have liked another opinion on him.

It was mainly the Lieutenant himself that they had talked about when they were together. Once Dolly had asked if he thought the Lieutenant was rather young looking. Joshua had not thought so. In fact, he had not thought about the Lieutenant's age at all. If anyone had asked him, he would have been hard pressed to guess how old the Lieutenant was. But when Dolly asked the question, Joshua felt no hesitation in asking her how old he really was.

'Twenty-five,' she had told him, colouring as she spoke. 'Aye. Only twenty-five.'

It seemed important to her, the fact that the Lieutenant was twenty-five. Or as she had said, 'only twenty-five.' That made her older than him. Usually women were younger than the men they went out with or married, Joshua had noticed. He hoped it would make no difference.

Now, since Rob had come, the Lieutenant was never mentioned. Dolly had warned Joshua on the night of Rob's arrival and he had kept his silence.

But he did miss the Lieutenant, just talking to Dolly about him. And she must miss him too.

And it was spontaneous really when on the Thursday morning instead of going straight to school, he set off early for the pier. Because he knew he would be there. He wouldn't want to be anywhere else for he was loyal and faithful. Joshua knew that. Lieutenant Samways was loyal and faithful like a knight. He would be there, on the pier, Joshua knew. Like keeping a vigil.

And he was there, gazing moodily at the sea, so wrapped up in his thoughts that he did not notice Joshua's approach, never heard him come to his side. Only when the boy spoke did the Lieutenant jerk in surprise.

'What are you doing here?'

The Lieutenant looked pleased to see him once he had recovered from his surprise. Questioning perhaps but pleased too.

'I've come down to see you,' Joshua said and came to a halt, unable to think of anything else to say, unable to find words to explain how sorry he was that Dolly and the Lieutenant were not meeting at the moment. He missed their meetings even though he was usually not present. He liked Dolly to tell him what they had talked about. And he wanted to tell him now about other things, about Rob, and the Augusta Tea Room and the Graysons.

'Well, Joshua, it's good to see you as well,' the Lieutenant said. He did not on the face of it appear to be in any way anxious but there was about him the air of a man waiting to be told something, given a message. Joshua wondered if he ought really to have come, asking himself if he should only have come if Dolly had asked him. Would he, should he, tell her when he saw her again that he had gone to meet the Lieutenant?

'And how is Mrs. Weston?'

It was courteously put as if the Lieutenant was asking about a distant acquaintance.

'She's very well, thank you.'

Joshua studied his boots, turned one foot on its side and looked at the shiny hob nails.

'You've seen Billy, then?' the Lieutenant asked him.

'Yes.'

'A good boy.'

'Yes.'

'He's had a very hard week. He's going back tomorrow.'

Billy would have had an easier time if he had gone to school instead of having a week of sermons and meetings.

'I see that Mrs. Weston's brother has made a name for himself.'

A name for himself? The newspapers had not said anything about what he had done at the Augusta Tea Room.

'Billy told me what really happened.'

Joshua pictured Rob sitting in the Augusta, his head back, while Mrs. Forster dabbed iodine onto his cut eye.

'They didn't catch the men.'

The Lieutenant shrugged.

'Well, that's a pity,' he said, 'but the main thing is that right triumphed over might.'

It could have been Mr. Pybus speaking, just the kind of words he would use. But Mr. Pybus would never have had Englishmen representing anything but right. And he would not have them fighting each other. There would have been no place in the story for the three soldiers, unless of course he changed their nationality.

'He's got the Military Medal, ye know,' Joshua announced. He was trying not to sound boastful. Rob was no boaster and Joshua had no wish to suggest by his tone of voice that he was.

'He got it at "Wipers" last year. He's been there over two years.'

'I know he has,' the Lieutenant said. 'Not much fun.'

Joshua knew the Lieutenant spoke very little about the war. Dolly had told him that he did not like to talk about it. He changed the subject.

'I might see Billy before he goes.'

The Lieutenant put his head on one side — a typical stance of his and pondered the possibility.

'There's a social tomorrow night at the Chapel Hall. He'll be there. His father is calling for him to take him home by the nine o'clock train. Why don't you come?'

Joshua's mind travelled back over the years. He had been in that hall many times when he was younger, less frequently in the past year or so, since his mother had been ill. Ill. He admitted it to himself now. She had been ill.

'If Mrs. Weston wanted to come could I bring her with me?'

The Lieutenant smiled.

'Of course. She'd be very welcome. And her brother too. Tell them, Joshua.'

On second thoughts he wondered about Rob. He couldn't really see Rob there, couldn't imagine him at a social in the Chapel Hall. Dolly had once hinted at why he used not to come home on leave but preferred to stay in France. Liked to enjoy himself. In a rowdy sort of way. Whatever she intimated by that Joshua was uncertain but he knew a chapel social was not rowdy. On the other hand, Rob had not seemed very rowdy since coming on leave. In over two weeks he had scarcely gone out. Even when he did, it didn't seem very successful. At the theatre he'd had trouble with his back and at the Augusta Tea Rooms, well. You could count the number of other times he had been out on one hand. He just sat most of the day, reading the paper, smoking, dozing.

'I'll ask them. They might come.'

Rob might even be grateful to come to the social.

'If they'd like to.'

And there might be another reason why he did not go out and Joshua had just stumbled on that the day before.

'Rob's a bit short of money, I think,' Joshua said. He wondered if he really should tell the Lieutenant this. 'He hasn't been paid in weeks. So he might just come.'

The Lieutenant's eyes narrowed momentarily.

'What d'you mean, not been paid in weeks?'

'The army. They've never paid him. They owe him a lot.'

If he'd had any money, he wouldn't have just been sitting round the house. Not a rowdy feller like him. Not from what he'd heard.

'How d'you know this, Joshua?'

'I've seen his pay book. He's not had any money since March.'

He hadn't been deliberately nosing round Rob's belongings, nothing like that. It was just that yesterday, his baccy pouch and pipe and a packet of 'Gold Flake' and his wallet and pay book were lying there on the mantelpiece. He wasn't being nosy, just curious. The embossed cover looked interesting. The Lion, the Unicorn. And he'd just looked. He thought it was wrong if Rob hadn't been paid but he had not said anything about it to him. He only mentioned it now because he wanted to explain to himself really why it was that Rob had turned so quiet and withdrawn in the last few days. It must be because he had no money. Looking at the Lieutenant's face now, he began to wish he had not mentioned it.

'I've got to get goin'. I'll be late for school,' he said.

But the Lieutenant appeared not to hear him and seemed quite distracted when he waved him off.

Diggle had read the account of Oscar Solly's meeting with Billy Moffat in the Aurora Tea Room as well. And Dexter had been with him. Alby Diggle, a man that few people ever took to, a coarse unfeeling sort of man you would have said, was consumed with shame and guilt at what they had made him do to Ernie Grayson. He thought about it every day. Poor Little Ernie, poor little sod. Well, Diggle thought, before he went back off leave he'd settle with Dexter. Because Dexter had volunteered for the job that day. He must have. Diggle would never forget that and now the bastard had skipped. I'll settle his hash, he told himself. I know where he lives now.

He'd had all day to think about it. Perhaps he shouldn't have told the Lieutenant about Rob and the fact that he had not been paid. Mebbes the Lieutenant would think he was being asked for money, as if he was being asked to sub Rob. He might even think that Dolly had sent him down. What if the Lieutenant thought Dolly was scrounging off him? What then? The Lieutenant might even change his mind about her.

By the time he reached home from school Joshua had made up his mind. He would tell Dolly what he had said. Then if she was worried he would go early the next day to the pier and explain to the Lieutenant exactly how things had come about. And he wanted to tell Dolly anyway about Rob's shortage of cash. He was leaving in three days' time and although he had a travel warrant — he had shown it to Joshua, stamped, signed — he would need money as well.

Rob was in his usual place by the fire when Joshua entered. A newspaper lay on the floor by the side of his chair. He had been sleeping. It was obvious by the way he shuffled in his chair and wiped the sleep from his eyes. If Joshua had not spent all the money in the box on his mother's funeral, he would have given it to Rob there and then. But now he could not stay in the room with him. He was too embarrassed to carry his secret knowledge.

'I'm goin' down to chop some sticks,' he told Rob and went down to the back yard to get the log and the small axe out of the wash house. Only half an hour or so later, long after the stick chopping was over, did he go back upstairs.

Dolly was chattering away, in one of her very cheerful moods, laughing, telling Rob about some incident during the day, though his replies showed little real interest. Rob had pulled his chair close to the fire, rubbing his hands in front of it as though in need of warmth. Even Dolly's animated chatter faded when she saw how little notice her brother was taking.

'Think I'll have a bit stroll,' Rob said quite suddenly. He stood up. 'I'm just goin' round the block. I won't be long.'

He put on his cap and fastened a thick wool muffler round his throat. With only the briefest of goodbyes, he went quietly down the back stairs, through the yard and into the back lane.

Dolly busied herself, peeling potatoes and turnips. Her face was set tight as though she was very unhappy. She lit the fire, putting up a sheet of newspaper as a blazer. The first sheet took fire and she wrapped it into a hasty ball and threw it into the grate. Somehow the sudden flames seemed to cheer her up and by the time a second blazer had got the fire going, she was a little more her old self. Only then did Joshua feel himself able to say to her what he had been thinking about all day.

'He's got no money,' was how he started.

'Eh?' Dolly was busy lighting the gas mantle and she looked over at him, the paper spill still alight in her hand.

'He's got no money. Rob. He's got no money. That's why he's so quiet. That's why he doesn't go anywhere.'

Dolly shook her head.

'I don't think it's that,' she said. She paused to blow the spill out. 'Those people the other night, the Graysons, I think that's what's upset him.'

Joshua remembered the old couple sitting there, how the old man had reached over and held his wife's hand.

'Well, anyway, he's still got no money. I know that,' he said. 'If he had some money, he could go out. Enjoy hisself.' In the way a rowdy feller might do.

'Has he said? Has he mentioned not having any money?' Dolly was looking alarmed now. 'We let'm pay for the tickets at The Imperial. They weren't cheap seats.'

'Best in the house,' Joshua reminded her.

She went through to the scullery. He could hear her there, moving pots around, running something under the tap. She had some meat left, not much; she would chop up some onions; she would make some gravy and they'd have panhacklety for supper. It wouldn't be as good as before the war, of course, what with the meat shortage, but it would be tasty.

'Anyway,' she called through, 'how do you know he's got no money? Has he been sayin'?'

That was the question he had not wanted her to ask. Really, given time, he could have told her. He could have led up to it, explained that he had seen Rob's pay book almost by accident, just lying there really.

'What d'ye say?' she called. She hadn't heard him, his voice had been so low. 'Has he been sayin' somethin' to ye?'

'I've seen his pay book. It was on the mantelpiece.'

Joshua's voice was louder than he had intended this time. It seemed to him that he had shouted to her at the top of his voice.

In the scullery, Dolly had stopped doing whatever it was she was doing. It was suddenly very quiet in there. She came to stand at the kitchen door, holding a saucepan by the handle.

'Ye've seen his pay book?'

She was puzzled.

'What d'ye mean, ye've seen his pay book?'

Joshua flicked a strand of hair away from his forehead, licked his lips. His throat was dry. He'd said it. He'd have to go through with it.

'I looked in it. I saw it on the mantelpiece and I looked in it. Yesterday.'

Dolly took a hesitant step into the room.

'Well?'

He didn't want her to think he did that sort of thing regularly, poking round in other people's belongings. Because he didn't.

'He hasn't been paid for ages. Not since March.'

'What d'ye mean?'

What could he mean? Nothing more than what he had already said.

'Just, he can't have any money if he's not been paid.'

'Since March?'

She went back into the scullery and he heard the saucepan being put down. She came back into the kitchen, wary-eyed, rubbing her damp hands on her pinafore. Joshua wondered if she was going to be angry with him.

'He hasn't been paid since March?' was all she said. She was frowning, anxious looking, quite unlike her usual self.

'No.'

She shook her whole body as if trying to wake herself up, as though she was in a dream.

'I told the Lieutenant,' Joshua told her after a long silence. The Lieutenant, he had never called him that to Dolly's face before and wondered if she would be annoyed with him.

But that was the last thing that concerned Dolly. 'Ye told Mr. Samways?' she asked. This was an even greater shock or so it seemed for now she put one hand to her mouth and with the other she balanced herself against the table.

'When did you see Mr. Samways?'

And her voice was sharp, harsh, like a teacher's. She was angry now.

'This mornin'.'

'Where was this?'

And he told her, down at the pier; he'd thought he would be there. He always was. He needed the exercise, the fresh air, because that was what the doctor had said about his lungs. He'd been wounded and they had said that he should get plenty of fresh air, fresh morning air. A good walk on the pier each morning ... they both knew that. He was always there. But also he was there because if ever Dolly needed him, that's where he was. Loyal. Faithful. Like a knight.

'And ye've told him our Rob's short of money?'

'Yes.'

She licked her lips, uncertain of what next to say.

'And ye mentioned the pay book? Ye told him ye'd seen the pay book?'

Joshua nodded and before anything else could be said, they heard Rob's footsteps coming up the back staircase. When he came into the kitchen he muttered something, gave a sharp nod of the head and went through to the bedroom. Dolly took a deep breath and followed him.

Joshua heard Dolly speak, knew she was asking her brother something even though he could not make out exactly what it was she was saying. But if she kept her voice low, Rob did not. Every word he said was clear enough.

'No money? What d'ye mean, I've no money?'

Then Dolly's voice, once more restrained, indistinct.

And Rob's.

'Where d'ye get that idea? Look. Here.'

Joshua imagined him bringing out a wallet, showing Dolly that he most certainly had money. And he hoped that he had. He did not want Rob to be worried about being short of cash.

'That's all right then.' Dolly's voice, louder now, came through into the kitchen. 'Just an idea he'd got.'

It was Rob's turn then to lower his tone, his turn not to be clearly heard. Something he said, his voice putting a question. And now Dolly's voice, quiet again, uncertain, faltering.

Then the angry shout.

'And I'm sayin' I want to know where he got the idea from!'

Rob came bustling into the kitchen.

'What's this?' he shouted, walking up close to Joshua, bending down to him so that their faces were on a level.

'What's this about?'

The angry eyes stared into Joshua's and then he felt Rob's grip on his forearm.

'Come on, lad.'

Now, tightening his grip, Rob shook Joshua to and fro.

'Leave him!'

Dolly was standing at Rob's side, her expression anxious and her voice shrill.

'Leave him alone. He's only a bairn.'

'I want to know what this is about,' Rob insisted, his tone fierce. He stood up now and released Joshua. 'I'm not satisfied. Ye just don't come up with some idea like that. Have ye been pryin' into things that don't concern ye?'

Joshua, transfixed, unable to speak.

'Come on, Rob,' Dolly said, speaking in a more reasonable manner. 'Come on. Forget it.'

But there was to be no forgetting it.

'You been stickin' your nose in where it's not wanted?'

Now the words came out cold and hard, more frightening to Joshua than the shouting.

'I saw it in your pay book,' he said.

He had just been looking at the cover, he told Rob. Then he had glanced inside just to see what it was like.

Rob nodded.

'Aye, well.'

His features relaxed, he drew a breath as though making himself ready to apologise. That is how he looked, like a man preparing to say that he had been rather hasty.

'That's easily explained. I'm lettin' it accumulate. Savin' it. I haven't been drawin' me pay.'

It was good enough for Joshua.

But that was not all. He had thought about it. He had meant it for the best but mebbes he should not have told the Lieutenant. It really was not his business, had nothing to do with him.

Joshua swallowed hard, clearing his throat.

'I told somebody.'

He sneaked a look at Dolly, wondering now if he had not made another mistake.

'Told somebody?'

Joshua mumbled something, made a flapping gesture with his right hand.

'He told somebody,' Dolly broke in. 'He didn't mean any harm.'

Rob stared at Joshua, his expression changing once more in such a short time.

'He didn't mean it,' Dolly insisted. 'Not the way you think. Really.'

Dolly pleading: Dolly being reasonable: Dolly trying to persuade her brother to be reasonable: Dolly ignoring what her brother had said about saving his pay, accumulating it, not drawing it. Could soldiers do that?

'I just wanted to tell him that ye had no money. I thought ye'd go to the social for a bit of entertainment. I though ye would be glad to go there,' Joshua paused, fidgeted a moment with the flap of his jacket pocket. 'I was sorry for ye.'

'Sorry for me?'

'Wait a minute,' Dolly interrupted. 'We might as well explain.' She stood up straight, facing Rob. 'Listen. I want you to be sensible when ye hear this.'

'Well?'

'Will ye be sensible?'

'Come on. Let's hear it first.'

Before Dolly had time to insist further, Joshua spoke, blurted it out.

'I told Mr. Samways.'

He saw Dolly's eyes close, her lips twitch. She would have explained it differently.

'It's not the Samways you know,' she said. 'Not him. His son.'

'He's a Lieutenant,' Joshua added.

'He's been kind to us,' Dolly broke in. 'I told ye how Joshua came here. His father got him here, away from the workhouse.'

'He's a nice man,' Joshua volunteered. 'He's very nice, Mr. Samways, isn't he?'

But Dolly was flustered now, picking with nervous fingers at her pinafore.

'Yes, very nice,' she agreed curtly, never taking her eyes off her brother.

'He really is,' Joshua went on. 'We've been on a picnic with him and other places.'

Then the silence fell. Joshua looked from Dolly to Rob, from Rob to Dolly, both standing motionless in the middle of the room. Dolly dropped her eyes at last and Rob, clearing his throat loudly, took a seat in the horsehair chair.

'So then,' he said at last. 'Ye've been out on a picnic and other places with this Lieutenant Samways.'

Dolly bit her lip, made no reply.

Joshua watched her, took her silence as his cue and made no attempt to speak even though he felt able now to explain this whole business. If only Rob could understand, the Lieutenant had been wounded, had fought in France. He had been decorated. He was sure that if Rob just listened to that, he would see matters differently.

'Have ye no memory?'

Just one sentence, a few words at a time, dripping out slowly.

'No pride?'

Let that sink in.

Should he say, Joshua wondered, that Dolly still went each week to clean at Mrs. Waterstone's house. It was empty. Even the housekeeper had left now. But Dolly went every Tuesday night just to keep it nice. The Lieutenant used to be there to let her in. Should he tell Rob that? But he remained silent.

'Can ye remember our mother? He broke her heart.'

'Not him,' Dolly answered sharply as if suddenly coming to life.

'Doesn't matter. That family.'

Dolly, ashen faced, went to the fireplace, moved the pan of potatoes and turnips, eased the coals with the poker. She had to keep occupied, think of other things.

'That family,' Rob repeated, emphasising both words.

'He's kind to Mrs. Weston.'

Joshua felt he had to protect her, support her somehow. He had always thought her strong, able to look after herself, but tonight she could not stand up to her brother.

'He's given her clothes. That's why she looks so smart. His sister's.'

Rob placed his hand on a chair back as if to steady himself, as if unable to believe what it was he had heard. His face was flushed, tense. He stood with his back to the fireplace, put his hands on his waist.

'This is disgraceful, woman,' he said.

Dolly remained silent, going to the cupboard to get out knives and forks, giving herself some activity to relieve the tension.

'He's been givin' ye clothes, has he?'

She placed the cutlery on the table with some deliberation, taking more care with their arrangement than usual. She went back into the scullery, coming back with the plates.

'Are ye his kept woman, then?'

Again she said nothing though she flinched as she heard the words.

'Are ye that to one of the Samways family?'

Before she had any chance to answer, he crossed to the table, gripping her by the arm, just as he had done earlier to Joshua. His face was bright red with anger whilst Dolly's remained ashen white.

'The family that treated you the way they did ... and your husband away in the army ... you foolin' about with one of them, one of those Samways ... after what they did ... and our mother ... have no memory? Can you not remember anything?'

It was not coherent but it was loud.

And Dolly, wrenching herself away, found the courage to shout back at him.

'It's not your business. You're a visitor here. You don't belong in this house. Nothin' in it is yours. You're a visitor. Behave yourself and let me alone.'

Rob pondered her words a moment, let loose her arm and went back to the fire. He stared into the flames for a moment, seemed to be closely inspecting a bubble of tar running down the bars. And then turned speaking much more calmly now.

'You've had the nerve to associate with a man who's givin' ye clothes.' He shook his head. 'If that's not bein' a whore I don't know what is.'

Dolly stood her ground this time, defying him, letting him have his say.

'But if that's not bad enough, it's one of that bloody clan that treated our mother so badly, stopped me and my brother from workin' in the shipyards.'

'Go on,' Dolly said. She was back to her old commanding form. 'There's more. I know the story, of course. I'm the point of it.'

'Enough's been said,' Rob answered her. 'I'm finished with ye.'

'Finish the story,' Dolly said. She was confident now.

'There's no story, woman.' Now Rob was on the defensive as if he knew he had said too much already. He sat down again, his head in his hands.

'There's a story, right enough,' Dolly went on. 'Ye can't just pick the bits ye want to hear.'

She went over to where Rob sat, stood over him. It was as if she had forgotten all about Joshua. As though only she and her brother were in the room.

'When I was goin' to have a baby you and Henry and mother stuck by me. I was grateful for that.'

'That's enough,' Rob snapped. 'No need goin' over past history.'

'It is past history. That's the point of all this. Past history. You brought it up. And what I'm sayin' to you is that ye can't just pick the bits ye want.'

'The lad's here. He's too young for this.'

'No, he's not. He's not too young.'

Dolly moved over to Joshua and in that old familiar way of hers she put her arm round him.

'I'd never want to hurt or upset him. He knows that,' she said quietly. She no longer had that hard, argumentative edge to her voice. Now, it was as though she was taking part in an intimate discussion. 'There's a reason for that,' she said.

Suddenly Rob made to leave the room.

'Wait. Don't you go runnin' off now,' she called out to him. She held out a hand though it would never have restrained him if he had been determined to leave. As it was, it was enough to stop him. 'I need this. I need to say these things. I had little chance all those years ago. Now please. Let me have my say.'

Rob took out a handkerchief, dabbing his sweating face. He was still angry, that much was obvious. But he looked exhausted too. He lowered himself slowly, feeling the edge of the chair behind him. When he was seated, he placed his elbows on his knees, his head in his hands.

'Sit down, Joshua,' Dolly said. 'Ye need to hear this partly because of your mam; partly because this man here has called me a whore and he says I've forgotten things about my past.' She drew a deep breath. Then she took a kitchen chair and drew it up to the

188

table. She rested her worn hands on the oil cloth and as she spoke she drew little circles with her finger tips.

'Your mam was so kind to me,' she began. 'She was a stranger in this town and I was born here but I had more comfort from her than most.'

'I was havin' a baby, and unmarried, and the father off out of the district,' she said. She looked first at Joshua and then at Rob. Her words did not come out angrily or bitterly, just rather wryly. 'It's a sin, ye know. Havin' a baby and not bein' wed.'

And Joshua knew it was, taking her words at face value. Dolly had been a sinner. He knew about sin. The chapel had told him: his mother had told him.

'He stood up in that chapel on the Sunday morning. That Samways. And my mother was there. And you, Rob, and Henry.' She nodded at Henry's photograph as she mentioned his name. 'And Samways stood at the front there and he looked at me and all of us, all the family. Looked at us and without flinchin' he told them, everybody there. I can remember it as if it had happened this mornin'.'

She glanced down at her hands, stretched out along her thighs. She drew a deep breath as though preparing herself to say something devastating.

'One among us has sinned!'

Dolly boomed the words out, stretching out from the edge of her chair towards Joshua. Rob, sitting now by the table, stared out of the window.

'That's what he said. "One among us has sinned."'

She clasped her hands together in her lap, gripped them tightly until her knuckles shone white.

'That's what he said. And it was me he meant. I hadn't even any idea he knew.'

She sniffed, gave a short laugh.

'The doctor. He'd no compunction about lettin' Mr. Samways know, the great Mr. Samways. No difficulty at all lettin' him know that one of the daft young lasses in the chapel had sinned. Can ye imagine it?'

Joshua could imagine it.

His mind went back to all those Sundays, sitting next to his mother in the highly polished, crowded pews. And some Sundays

Mr. Samways would stand up in front of them and say exactly those words that Dolly had just uttered. 'One among us has sinned!' Fornicators, adulterers, loose livers, intemperate men and women given to drink, lust, passion and Mr. Samways would identify their sins, name them sinners. He wouldn't shout out their names. Rather he would stand there, fixing his pince-nez more firmly on the bridge of his nose and would call out the names and the offences calmly and quietly. And Joshua had seen the guilty identified, had seen them stand up, their heads bowed, their stricken faces pale or scarlet with shame, the tears chasing down their cheeks. At Mr. Samways' urging they would stumble forward down the aisle, every eye upon them, right to the front where, agonised, they would admit all that they were guilty of. And not one, at least not one in Joshua's experience, ever claimed his innocence.

'I've beaten me wife.'

'I've committed adultery.'

'I've drunk to excess.'

Mostly the men.

But sometimes the women.

And all the greater the sin for that.

'He said I should come out to the front and confess me sin in front of everybody,' Dolly's face revealed the horror of that long ago event. 'Even you were there that day, Joshua. You were there with your mam. But ye were too young to remember it. You were in a shawl in your mam's arms.'

He had seen her, had been there.

All those years ago. But he had no memory of it.

And he felt ashamed that he should have been there to see her, a young girl, brought out like that in front of all the people in the congregation.

'I was just a young girl. I'd no idea he knew. Didn't know what he was goin' to say. Only my mother knew, so I thought. And she'd been good and understandin'. And the doctor, of course. He knew.'

Dolly ran her hand over her mouth and looked at Rob, still motionless in his chair.

'You two, you and Henry, knew nothin'. It must've been an awful shock, I'm aware of that and I said sorry at the time. Sorry to you two.'

In his seat, Rob gave no indication that he had heard her. His bony face was still.

'Anyway,' Dolly went on. '"Come forward, girl," Samways says. I didn't know what I'd do. I was gettin' ready to go out, up to the front, just as he said. I felt terrible, all those people, everybody watchin'. And ashamed. Then our Henry stood up.'

Again Dolly's eyes travelled across to the photograph.

'"She's not comin'," he said. He was only a young chap but he stood up in that chapel that day. "Ye can forget about it, Mr. Samways," he said and his voice — I'll never forget it, his voice — it carried to every quarter of that buildin'. He was a quiet lad, Henry, but that day he spoke up. He spoke up for me.'

Joshua could not imagine it, somebody standing up like that in the chapel and defying Mr. Samways. It had never seemed possible that anyone would ever answer him back. He remembered how his mother had always been in awe of Mr. Samways, of how she spoke about him, always as if she was frightened of him.

'And he marched us out, our Henry. Him and Rob and my mother and me, we all just went out.'

Just at this moment there was a hint of triumph in Dolly's voice.

'And we never went back.'

Only the hiss of the gas, the water bubbling in the pan on the fire, the collapse of some coals at the side of the grate — a silence now as though Dolly was awaiting some kind of judgement from her two listeners.

'No, ye haven't forgotten,' Rob said. He did not sound angry now, just calm. And bitter. 'That's why it's so mad, you goin' out with this feller. Him a Samways. And lettin' him give ye clothes. It's inexcusable, Dolly.'

'What's inexcusable,' she said, her own voice equally level and calm, 'is your inability to recognise that Hector Samways isn't responsible for his father's acts.'

'Same blood.'

The gaslight behind her seemed to make the ends of Dolly's hair shine as if they were the finest wires of gold. Usually she looked so strong and cheerful. Now that her story was over she looked ill, shrunk into herself. Then she appeared to summon up all her strength as if there was more that she needed to say.

'It broke us up, Joshua, as a family. Mebbes it was my fault gettin' pregnant. It all sprang from there. It started with me. Perhaps I'm the one that ought to be blamed. Mr. Samways wouldn't have had to call me up in front if I hadn't've been pregnant.'

From Rob, standing in front of the fire, came an unexpected snort.

'Aye. And we'd all be goin' to the chapel to this day. All good members.'

'Rob thinks Mr. Samways was responsible for all of it.' She shook her head. 'He wasn't. Bits, mebbes. But he's not God. Mebbes he thinks he is. But he's not. He made life difficult for us. But not impossible. Me mam's rent went up. Wasn't his house. One of his pals owned it but we've no proof that it had anything to do with Samways. And we managed.'

'Managed?' Rob again. 'Henry was a skilled man but he couldn't keep a job. Not in the yards. They hounded him out. All Samways' work. He joined the army because of Samways.'

Dolly made no reply. She had said all she felt able to say. She was exhausted.

'Ye've a lot to learn,' Rob said, shaking his head slowly as if he could not understand his sister. 'I went south as well.'

He walked over to where Dolly had sat down on one of the kitchen chairs. He was not angry any more. It was as if he suspected that Dolly had no stomach for any further argument.

'I'm sorry, Dolly,' he said. 'We're not goin' to agree on this. Just let's leave it.'

He crossed the room and went through to the bedroom. After a couple of seconds he came back in pulling on his jacket.

'I'll be leavin' on Monday,' he said. 'It's nothin' to do with me how ye conduct your life. Perhaps you're right about young Samways. I doubt it but that's up to you.'

Dolly began sorting the cutlery on the table again although it was not necessary. It had already been put in place.

'Are ye goin' out again? Ye haven't had anythin' to eat.'

They couldn't look at each other.

'Come and get yourself something to eat', she said. 'It won't be long.'

She was struggling to speak in her normal voice, as if no angry words had been exchanged.

'Keep some. I'll have it heated up later. I'd just like to go out.'

Rob paused at the door, struggled with a brief smile and left.

'Why's he gone out?' Joshua asked when he heard the front door close.

'I think he's a bit embarrassed. He's not an argumentative man.'

She walked across to the window, looked down at the yard below where Mrs. Rimmer's chickens busily pecked their way through life.

'Can I ask?' Joshua said to her back. 'What happened to the baby?'

He did not know if it was the sort of question he ought to ask. He had had to steel himself to ask it.

Dolly turned, her face flushed. She brushed her forehead with the back of her hand. Then she inspected the back of both hands, then the palms. When she spoke it was to them that she addressed herself.

'I went to Carlisle to live. Stayed with a nice woman, friend of me mother's. I had the baby, went to work and this woman looked after him during the day. And it was George Weston's mother's home. She didn't look down on me, didn't think I was shameless. Just as well. Anyway, the baby died after five months. I didn't know what to do. Then George asked me to marry him. We lived there in Carlisle for several years. Last year I came back here. After I'd heard George was missin'. No reason why, really. I just felt I wanted to.'

Yet again Dolly appeared to have come to the end of her story. Without a word she left the kitchen and Joshua heard her pick up the bucket in the scullery. She went downstairs into the yard. The sound of her filling the bucket in the coal house drifted up the stairway. Then the coal house door was sharply shut and Dolly climbed the back stairs. She hesitated on the top stair to catch her breath. Then he heard her put the bucket in its place in the scullery. She came into the kitchen again, rubbing her hand, trying to ease the marks made by the handle. Joshua wondered if she really needed to go for coal then. Had she gone just to have a few moments to herself?

As if there had been no interval, Dolly took up the story again.

'Your mother was a friend to me in those days after that business in the chapel. She'd just had you and your dad had been killed in the yards.'

Dolly smiled.

'She wasn't taken over by the chapel in those days. She came round to see me, give me a bit of comfort. I'll never forget it.'

Then the smile left her face. Her eyes brimmed with tears.

'I never forgot it. But I wasn't grateful enough. When I came back here, we did a few jobs, cleaning, together. But I found her difficult, changed. D'ye understand?'

Joshua's put his hands in Dolly's. 'I know ye didn't see her much after ye came back. And I understand why.'

He could understand it, why a kind generous woman like Dolly could not forget his mother's kindness and yet did not wish to see her any more. He knew his mother had changed.

Dolly freed one hand, wiped a tear from her cheek.

'What I do know is that the day ye saw her bein' taken to the workhouse, ye decided to do something really kind.' Joshua felt strong, protective. He stroked her cheek. He wished he could say more but he did not have the words.

9

Dolly was glad to have the place to herself. And Joshua had looked forward to going to the social, she knew that, could see how excited he was as he left the house.

With Rob about, after the row, she was uneasy. He was her brother. They had tried hard since last night to make things up. Not in any sloppy kind of way. But they tried to talk and act normally, as if nothing had been said. But, of course, there was a tension between them, an atmosphere. And they were trying too hard to pretend it did not exist. She was glad when Rob had said he would be going out. He had been out most of the day and he'd decided to go out again before his supper. She tried to stifle the thought that she would be glad when he went back. She mustn't think such things, she told herself, mustn't wish him back in the trenches. She thought again about his pay book, what he'd said about it. It made her uneasy but she told herself she was being silly, over-dramatic, looking for trouble.

She sat in the chair by the kitchen fire, pulling a rug over her knees. It was cold, the draught finding its way through the window frame, searching its way up both sets of stairs, front and back. She reached forward, warming her hands. The chapel hall would be freezing. She had made Joshua put an extra vest on before he went.

It had been a hard week, she thought. Mostly because of Rob but because of work as well. She had worked every morning and all but one of the afternoons. She had done two nights as well, laundry work in a house where the woman was sick. Sheets and blankets, boiling, scrubbing, ironing. That house wasn't even on the tram route and she had had to walk a couple of miles each way.

Beggars can't be choosers, she told herself. No George now with a pay packet to look forward to when the war was over. When it was over? If, more likely, the way things were going on. Strange though, she often thought of George, that she ought to weep for him, mourn for him. She never had. Not enough, anyway. What would she have done if he had turned up one day, just out of the blue? What would she have thought if she had found him standing on the doorstep a fortnight earlier? How would she have felt, seeing him standing there instead of Rob? The questions were insistent, always there, never answered. She tried to persuade herself she would have been glad to see him.

Dolly stood up from the chair, uncomfortable with herself. She'd tried to be a good wife. She was sure of that. Could she not sustain love? Would what she now felt for Hector pass away just as easily? In two years' time would she be just as indifferent to him? She wasn't indifferent to George: she just didn't love him. Or rather, she was no longer in love with him. That was more like it, she told herself. She loved him all right: she wasn't in love. Even to realise that gave her little comfort. Was it her? Was there something wrong with her?

She drew her shawl around her shoulders, shivering. She went through to the front room which was colder still, a room deep in shadow, only a faint streak of moonlight lighting up one wall. She looked out onto the brick terrace opposite, almost black now, occasional windows faintly lit by flickering gas jets turned down low. The cobbles of the street had a kind of dull patina from a light drizzle. The wind was rising. It was the kind of night when, later, chimney pots would rattle, when loose slates would fall, when zinc baths would be wrenched off back yard walls and dustbins would tip out bucket loads of ash from countless fires.

She hoped Joshua would get back dry. And Rob too. He said he had somewhere to go, but he had not said where. He had not been surly or anything like that. He had just said, 'I'm off out. Got to see somebody. I'll be back by nine.' Perhaps earlier during his leave he might have said where it was he was off to. She was not sure.

She fidgeted, standing by the window, gazing out into the deserted street. What if she had never come back here from Carlisle? No Joshua; no Hector. Mebbes it would have been wiser, she thought at first. Yes, it might have been wiser not to get mixed up with a ten year old bairn and a man from the wrong family. But staying in Carlisle wouldn't have brought George back.

It was getting cold standing there at the window. Nothing to see. She tugged her shawl more closely around her shoulders, picked her way out of the front room and went back into the kitchen. She sat down and the heat of the fire enveloped her.

She might have dozed ten minutes or so. Not much longer. A knock at the door. She was unsure if it was the first knock. Maybe whoever it was had been knocking for ages. She stood up unsteadily, stifling a yawn. Only quarter to eight? Was that Joshua back already? Surely not. Or perhaps Rob had decided to come home early. She glanced at herself in the mirror.

'I'm a mess,' she said, scowling at the woman in the mirror.

Another knock.

Couldn't be Rob. He had a key anyway. Unless he'd left it behind, forgotten it.

By the time she reached the bottom step she heard men's voices outside on the pavement.

'Now who?' she asked herself.

For a moment she wondered if Rob had brought some fellers home. Met them in the pub, saying, 'Come on back, lads, have a drink in the house.' Had he given out some kind of invitation? But she knew he hadn't as soon as the thought came to her. In any case, there was never a drop of anything like that in her house. Never had been in her mother's either. She'd seen too much, the old woman.

Dolly opened the door to a huge policeman, his helmet and cape beaded with rain. Behind him stood three soldiers, one of them a corporal. Each one of the four looked serious.

'I've come to see Corporal Dexter, missus,' the constable said. Evidently he was in charge. 'Can I ask ye if he's in the house?'

Dolly shook her head. Her throat was dry. She knew. They didn't have to tell her.

'You're tellin' me he's not home at the moment?'

'He's not home, no.'

Could the people over the street see what was happening? Did the people next door? Policeman at the door; soldiers. Two of them, by their hats and armbands, she recognised as military policemen. The third soldier, standing at the back, gave the appearance of a hanger-on. He looked from one to the other as they spoke but never offered any remarks, just stood there sucking his large misshapen front teeth.

'Can I ask ye,' the policeman said, 'can I ask ye if he is stayin' here at the present?'

'He's gone,' Dolly blurted out.

She'd known since yesterday, when Joshua told her about the pay book. She had known something was wrong, had known exactly what it was.

'Gone?'

It was the corporal's turn now. He half thrust himself in front of the constable.

'Where's he gone, missus?'

'I've no idea.'

What if he came up the street now? What if Rob just walked up to the house? She looked at the man waiting on the step. The constable sniffed, rubbed the side of his nose with his forefinger, cleared his throat. He was embarrassed.

'I'm afraid we're goin' to ask ye if we can search the house for him,' he said, not looking at Dolly but rather staring over her shoulder and up the stairs.

Her brain was numb.

'What's he done?'

Even as she spoke the words she realised she should not waste time. If she held them up he might come along slap-bang into their arms. Don't argue, don't question, get it over with. Let them in and get them out quick as possible.

'He's deserted, pet,' the constable told her. 'At least, that's how it seems.'

The soldier at the rear shuffled on the pavement.

'Deserted?' She wondered if she was convincing enough, if she sounded surprised enough.

'Well, ye know. We're not sure altogether. Might be an explanation. Easy enough explanation,' the policeman said.

'But he's been given a medal,' Dolly said. 'He won a medal. For bravery. It was in all the papers.'

The constable gave her a sympathetic look, smiling quietly, nodding at her, as if he was confident that such an explanation would be forthcoming.

'Might just be a misunderstandin'. Best clear it up, eh?'

At the constable's side, the corporal was impatient.

'Can we come up?' he asked abruptly.

Dolly stood aside and the four men went carefully upstairs. What are they expecting? she wondered. Do they expect him to come out and attack them?

They went cautiously from room to room; two of them went down the back stairs and searched the back yard, the coal house, lav and wash house. Dolly remained in the kitchen. When they came back to where she was standing close to the window, they had found not a sign of him or his belongings.

'Ye say he's gone,' the corporal said. 'When did he go?'

Her hands were shaking and she attempted to still them, gripping tightly at the seams of her skirt. She knew she must look guilty.

'He went yesterday,' she told them, knowing that she sounded as if she was lying, and only realising now as she spoke why he had put his rifle and his uniform and his boots in the attic space.

'They'll take less room up,' he had said.

If they looked up there, they would know he had not gone back.

'Right then,' the policeman said. He put a hand on her forearm. 'Don't worry, hinny. I'm sure it'll work out. There'll be an explanation.'

'He was on leave,' Dolly faltered, hanging on to one small straw of hope.

'He's been missin' from his unit for several months,' said the corporal. 'At least that's what we believe. We don't believe he was on authorised leave.'

'No,' Dolly said. 'He's been here only a couple of weeks. Just a bit longer. Not three. He hasn't been here three weeks yet.'

There was obviously a mistake somewhere, she told them, trying hard to convince herself.

'Aye, missus,' the corporal replied. 'He might've been here only a couple of weeks or so. But he's been somewhere else an' all.'

'Or so it appears,' the constable added, still sympathetic towards Dolly. 'Mebbes it's all some kind of mistake.'

But Alby Diggle, the only one who had not spoken, had a smirk on his face.

Dolly saw them downstairs. Now she was anxious for them to get away from the house before Rob returned. It was nearly twenty past eight. He might already be on his way back. They might even bump into him.

Dolly opened the front door and they trooped out into the street. The constable smiled encouragingly, reinforcing yet again his idea that it was all a mistake, a silly misunderstanding that would easily be cleared up. But the soldiers were surly, stone-faced. It was really to them that Dolly, already closing the door on them, addressed her last remark.

'He won a medal. It was in all the newspapers,' she told them again as they turned to walk away.

Even the grown-ups had joined in — Winky, Blind Man's Buff, King Tut and the Queen of Sheba (oh, the shrieks at that one when the blindfolded woman put her finger in the peeled tomato 'And here's his eye,' Mr. Ainscough had said to her, guiding her hand), Trencher, Musical Chairs — and there had been some dancing. Joshua had joined in the dancing, the Eightsome Reel and Stripping the Willow. He had not known always what to do. They had shouted at him, the old 'uns, 'No. Not that way, man' and 'Now, down with your partner. That way, lad' and 'Go on. Down the middle. That's right.' And they had laughed at him not knowing which way to go and what to do next. But he was not the only one.

Now he sat at the side waiting. It was all over. People were on their way home now, pulling on their overcoats, their mufflers, saying goodbye to each other, roaring with laughter, some exchanging whispers, glances, I-told-ye-so sniffs. But none of that concerned him. He was just hanging on to say goodbye to Billy, wondering if ever he would see him again. Billy and his dad were talking to Mr. Samways, shaking hands. You'd think their conversation was nearly over. The two men would tap each other on the arm and then would step back a couple of paces so that you'd think, Yes, that's goodbye, that's the end. But it wasn't. The talk would start up again.

More and more the hall emptied so that eventually there were only a few stragglers left, half a dozen men putting the chairs away in the store cupboard and some of the womenfolk washing up in the kitchen. The Lieutenant was on the other side of the hall talking to an old couple, smiling all the time at them as if he was really interested in what they had to say. When Joshua had first come in the Lieutenant had come over and he had said he was glad to see him. He had helped Joshua off with his coat. Then Billy had come over. He'd felt so proud. Two of the people he most admired in the world were there, under the same roof, and they had both spoken to him. Billy had been with him most of the evening. They'd danced in the same groups and during the games they'd sometimes partnered each other. Billy wasn't all that good at some of the games. He wasn't quick and nimble and although Joshua liked him enormously, he was pleased that Billy was so awkward and ungainly. Just as all those months ago, when Billy had had his accident, he was awkward and ungainly.

Now he looked across at Billy again. This time, it really did look as if they were saying their last words. Old Mr. Samways — how long ago it seemed since that Sunday morning when they had gone to the hospital to see Billy — old Mr. Samways had shaken hands with Billy and was turning his attention to Mr. Moffat. He hadn't really been too bad tonight. Joshua remembered how his mother had talked constantly about Mr. Samways, about how frightening he seemed, but he really had been quite nice. When he had time between one of the games he had come over to where Joshua was sitting. 'How're you getting on?' he'd asked. 'D'you like it where you are now?' Very nice of him.

And now Joshua stood, readying himself to go over to Billy, when he heard the resounding slam of the outside door. Such a slamming noise that the woman talking to Lieutenant Samways jumped and then giggled at the shock it had given her. Then Joshua saw Dolly coming through the door at the top of the hall, hesitating and looking round. When she saw Joshua, she came over to where he was. At the same time, Joshua saw the Lieutenant making a hasty farewell to the old couple and walking across in his direction too.

'Joshua,' Dolly said, her voice a hoarse whisper, 'for goodness sake, listen.' She had half run across to where he was sitting and now, bending over him, she put her hand on his arm.

'Dolly,' the Lieutenant's voice cut across hers. He was worried: he knew that only rare circumstances would bring her here. 'What are you doing here?'

'I can't say,' she said, looking over her shoulder, eyeing him stonily as if he was some impertinent stranger. 'I want a word with

Joshua. D'ye mind leavin' us alone?'

'Is there anything I can do?' He knew from her anxious expression that something was wrong. Something serious.

'Please,' she said. Her voice was breathy with impatience. 'Will ye leave us? Go on. I've no wish to speak to ye.'

She bent closer towards Joshua.

'Ye've got to help,' she told him, gripping his arm. 'Quick. Get your coat on. I want ye to find Rob.'

Find him?

Find him where?

At this time of night?

What's up? What's up with Rob?

'I don't know where he is,' Joshua stammered, astonished. 'I've no idea.'

'Listen,' Dolly urged him, tightening her grip. 'Rob's in bad trouble. Serious. We've got to find him.'

Before he had any chance to reply, Joshua caught the vague shape of someone standing next to the Lieutenant. Looking up he saw Mr. Samways staring down at Dolly, with that same expression that he remembered from that Sunday in the hospital all those months before. He was angry and it was apparent even before he spoke.

'What are you doing here?' he asked Dolly. 'With this lad?'

'I want to speak to him. Leave us alone. It's important.'

'I'm sorry,' Mr. Samways said. 'It's not possible. You'll have to leave. You're not welcome here.'

His mouth shut firmly. As far as he was concerned the matter was at an end.

'Father!'

The Lieutenant was puzzled.

'Father. Mrs. Weston is Joshua's guardian at the moment.'

Now it was the old man's turn to look bewildered and to fall silent momentarily.

'She's who?' he said at last and it was as though everyone had waited to give him his turn to speak. 'This lad's guardian? Joshua Slater? His guardian?'

Dolly held out an impatient hand, waving it at both men, to rid herself of them. She manoeuvred herself so that her back was to them. She peered into Joshua's face.

'Listen.'

She had put no lipstick on, no rouge, so that in the gas light her face was shiny and pasty. It was apparent that she had been weeping. She was not the small, neat, jolly woman that Joshua was accustomed to seeing. Tonight she looked ill.

'I can't do it. I can't look for him. They were waitin' outside the house. They've followed me.'

In the doorway three soldiers were standing in a self-conscious huddle and a constable, in cape and helmet stood apart from them.

'You go. Find him. He'll be on his way home,' Dolly whispered. 'He'll only come one of two ways. Either along Huskisson Street or down Alma Lane. If ye see him, tell'm not to come home. And give him this. Tell him to catch a train. Any train as long as he gets away.'

She thrust a bulky envelope into his hand.

'Get your coat on now.'

'What if I don't find him?' What were the chances on this dark night of finding one man who might already have gone home. And how long would he have to stay out? And worse, what had happened to Rob? What was the trouble?

'What if he's not about?' Joshua asked in desperation. 'What if I can't find him?'

'Ye must,' Dolly said, patting his shoulder to encourage him. 'Ye've got to try anyway. Do your best. Please.'

Joshua ran to the end of the hall. Dolly had told him what she wanted him to do. He'd do it if he could.

'You, boy.' It was Mr. Samways shouting. 'You, boy. Where are you off to?'

He heard Dolly call out.

'None of your business. It's nothing to do with you.'

Mr. Samways' voice got mixed up with hers. The few others in the hall were reduced to sudden silence.

'I'd never have done it. Never have agreed,' Mr Samways had turned to his son now. 'You never said it was that woman. I didn't recognise her name when you said she was going to take the lad in.'

It was not clear to Joshua who the old man was shouting at now. He seemed to be addressing both Dolly and the Lieutenant.

'I'll stop it though. I'll stop it tomorrow. I remember her, all those years ago. There's no mistaking her. I knew her the minute she stepped in here.' Mr. Samways' voice was quivering with rage.

Joshua went into the store room, came out struggling with the sleeves of his coat. He looked up at the top of the hall and the constable and the soldiers, still in the same positions.

'You, boy.' Mr. Samways shouted at him again. 'Come here.'

'Go, Joshua. Off you go,' Dolly screamed.

'Dolly Dexter,' Joshua heard Mr. Samways shout in a piercing yell. 'You are not welcome here.'

Then Dolly's voice took over.

'No. I know that. And I don't care.'

Even as he slipped out of the kitchen, past the astonished women washing cups, and even though his mind was concentrating on what he had to do, Joshua was aware of how everyone in the hall, policeman, soldiers and those others who only shortly before had been enjoying the social, all were now focused on just two people. The constable and the corporal were walking over to them.

'She was the kindest of women,' he heard Dolly saying. 'D'ye wonder I wanted to look after her boy? D'ye wonder?'

And Mr. Samways was saying, ignoring Dolly, 'I knew her the moment she walked in. A scarlet woman. She is totally unfit to look after that boy.'

And as he went up the path by the side of the kitchen, Joshua had just a tinge of regret. He had not said goodbye to Billy.

Joshua.

He's out that back door fast and into the back lane behind. Quick as anything. Like a flash. As he would say, 'like a linty'. And even though he's running fast, he's making as little noise as possible. He's not sure what's up, not exactly, but he knows that those fellers inside, the constable and the soldiers, will probably listen to Mr. Samways and try to stop him. Or they might try to follow him. Just as they have followed Dolly. They'll soon twig what's happening. That Dolly's trying to put them off the trail. So off he goes, fast but quiet.

These boots of his — Dolly lets him replace the hob nails as soon as they are worn out; she gives him the bag of studs and he goes down to Mr. Charlton and asks to use his hammer and last. These boots could make an awful clatter, do make an awful clatter when he gets going sometimes, when he bangs his feet down as hard as he can or when he slides along pavements. And you should see the sparks when he does that. But not tonight. Because tonight, though he's running as fast as he can, he's putting his feet down as quietly as possible.

When he gets to the lane end he comes to a stop, chancing his head round the brick wall, weighing things up because if those fellers have tumbled to what's on, they will have left the chapel already. They could be on the pavement even now, not yards from him. So he has this darting glance round the corner, a look to the left, to see if they are anywhere to be seen and there's never a hint of them in the drizzle-shrouded street. He's lucky as well with this drizzle, and fog now, and the mixture getting thicker by the minute. And you can taste the night air, its thin, sharp sourness from the river, and all the factories and the workplaces along it. They're going to have a devil of a job seeing him in this because even though the moon's up, a full moon, there's thick cloud as well.

And he thinks, crossing the road which hasn't a soul in sight and not a van or a lorry in it, never a cyclist nor a pony cart — he thinks to himself, No, they'll never see me but it's not lost on him that it's going to be just as hard for him to find Rob, now on his way home, but who mustn't reach home because somebody, the police, soldiers, are looking for him. And the ones in the hall might not be the only ones. There might be others waiting at the house.

He's got to cut up right now, make his way up these next two, three hundred yards and he's running easily between the unlit street lamps. Never gives a thought to oases. That's over now: that's a game. This isn't. He's got to work out how he's going to find Rob because that is what he has been told to do by Dolly. He mustn't fail and the thought of that, the notion that he must not fail, rather than deter him, elates him. And he feels the excitement in his stomach as he runs and it rises to his chest, almost a tickling sensation, and into the back of his throat. And as he runs, he expels the excitement; with each thudding step he says, 'Rob, I'm comin'. Rob, I'm comin'.'

He cuts through one lane, crosses John Ferris Street at an angle and another lane leads him to the top of Stanhope Street. More like it here, more people about. Not as many as on a Saturday night but for some of them this is pay night and they're out to enjoy themselves and to blazes with the drizzle and the fog and the darkness. So how to find Rob in this crowd? And how to make any good progress when he's constantly having to get off the pavement? At least, here, the fog has lifted and he can see a bit better. And then it closes in again. Sometimes he finds himself in this endless woolly space where he scarcely believes himself to be moving save for the motion of his legs and the fact that he keeps bumping into other people, all of them taking more care than he is. Because Joshua cannot waste time being too careful.

Why has Rob got to catch a train, the first one? Why are the soldiers after him? He's a hero; he has a medal.

Up there, after a couple of minutes or so, he'll come to the bottom of Alma Lane. Rob's not far off, he's sure. He'll go up there because that's one of the ways Dolly said he'd take to get home. He'd get off the tram in Stanhope Street and walk up Alma Lane and he'd soon reach the house. On the other hand it would be just as easy to stay on the tram to the next stop. And even now, a tram comes jolting by, sparks jumping from its overhead rail, sparks from its wheels as well, and it's slowing for the Alma Lane stop and Joshua puts a spurt on. He's just getting his second wind now and there's no tightness in his chest and no tiredness in his legs. As the tram pulls up, only a hundred yards ahead, out they get, three, five, a dozen folks. And he can't be sure yet but as he gets closer, nobody really looks like Rob, who could of course stay on to the next stop, get off at Huskisson Street, walk up from there and be home just as quick. But there's no knowing if he's on that tram. He might have gone up ages ago. And if so he might already have walked in to whoever it was that was waiting for him.

If he's trying to escape from the soldiers, what has he done wrong? Whatever it is, he's a brave man.

Dolly, he thought, is she still rowing in the hall? Is she still arguing with Mr. Samways? Are they both raising their voices and are people still staring at them? And is Mr. Samways still staring at Dolly and repeating what he had said? He was not cold this time as he had been that morning when the spittle had fallen from his mouth onto Joshua's mother's coat. Tonight, when Joshua had last glimpsed him, he was fierce, red-hot angry.

Joshua passed the Alma Lane stop and did not waver, didn't think about going up there. Straight on to Huskisson Street. He could see the tram beyond, getting smaller, its hooded lighting speeding away from him. Then it stopped. It never gave the appearance of slowing down, didn't glide gently to a stop as he knew in reality it must have done. But to him, it appeared to come to a sudden halt. He could make out distant shapes of people coming downstairs and getting down onto the roadway and crossing to the pavement. He wasn't sure, but he didn't think Rob was there. Some of them were going up Huskisson Street but he didn't think any one of them looked like him.

When we went on that picnic ... it was no better than the one with the Lieutenant ... but the picnic and the visit to the theatre. Rob had been so happy ... it was after that he had his back trouble. Everything changed after that.

But what did Rob look like, way ahead in the dark drizzle, in the fog that disturbed all shapes on this Friday night? Easy enough to say that's not him, but it could be and the thought urged him on. Because he had to do something to stop Rob getting home. And he wondered what Rob might have done? What could he have done? Why were they wanting him as urgently as this? Something had gone wrong. But he couldn't work out what and he couldn't work out why they would so desperately seek a hero as if he was a criminal.

Not a criminal, he thought. Not a robber or a murderer. Rob wasn't like that. He was a hero. Like the Lieutenant. It is something to do with his back. That's why they've come for him.

Now Joshua turned up Huskisson Street, going fast, his boots clattering, the sparks flashing. He could imagine the people he passed seeing him giving off these sparks.

The Lieutenant was kind tonight. He came over ...

Suddenly he was lit up from behind and the light cast his shadow against the wall of fog, there was the loud honking of a motor car. 'I'm not in the middle of the road, am I? I'm on the pavement, man.' And as the second honk came he cast a glance over his shoulder, never losing the rhythm of the running, never missing a step, just edging himself further towards the little low walled gardens of the terraced houses on the inside of the pavement. The masked headlights cast their beam beyond him until the light lost itself in the cottonwool fog.

'Here, Joshua.'

Billy's voice. He'd not said goodbye to him. Joshua had been waiting to say goodbye but Billy and his dad had been talking to Mr. Samways but then he'd had to dash away, to look for Rob. And now here was Billy, leaning out of a taxi cab window. It had come to a halt only yards away.

'Get in.'

Now it was Billy's dad, opening the door and getting hold of him by the shoulder.

'I'm looking for somebody,' Joshua shouted into the shadows of the car, and trying to shrug off the man's hand.

'Yes. I know that. Now, get in. We'll give you a hand.'

And Joshua scrambled into the back of the taxi cab with Billy and his dad.

'I'm lookin' for somebody,' Joshua told them again.

'We know that,' Billy's dad said. 'What's he look like? This feller. What's he wearing?'

And he couldn't say. Rob. He was just ordinary. Tall. High cheek bones.

'You know Mr. Dexter,' he said to Billy. 'You know what he looks like,' as if that excused him for giving such an impossible description. 'He's got a suit on.'

'Ye want us to go up Huskisson to the top?' the driver shouted back.

'Do we?'

'Yes,' Joshua replied. 'Go to the top and then ye turn left and come back down Alma. That's the best way.'

And it was.

The driver went to the top of Huskisson Street, turned left, came back down Alma, and there he was, Rob, striding out, his head down against the drizzle, his hands in his pockets.

Billy's father rolled down the window.

'Mr. Dexter,' he shouted and Rob unable to believe that anybody in a car would be shouting his name, took no notice until his name was called again and he came to the pavement's edge. But he didn't know Billy's father and his face in the moonlight was creased with wariness. Only when he recognised Billy and then beyond him, Joshua, did he relax and smile.

'Wait a jiffy,' Mr. Moffat said, opening the door. 'Don't come in yet. Joshua wants a word with you.'

Billy's father pulled his legs in and let Joshua past, kept his hand on the boy's elbow until he was out of the car.

'Tell him what Mrs. Weston told you,' Mr. Moffat said, keeping his voice down because he did not want the driver to know that there were some difficulties.

'Mrs. Weston. She came to the chapel,' Joshua said, more out of breath now in his anxiety than he had been in the twenty-five minute run he had finished only a short time before. 'There's a policeman looking for ye. And some army police.'

Rob didn't look frightened. He was not in any way alarmed. His face didn't change really, just kept the same thoughtful expression.

'Are they at the house?'

'They might be. She sent this.'

Joshua took the envelope from his pocket. He hadn't given it a thought since Dolly had handed it to him. He could've forgotten it altogether.

Rob looked inside. Money, his army papers, his leave pass, his travel warrant. Dolly had found them in the loft.

'Aye, right,' he said.

Now, Mr. Moffat had climbed out of the taxi cab.

'Come on. You'd better get to the station. They'll not be looking for you there.'

'Who are you?' Rob asked.

'I'm just a simple man who wasn't very impressed by a chapel trustee tonight. At the same time, a lady I've never seen before did impress me and she was in some sort of trouble. Last time she was in trouble it seems this boy's mother helped her. I'd like to help her now.'

Billy's father was just like his son. No wonder Billy was such a preacher with a father like that.

'I know it's not murder. I know you've been in France and won yourself a medal. And I've learnt from my son,' and here he pointed inside the car to the corner where Billy was sitting, 'that you did well helping a couple of old folks in a cafe the other day. That's good enough for me.'

The drive from there was quiet enough. No-one was ready for conversation and they felt obliged to be careful in front of the driver. When they reached the station, Billy's father got out first.

'You lot hold on here,' he told them.

He went into the booking hall and on to the platform.

'Right,' he said when he came back. 'Out you get ... No, not you, Joshua.'

Billy and Rob got out of the taxi standing on the pavement while Billy's father paid the fare.

'He'll take you home, son,' Mr. Moffat told Joshua. 'It's taken care of.'

Billy put his head through the open window.

'I'll come down again, Joshua. But I won't be staying at the Samways, I don't think. My father doesn't care for him very much.'

And then Rob looked in.

'It'll be all right, tell Dolly. Tell her not to worry. Everything'll work out.'

Joshua heard the message though when he later thought about it he was unsure of what it meant.

'And you take care of her, eh? I'm meetin' a feller called Dickie O'Hara. That's all she needs to know.'

They shook hands like two grown men.

'Good lad,' Rob said to him and then he turned away.

The taxi moved off. Joshua swivelled in his seat to watch them go into the booking hall and as he did so, all three of them had stopped and were waving goodbye to him.

They had sat up late, thrown more coals on the fire, wrapped blankets around their shoulders and knees as the house grew colder.

They talked about Rob, tried to understand, to piece things together, tried to accommodate themselves to the idea of him as a deserter. And what that meant to both of them. And to him, Rob, somewhere in Newcastle or on a train to some other part of the country. They had no idea of his plans except that he was going to meet someone called Dickie O'Hara.

But whatever it was, Dolly told Joshua, it wasn't his back.

Can a man be a hero and a deserter? Is Rob a hero? Is he a deserter? And if he is, does that wipe out all the bravery of the past? They were terrible questions for both of them. But no, Joshua was increasingly certain, it didn't matter what he was doing now. Rob was a brave man.

They talked about old Mr. Samways; even laughed about the constable and the soldiers for a brief moment.

But Joshua never spoke of the Lieutenant and Dolly made no mention of Hector. Nor did either of them dare to play with the idea of who had betrayed Rob; fugitive, deserter, hero.

For the truth of that might be unbearable.

'I wonder if he's all right.' Dolly sat with her head in her hands, never moving. In the chair opposite Joshua wished he could answer her.

If an answer was required of him, none came even when she whispered the query only seconds later. Instead there was a loud knocking at the front door. Joshua looked up at the clock. Quarter to twelve. Whoever would want to come at this hour? Had Rob been taken? Had they been waiting for him at Newcastle when he stepped off the train? And what about Billy and his dad? Were they in trouble?

'I'd better go an' see,' Dolly said, throwing her blanket down on the chair and she left the room tugging nervously at her skirt.

Joshua heard her make her way cautiously down the dark stairway, heard her turn the key in the lock.

'I hope it's not too late.'

Joshua recognised the voice.

'May I come in?'

He was uncertain of what Dolly answered. She was speaking quietly, in a low monotone. But she made no attempt to stop the visitor coming up. Joshua heard the Lieutenant's tread on the stairs and Dolly closing the front door.

The Lieutenant was surprised to see Joshua sitting there.

'I thought you'd be in bed,' he said almost accusingly. He had never spoken so sharply to him before.

'We've had a busy night.'

Dolly's voice from the doorway behind him was cool.

The Lieutenant sighed.

'May I sit?'

211

Dolly, her lips taut, motioned with her head towards the chair she had been sitting in. The Lieutenant took his seat, folding the blanket carefully and handing it to Dolly. He kept his overcoat on, his homburg perched on his knees. Dolly sat on one of the wooden kitchen chairs.

'It's rather late,' the Lieutenant said again looking at Joshua.

'We're not usually late like this,' Dolly replied but offered nothing more.

'I thought I'd have a word with you.' He was uneasy, unable to look her in the face, kept his eyes constantly on the move but never on hers. 'I had an idea you' — and he emphasised the 'you' — 'I had an idea you might still be up.'

Dolly's face was a mask.

'I wouldn't have called usually,' Hector went on, 'but tonight ...' and here his words faltered.

'Did you tell them?'

Joshua could not wait any longer to ask. His words came out in a husky rush. He feared the answer, feared that the Lieutenant could have betrayed Rob. The Lieutenant, a betrayer. He did not think he could live with that.

'Joshua says he told you about the pay book,' Dolly put in. 'That's how you knew.'

The Lieutenant turned a pained face towards her.

'He was reported by someone who recognised him. He'd been seen. His name was in the paper. Somebody recognised him.'

The Lieutenant's voice was irritable now. They could blame him for a lot of things but he was not responsible for that. But his answer had not satisfied Dolly.

'Joshua told you about the pay book,' she repeated. 'Did you do anythin' about it?'

'No.'

The relief flickered momentarily in her eyes but her expression did not relax.

'Were you goin' to?'

The Lieutenant shook his head impatiently.

'No.'

Joshua could have run across to hug him then, wanted to. The Lieutenant had not betrayed the hero.

'But I should have done. That's really what I ought to have done. What I wanted to do.'

The Lieutenant turned his wretched face not to Dolly but to the boy sitting facing him.

'I should have done my duty, shouldn't I? We've talked about it often enough.' His face swivelled back to Dolly. 'All those mornings, walking on the pier, we've talked about duty, haven't we?'

They had.

Duty to parents, to husbands, to friends.

All sorts of duties.

Duty and no excuses for not doing it.

Duty to country.

They had not always agreed on that, Dolly and him.

The Lieutenant wrung his hands agitatedly. Joshua had never seen him like this before.

'So,' the Lieutenant was saying, 'I have to hope that the deserter is caught.'

He sounded so bitter as if he was wanting to condemn himself totally in Dolly's eyes.

'I suppose ye must,' she spat across the room. 'That's where your ideas are leadin' you.' Then she paused and drew in her breath before going on. 'You lot might be fightin' for your big houses and your fathers' businesses. And then there's your fancy schools. But all that Rob and Henry seemed to be fightin' for was to send bairns like this' — and here she pointed at Joshua — 'to the workhouse.'

Dolly put both of her hands on the table for support. Her face was ashen white and she was trembling. Joshua had not wanted her to say that about the workhouse, had no wish to be drawn into this as if he was against the Lieutenant. He did not want Dolly to use him this way.

'Ye think these lads, like my brothers and Ernie Grayson and thousands of others, want to stand in the mud for months and years? What for? What did they leave behind that's so much worth fightin' for? And what are they comin' back to? Jobs in the pits, if there are any? Work in the shipyards until your lot gets rid of them for talkin' out of turn?'

Dolly clamped her jaws together as though she had nothing more to say but before the Lieutenant could find words to answer, she started again, less fiercely now, more scornfully.

'And what are you comin' back to, Lieutenant Samways?' Dolly's voice had a sneer in it now. 'What have you left and what are you comin' back to? I suppose whatever it is, it might be worth fightin' for. But for God's sake, don't wrap it up in duty. Don't tell me about duty.'

The Lieutenant studied the palms of his hands soberly.

'I don't really want him caught. Not personally,' he told her. He sat back in his chair as if he had suddenly laid down a heavy burden. 'In any case, I didn't come about that.'

For a moment there was a silence between them as though they were both regrouping their thoughts. The coals stirred in the grate, sagged as the ashes fell into the pan below. An unexpected spark flew out, glowed, a smouldering cinder on the fender top. Joshua got out of his chair, licked his finger ends, picked it up and threw it back.

'I'd like to speak to you, Dolly, in private,' Hector said quietly. Her firm expression never changed.

'You can speak in front of him, can't you?' she asked, her voice sterner than Joshua had ever heard it before.

The Lieutenant paused, reflecting, then resumed.

'I'm going back to France,' he said. 'The Board. I heard yesterday. I'm fit.'

Only the slightest flicker at the corner of her mouth betrayed the fact that Dolly had taken in what he had said.

'I'm due to leave here on Wednesday.'

It was like a replacement, he thought. It would make up for Rob Dexter. He'd have another hero there, fighting for old England. In a curious sort of way, it made up for Rob. It might almost be said to wipe the slate clean. So he told himself anyway.

'I wondered if you would marry me?'

Hector was sitting bolt upright, his fingers stiff against the brim of the hat on his knee. He looked like a man awaiting sentence.

Before he had a chance to hear Dolly's response, Joshua played with the idea of what this meant. The Lieutenant would be his father. Like his father anyway. That is if he could count Dolly as his mother as he almost did now. And would he come to live here? When he came back from France, would they all three settle down together here?

But Dolly's voice was just above a whisper.

'I'm sorry, there's no point in discussin' it.'

'None?'

Hector's still expression had not changed. His voice carried no note of disappointment.

He stood up, nodding more to himself than to her. It was as if he was digesting her answer, agreeing with it.

But no. Don't just go. Don't just get up like that just because of what she's said. Ask her again.

'I'm sorry,' Dolly said. 'I'll see ye out.'

No, please, Dolly. Please, Mrs. Weston. He's asking you if you'll marry him. One sentence was all he said and you answered back in one sentence. Ask her again, Hector. Tell him you'll change your mind, Dolly. Mrs Weston.

'Will you not give it some thought?' His voice was hesitant.

'No,' she said very calmly and added quite formally, 'Thank you for comin'.'

The Lieutenant paused as if what she said needed deep consideration. He looked as if he intended to speak again and then appeared to think better of it.

Dolly stood by the door, her hand on the handle.

Perhaps she will change her mind. Please. And why won't he speak up, ask her again?

The Lieutenant goes to the door, fastening the belt of his heavy overcoat. He raises his hand, the one holding the homburg, towards Joshua.

'Goodnight,' he says and goes out, down the stairs, following Dolly. There is the usual pause, the interval, while Dolly unlocks the door. At the head of the stairs, Joshua waits in the shadows, hoping to hear something, hoping Dolly or the Lieutenant will even at this late stage change their minds. But then the door opens and after the briefest 'goodnights', it closes and Dolly climbs back upstairs again.

But why, Mrs. Weston? Dolly, why?

He has the question but cannot bring himself to ask it.

'Time for bed,' is all she says wearily.

Since he had gone to bed, well past midnight, he had heard her moving about the house. She had done some ironing. He recognised the sounds. Then she had riddled the ashes and shovelled them into the bucket. Now she was laying the fire ready for the

215

morning, carefully placing the sticks he had chopped the day before, tucking in the firelighters he had made from newspaper before leaving for the social.

The social. In a few hours, everything had changed. Life before the social was different from life after. It was a happier time then, a time for heroes. It had really changed the moment Dolly had bent over him, when he had become aware of her white face, her strained voice. She had almost pushed old Mr. Samways aside. And as he left the hall by the back door, he had heard their angry voices.

Poor Dolly.

Poor Dolly and her dead baby. Once, the night he had come to this house, she had told him about the baby. She'd said she'd once had a baby. She would have been a wonderful mother to have. He could almost envy that poor, dead baby having Dolly for a mother. But he shouldn't think like that, shouldn't be envious of a poor, dead baby.

And Henry sticking up for her in the chapel ... and Rob ... Rob whose hands would shake sometimes ... one day, a packet of cigarettes fell from his fingers and scattered across the floor ... another time, the same happened with the matches ... can you be frightened and a hero at the same time? Mebbes you can only be a hero if you are frightened ... and the Lieutenant ... he didn't deserve it, didn't deserve to be sent away into the cold, misty, blacked-out night.

Funny, till now he hadn't thought about the taxi ride, only his second ride ever in a motor car. And not till now, when he was on the verge of sleep, did its rumblings, creaks, lurches, its smells ...

Rob on a train, going to find Dickie O'Hara.

Dolly in the kitchen, staring at the cold grate, through swollen eyes.

The Lieutenant walking home. He shouldn't have asked her. He'd been selfish. She'd already been widowed. If he survived ... Dolly ... Rob ... George ... and a soldier drowning in the slime of a shell crater. No sound, no scream from his terrified mouth. An Englishman perhaps; possibly a German. Whoever he was, he couldn't be saved. The Lieutenant pulls up the collar of his overcoat, walking home.

Joshua, in bed, dreaming about all of them. About Rob and the Lieutenant and Dolly and himself.

10

In the frosty air Joshua's breath shoots out in a column. Now on these winter mornings it is no longer dark, not yet light, and he sucks the air into his lungs and only after long seconds, several paces along the icy, snow-packed pavement, does he release it. Smoky, milk-white. And satisfying.

The grown-ups, fellers, old women, they do not like it, this weather, this harsh February of 1918. They huddle into themselves as they walk. They do not often lift their eyes from the pavements, anxious they might fall. Only occasionally do they look up, scowling at the passing schoolboy, crunching his boots in the snow, sliding, where it is thin.

'Somebody'll have an accident,' they grumble at him. 'Making the paths slippy like that.'

They could slide at school in the yard. Always had done. Not that the girls did it much except in corners where they screamed along their short narrow glassy tracks, not like the boys along their great long snaking slide where they slid in groups, where at the end they tumbled and sprawled in yelling confusion.

Until last week that is, last Wednesday, when Wilfy Errington, too enthusiastic, took himself to the girls' slide and brought them all down in a random sprawling which when they sorted themselves out, revealed Ada Chapple with a broken leg.

'No more sliding in the yard,' Mr. McKie had pronounced when he had trooped them all into the Seniors' Room. They stood there in their classes, row by row, infants on the left right up to the oldest boys and girls on the right.

'No more sliding. Don't let me catch anybody in that yard even thinking about sliding.'

And the infants rustled guiltily because they could not get the idea of sliding out of their heads.

'I hope that's understood,' Mr. McKie had said before he turned his back abruptly on them and left Mr. Pybus and the other two teachers to reinforce the message.

But on the way to school this hard January morning Joshua slides. And wonders, in the joy of it, what by the winter after next he might be doing. He'll be nearly thirteen then.

Work?

He's thought about it. Naturally.

Joshua, now with his hands in his pockets, his cap pulled down well over his eyes, his muffler three times round his neck, skips gingerly across an especially icy patch, where Henderson Lane cuts into Alma Lane, where the cars and lorries and the horses and the pony drawn carts have passed and repassed these last five weeks, packing the ice so hard, so black-glass shiny, that it has to be negotiated with care. Even he feels relief when his feet come into contact with the deeper, softer snow in the gutter.

Could go down the pit. He knew a lad, left school last year, who went down the pit. And liked it, though he never saw winter daylight for weeks on the shifts he worked.

Dolly wouldn't like it though. They had talked about it, what he'd do when he went out to work. She seemed to favour the shipyards. Plenty of opportunities there. Ships would always be wanted. Great ships for the greatest navies and mercantile fleets in the world. Henry had been a tradesman in the yards. She often talked about how he'd started there. She would point at the photograph.

'He was only a couple of years older than that when he went to work in the yards.'

She used to describe him, in his new work boots and his man's cap and his bait tin and his bottle of tea. Those days, the knocker-up used to come round at God knows what hour.

'Poor bairn,' she would say. 'First couple of months he was still asleep when he went out the door. But he loved it.'

Rob, as well. He worked in the yards.

Funny. Rob didn't come into her conversations as often as Henry. Never had since Joshua had first stepped in the door all those months ago.

Rob.

There'd been a postcard, a month or so ago. It had come from his old sergeant in London. He hoped they were well. He'd heard from another old friend, Dickie O'Hara. Dickie was in the best of health. No complaints at all, Guthrie wrote.

From Billy's father they learnt some more. When Rob went into the railway station that night, he'd stayed on the train until they got to Newcastle. Then, Billy's father told them, when he came down a couple of days later, Rob had just disappeared over the railway bridge inside the station. Off to some or other platform. Going north or south or even west. Whenever he heard that somebody had gone west — and he heard that expression often enough in these days — he thought of Rob. Though, of course, he might have gone north or south.

And another thing they knew. About his last night, the night when the soldiers and the policeman had called and Dolly had come to the chapel hall. They knew where he went earlier that night when he went out, just before Joshua went to the social.

Because several days later, when the news was out about Rob and everybody seemed to know, the Graysons came back to see Dolly. They didn't stay long. But what they said stayed with Joshua.

'He came to us that night, the last night he was here. Came to tell us what a grand lad our Ernest was. Thought he hadn't praised him enough when we came here that time. Gave us a lot of comfort, that.'

And as they went out the door, Mrs. Grayson, that sour-faced little woman, had turned to Dolly.

'I hope they never find him, dear,' was what she said. 'He's a grand young man and I hope they never find him.'

And her husband had laid his hand on the old lady's shoulder.

'I sometimes wish,' he said, and he did not sound bitter, 'that our lad, rather than be killed, had run off. He'd be alive today.'

They were making an effort in Stanhope Street to keep the roads clear, to keep the trams running. This morning Joshua could make out a dozen or so working beyond the railway bridge. He hadn't been up that way for months now. He'd loved to go up there at one time, waiting for the trains to thud overhead, keeping his ear pressed to the juddering supporting pillars. That night — it seemed so long ago now — when Billy had come to stay was the last time. That was the last time ever he had put his ear to the pillar. And now, Billy was coming tomorrow to stay with him and Dolly. It was nothing to do with Mr. Samways or the chapel. It was just an ordinary visit and Joshua was looking forward to seeing him. But when he looked up at the groups of men, or more to the point, when he looked up at the railway bridge, he knew he wouldn't be going out of his way, taking Billy up there just to feel the train passing overhead. That was gone. He didn't want to do that any more.

Ahead of him now he sees Freddy Forster, struggling to keep his feet. He puts a spurt on, trying to catch him up. Weeks ago he wouldn't have bothered. But nowadays he thinks quite a bit about what Freddy Forster had said to him that day, about him being brave. But he wasn't brave; he hadn't been brave that day. And when Mr. McKie had asked to see him he'd been frightened. Same that day in Mr. Fraser's office. His knees had jerked in fear. So how could he be brave? Unless — and this sometimes occurred to him — unless you couldn't be brave unless you were afraid. Now there was a puzzle.

Freddy was making quicker progress now. Where he was, the pavements had been cleared. If Joshua wanted to catch him he'd have to hurry. But when he got to the main road which was still icy, he just had to stand and watch Freddy going on ahead quite quickly now.

He waited for a slow file of army lorries bound for the docks to pass by before he jog-trotted across the road. He wanted to be early to school. Mr. Pybus had brought in two white mice the week before as part of his new science lessons. This week he had appointed Joshua to look after them. The tasks were few but they had to be done to Mr. Pybus's liking. The cage had to be cleaned out each morning and new water and grain put in. Joshua liked the job, liked the feel of the mice in his hands, liked to see their pink snouts and tiny paws. They were warm in his grasp these cold mornings.

Joshua wondered how they would be, wondered if they were looking forward to him coming, if they were waiting for him to whisper softly to them as he put his cold, red hands into the cage.

But he wanted to do the job especially well for Mr. Pybus. When his wife had died at the beginning of winter — the influenza, it had been bad — Mr. Pybus had been off school for nearly two weeks. He had been very cut up, they said. And he had no children, no sons or daughters, to comfort him. Mr. McKie had taken the class and he had been very nice. But Joshua and everybody felt sorry for Mr. Pybus, so naturally he wanted to do the job well.

He would be glad to get into school today, get those mice in his hands. He was always warm when he left the house. At nights, Dolly used to heat up four bricks, two for each of them, and she'd wrap them in flannelette and put them in their beds so that for the first hour or so anyway, he was as warm as toast. Just like the mice always seemed to be. Then, though it was freezing when he first got up, Dolly would light the fire and make a pot of tea and they'd give themselves plenty of time and they'd sip their tea and get warmed up, their fingers grasping the hot mugs. Dolly, he thought. Dolly, I love her.

The Lieutenant ...he often thought about him ... and about Rob. He wondered about both of them, asked himself if they had sometimes been afraid. Neither of them had said so, never even suggested it. But even now, at this very minute, the Lieutenant could be doing something courageous. If he was, could he be afraid at the same time? It would make a man doubly brave if that was so.

He wished that night, months ago now, she had said that she'd marry Lieutenant Samways. But they never talked about the Lieutenant. Not till this morning.

'Those poor lads,' she'd said. She was standing at the window, staring up at the leaden sky, promising more snow. 'Dreadful for them in those trenches this weather.'

She had given a great sigh.

'He's not dead, ye know,' Joshua had told her.

Dolly had spun around, her eyes puzzled and her mouth half-open as if she intended to ask him who it was he was telling her about.

Joshua forestalled her question. 'The Lieutenant,' he said. 'He's not dead. I know that. Least he wasn't last Sunday.'

She put her hand out, almost as if she was going to fall and then pulled herself together.

'What d'ye mean?' she asked Joshua. She wasn't angry with him as he almost feared she might be because the Lieutenant had seemed a forbidden subject since that last night she'd seen him down the stairs and out into the empty street. 'How d'ye know?'

There was a girl. She was only nine, much younger than Joshua. But he had always known her at school and at chapel. One day, he had asked her, did she know Mr. Samways. And she did not know how to answer, perhaps afraid Joshua was a friend of the great man. So she just nodded to acknowledge that she knew who he was.

'Do ye ever hear about soldiers at the chapel? Being killed?' he had asked her. He knew of course that there was a Roll of Honour made out of a large sheet of white cardboard. It hung on the wall and was added to weekly. And there were prayers for the dead every week. Each new death was solemnly, sadly announced, between the denunciation of sinners and the sermon.

'Mr. Samways, he's got a son in the army,' Joshua had told the girl. 'He's in France and he's a Lieutenant.'

The girl had listened to him gravely as he measured out his words. Then she had shaken her heard.

'No, he's not,' she answered. And Joshua's stomach churned. What was she going to tell him? 'He's a Captain now,' the girl told him, 'and he's in Belgium.'

He'd questioned her further but she was immoveable. She knew Mr. Samways had a son. And she had heard it announced only a week or so earlier that he had been promoted to Captain. And he was in Belgium. Mr. Samways had made the announcement himself.

And every Monday morning after that, for the last six weeks or so, Joshua had questioned her. Was there further news of Captain Samways? He was still alive, wasn't he?

So that, this cold winter's morning he had quite out of the blue been able to tell Dolly that to date, anyway, Hector Samways was still alive.

And Dolly had kissed him. Well, she always kissed him when he went off to school. But this morning was different. The way she held him was not the same. Nor was the way the tears slowly ran down her cheeks.

So that on this morning, Joshua has some hope. There is a chance that what he wishes for might come true. If only he holds out, goes on hoping, never gives up hoping. Never gives up.

Staying power, Mr Pybus had called it.

He's catching up on Freddy Forster as well.

'Hey, Freddy,' he shouts. 'Hold on.'

The pavement here is clear of snow and ice and he breaks into a run.